TWO ON ONE

Lando picked out the leader, got it in the canopy crosshairs, and stomped on both pedals. He kept the fighter centered, kept the guns going. The enemy's nose-cowling disintegrated before the small craft burst into flames, showering debris over the *Falcon*.

Suddenly the *Falcon* lurched, then stabilized as Lando applied counterthrust. Something solid had smacked her hard. He skated her in a broad horizontal loop, gave her half a roll as she came around, and there it was—another fighter, its fuselage accordioned, its engines spouting flames.

Ramming? In *this* century? They must be pretty desperate...

Also by L. Neil Smith
Published by Ballantine Books

Lando Calrissian and the Flamewind of Oseon

A NOVEL BY
L. NEIL SMITH

BASED ON THE CHARACTERS AND
SITUATIONS CREATED BY GEORGE LUCAS

A Del Rey Book

BALLANTINE BOOKS • NEW YORK

A Del Rey Book
Published by Ballantine Books

Copyright © 1983 by Lucasfilm Ltd. (LFL)

Lando Calrissian is a trademark of Lucasfilm Ltd. (LFL). Used under authorization.

Library of Congress Catalog Card Number: 83-90768

ISBN 0-345-31163-9

Manufactured in the United States of America

First Edition: October 1983

Cover art by William Schmidt

AND *THIS* BOOK is dedicated to J. Neil Schulman and Victor Koman, a pair of cards if there ever was one.

ONE

He was slightly over a meter tall, from the faceted wide-angle lens glowing redly atop his highly polished pentagonal body to the fine feathery tips of his chromium-plated tentacles.

Of these, there were five, which he felt was as it should be. After all, hadn't he been created in the image of his manufacturers?

He thought of himself as *Vuffi Raa*, an unsentimental designation from a different numbering system and a different language, half a galaxy ago. It served well enough as a name.

At the moment, he was in a hurry.

The tree-lined Esplanade of Oseon 6845 was a broad,

jungly, cobblestoned thoroughfare built exclusively for pedestrian traffic, no matter what the individual sentient's personal means of locomotion. It was equipped with an artificial gravity field three meters deep to accommodate the most attenuated of species. It was lined on both sides with elegantly restrained shops to accommodate the very richest.

It has been said that the commercial footage along the domed Esplanade of Oseon 6845 is the most expensive in the known universe. And that the patrons strolling its landscaped and sculptured kilometers are the wealthiest. Vuffi Raa didn't know about that—a rare failing of information on his part. In the first place, he hadn't the appropriate statistics ready to hand (in a manner of speaking). And if compelled to base his opinion on an *n* of one—the single case with which he was intimately familiar—he'd have had to hold the opposite was true. Not everybody there was rich. Not everybody there had come to buy and sell.

Which conclusion neatly brought his musings back around to the reason for his present urgency: his current master, latest of what had been, until recently, an embarrassingly lengthy list of thoroughly dissatisfied customers.

Freeble-reeep!

From the heavily planted median of the Esplanade, an entity that might have been a songbird warbled noisily in what may have been a bush, momentarily distracting the little robot. You could never tell. In the plush, cosmopolitan resort, the creature doing the singing might well be a photosynthetic vegetable attempting to attract pollen carriers, and the foliage it perched in, a soil-rooted animal. The entire Oseon System was like that, a richman's playground, cleverly intended by those who had ordained its construction to be full of surprises.

But then, so was life itself. Their very presence in this overstuffed watering hole, his and his master's, was ample testimony to that.

Vuffi Raa forced his jumbled thoughts back into relevant channels. He was a Class Two droid, with intellectual and emotional capacities roughly equaling those of organic sentients. And an uncorrected tendency in his programming to let his mind wander and to mix his metaphors on occasion. It was a price he paid for being one of the rare machines abroad with an imagination.

At the moment, it was a luxury he couldn't afford. He held the blackened evidence before his eye again as a reminder. It was a fist-sized chunk of scorched metal and fused silicon. A few hours ago, it had been a neutrino hybridizer, a delicate and critical component in the sublightspeed drive of a certain class and vintage of starship.

Now it looked like a microcredit's worth of asteroid mine-tailings.

Unconscious of a gesture he had acquired from long association with human beings, Vuffi Raa raised his free tentacle to scratch at the upper portion of his five-sided torso—the closest thing he had to a head. The little droid was pentadextrous, having no preference as to which of his five sinuous limbs he used for getting around on, which he used for holding, carrying, or manipulating objects. Such as treacherous lumps of recently molten quartz and platinum.

A well-rounded, versatile, and radially symmetrical fellow was Vuffi Raa.

And a very worried one.

His brisk but absentminded pace carried him past a leaf-shaded decorative pond where something between a green mammal and a small many-jointed insect dabbled a line—actually an extension of its right front leg—into half a meter of water. There was a modest ripple, a splash, then a *snap*! The creature reeled in a tiny, colorful fish, devouring it on the spot and spitting the bones back into the water.

Vuffi Raa never even noticed.

At long last he reached the expensively decorated surface entrance of the exclusive Hotel Drofo. With a brotherly salute, Vuffi Raa strode past the door-being, a robot painted in the garish gold and purple livery of the establishment, and went directly to one of eight down-shafts leading into the hotel proper.

On an asteroid, even one like Oseon 6845, and even where a first-rate hotel is concerned, surface area comes dear. Volume is cheap.

Selecting LOBBY on the miniature display beside the entrance to the down-shaft, he waited for the elevator to take his measure, then fell—"drifted" might be a better word—at a fraction of the augmented surface acceleration of the asteroid gently downward several dozen meters, coming at last to a cushioned rest at the bottom of the shaft. He stepped out into the whispery bustle of the underground hotel.

Plenty of other droids were in evidence, mingling freely with the humans, humanoids, and nonhumans present. Most of the automata here were in service of one sort or another; they were unusually conspicuous in their number and visibility.

The galaxy over, robots were the object of harsh and persistent prejudice. The Oseon was different, however. Cynics pointed out that neither its current inhabitants nor their ancestors were ever likely to have worried much about losing a job. The place was filled with exiled and vacationing nobility. Captains of industry, active and retired, gravitated here, along with majors, colonels, and generals. Mercantile—and literal—pirates who had purchased themselves a little class, sometimes from that selfsame deposed aristocracy, rubbed shoulders and less human body parts with media stars from a million different systems.

The little droid knew the man he was seeking would be in one of the small, comfortably furnished gaming salons just off the Grand Lobby, here on the first, or bottom, floor. Finding the room wouldn't be any problem, but getting in might be. Gamblers tended to be jealous of their privacy. He "shouldered" his way through the richly dressed crowd, thinking about the news he had for his master—and how very reluctant he was to deliver it.

A human being can only stand so much bad news.

It had begun with an adventure. His master had won a starship—a small converted freighter, actually, called the *Millennium Falcon*— in yet another card game, and had whimsically decided to add "captain" to his other professional titles: gambler, rogue, and scoundrel. He was proud of every one of them, though he preferred "con *artiste*" to what the authorities usually had upon the tips of their sharp and unforgiving tongues.

He'd been a perfectly terrible pilot in the beginning. Vuffi Raa, an accomplished ship-handler by virtue of inbuilt programming, was gradually taking care of that in two ways: piloting the *Falcon* when the need arose; teaching his master to do it for himself whenever they had time.

He'd won Vuffi Raa in a card game, as well. That had triggered a series of events that culminated with their leaving the Rafa System with the very last full cargo of the fabulous life-crystals ever harvested there. The only load ever removed from the system legally by a private cargo vessel.

And they were rich.

Temporarily.

Yet his master hadn't seemed very happy, filling out landing-permit forms, going over bills of lading, figuring overhead and profit margin. Even with Vuffi Raa along to make the workload lighter...It was too much like going straight. The gambler yearned to practice his original profession once again.

Thus, when the invitation had suddenly arrived out of nowhere to come and play *sabacc* in the Oseon, where the pickings were the richest in the galaxy, the pair's free-lance cargo days had come to an abrupt and highly welcome end. They'd blazed across a hundred parsecs to be here on time. The *Falcon*'s speed, in competent tentacles, was legendary. And here they were.

Trouble was, someone had attempted to assure that they be not only here, but also back in the Rafa, out on the Edge, down at the Core, and everyplace else tiny little pieces of their respectively organic and mechanical existences could be scattered.

That someone, it would appear, didn't like them very much.

Vuffi Raa approached the heavy antiqued wooden double doors. Standing before these was an enormous humanoid in an elegantly tailored groundsuit at least four sizes too large for any other two men in the hotel. Beneath the hulking fellow's stylish armpits the robot could make out the twin bulges of a pair of Imperial-issue blasters.

"Excuse me, gentlebeing," offered the little droid, "I have a message for one of the players inside." He produced a card his master had given him for use in just such a circumstance.

To Vuffi Raa's overwhelming relief, the bouncer/bodyguard looked at the holocard as the letters of instruction danced across its surface, nodded politely, and stepped aside. The doors parted slightly; Vuffi Raa squeezed past them.

The air inside the small, luxurious chamber was full of smoke, at least a dozen different, mingling odors, despite the best efforts of its starship-class life-support systems. In the center, seated at a table ringed with players and kibitzers, lounged his master, resplendent in tasteful and expensive velvoid semiformal shipclothes.

The robot approached, waiting until the hand was finished—his master raked in a substantial pile of credit tokens—then tugged gently at the hem of his short cloak.

"Master?"

The figure turned, looked down. White teeth in a dark face, irresistible smile, intelligent and mischievous eyes.

"What is it, Vuffi Raa—and how many times have I asked you not to call me master?"

They were both whispering against a noisy background.

The droid held up the oddly shaped clump of debris for his master's inspection. "There wasn't any spontaneous breakdown in the phase-shift controls aboard the *Falcon*, Master. I'm afraid you were right, that this makes two such incidents."

His master nodded grimly. "So it was a bomb."

"Yes, Master, someone is trying to murder you."

TWO

Lᴀɴᴅᴏ Cᴀʟʀɪssɪᴀɴ sʜᴏᴏᴋ ʜɪs ʜᴇᴀᴅ ɪʀᴏɴɪᴄᴀʟʟʏ ᴀɴᴅ grinned.

He had good reason. His first evening in the Oseon, his first *sabacc* game, and already he was ahead some twenty-three thousand credits.

The dashing young gambler stood, dressed impeccably at an hour when most people were rumpled and tired, before a full-length mirror, stroking the brand-new mustache he'd begun only a few weeks ago, when things looked so much bleaker. Yes, by the Core, it did give him a certain panache, a certain elan, a certain . . .

And without filling out so much as a single form in triplicate (if that was logically possible)—his mind was drifting back again to the money tucked into the pockets of his velvoid semiformals — without acquiring a permit, easement, license, variance, or Certificate of Mother-May-I.

Here was one fat bankroll that wasn't going to evaporate when he wasn't watching it!

What added amusement to triumph was that *sabacc* was a game considerably more complex and infinitely riskier than the entrepreneurship he'd been attempting since he'd acquired the *Millennium Falcon*. It called for quicker judgment, greater courage, and a more sophisticated understanding of human (in a broadly tolerant manner of speaking) nature.

So why was he so casually accomplished at the former and so miserably rotten at the latter?

He shrugged to himself, crossed the hotel room from the door he'd closed and locked securely not very many moments before.

Let's see — just the most recent example. He'd won the *Falcon* and Vuffi Raa, then proceeded to earn a handsome fee (work he'd been coerced into doing) that, by all rights, ought to have set him up for life. Orchard crystals from the Rafa System had never been cheap to begin with. Humanoids who wore them found their lifespans extended, their intelligence somewhat enhanced. They were both valuable and rare. They grew in only one place in the universe.

Lando had known, when he and the bot had quit the Rafa, that there would be no more life-crystals, at least for a while. The colonial government there had been overthrown by insurgent natives. Thus, he'd held out for the highest possible prices. Yet, somehow, the money — several millions — had seemed to disappear before his very eyes, eaten up in spacecraft maintenance, docking charges, taxes, surtaxes, sursurtaxes, and bribes. Every time he closed a deal, no matter what margin he'd built in at the beginning, he wound up losing. It didn't seem sensible: the more money he earned, the poorer he became.

If he got any richer, he'd be broke.

Perhaps he simply hadn't been playing in the right league. One of the rules of this new game (new to Lando, anyway) was that they didn't tell you the rules until it was too late. His figurative hat was off to anyone who could *survive* in the world of business, let alone prosper.

A small noise in the next room alerted him. He peeked in: Vuffi Raa was laying out tomorrow's wardrobe for him. He'd told the little fellow a hundred times that it wasn't necessary. He needed no valet, and long ago had begun thinking of the robot as a friend more than anything else. But exactly like a good friend (or consummate servant), the droid understood the gambler's need for some time alone without conversation, while he unwound from the evening's tense preoccupations. Lando suspected that Vuffi Raa actually wanted to discuss the bomb he'd discovered—the second since their last planetfall. Well, morning was time enough for that. He closed the connecting door softly and returned to his private thoughts.

A second irony struck him as he watched the bed turn itself down. He shucked out of his dressy Bantha-hide knee boots and reclined, one foot dangling over the edge of the bed to the floor.

The very individuals who had prospered most, either at legitimaté businesses like freight hauling, or shadier ones such as smuggling (the avocation, in fact, for which the *Falcon* had originally been constructed), those who had made their way to the top, lived here in the Oseon, where one Lando Calrissian, a dismal failure by their standards, experienced little difficulty at all separating them from their hard-won money.

It was their own fault. They'd invited him . . .

Fire streaked from the starboard weapons turret of the *Millennium Falcon*.

In desperate haste, Lando swung the quad-guns down and to the left as the drone squadron whooshed by, their own energy-guns coloring the misted space around the freighter.

"Missed! Vuffi Raa, hold her a little steadier!"

The ship ducked and swooped, narrowly avoiding being skewered in a cross fire as the drone fighters split up, attacking from both sides.

"Master, there are too many of—good shooting, *sir!"*

The little droid's voice issued from an intercom beside Lando's ear. The gambler made an imaginary chalk mark on a purely mental scoreboard, manhandling the guns around for another shot. The drone he'd splattered was an incandescent and expanding ball of dust and gas, augmenting an already dirty region of space.

Anyone else might have whooped! victoriously.

Lando fumed in the transparent gun-bubble.

All right, so it *had* been his idea to shortcut through this small nebulosity on the way to the next port. Blast it all, he was carrying valuable, somewhat perishable cargo. Crates of wintenberry jelly. Stacks of mountain-bollem hides. Expensive tinklewood fishing rods. In short, the produce of a frontier planet. His corner-cutting could save them precious days, compared to routes preferred by scheduled cargo haulers.

The shields pulsed with coruscating brilliance. They were taking hits again!

He slewed the quad-guns hard, pressed the double triggers. Bolts of ravening energy rammed directly into a pair of tiny unmanned fighters screaming toward the ship. One exploded, the other, severely damaged, cork-screwed crazily out of Lando's line of vision.

Vuffi Raa rolled the ship, skated into a wild, stomach-wrenching yaw, adroitly avoiding a direct hit. They were a good team together, Lando thought.

Besides, it wasn't much as nebulosities go. Even deep inside the scruffy patch of gas, a few molecules every cubic meter produced very little visible clouding. They did slow a ship down, however, making it dangerous to use the faster-than-light drive. That's probably why the regular lines avoided the place. But Lando, calculating distance over time, had figured that, even at a substantial reduction from lightspeed, they'd still gain time and profit thereby.

He'd been wrong.

Six more meter-diameter drones bore directly for his turret. The enemy seemed to have an endless supply. Lando caught a glance of their mother vessel, a pirate lying off and directing the attack in relative safety. She was approximately four times the displacement of the *Falcon*, clumsily built, a large sphere attached to a slightly smaller cylinder, the whole awkward assembly patched and mottled by hard use and long neglect.

He could imagine half a hundred crew-beings, hunched over their drone panels in a dimly lit control center. They were probably as broke and desperate as he was.

Waiting until the last possible moment, he let loose all four barrels on maxium power and dispersal. Lights dimmed aboard the *Falcon*. Two saucer-shaped drones blossomed into fireballs, the third was holed severely. The fourth, fifth, and sixth zoomed over his head in ragged formation, past the gun-blister, and out of his visual range before he could tell what he'd done to them. He released the triggers.

Full illumination sprang forth again.

Nebulosities *were* good for hiding spaceships. The gas, dust, and ions, the magnetic and static fields made a hash of long-range sensor instrumentation. That's how they'd wound up in this confounded—

"Vuffi Raa!" Lando shouted suddenly. "Close on the pirate herself! I've had enough of this. Give me a pass at her reaction-drive system!"

"Very well, Master."

There was doubt in the robot's doubly electronic voice—not concerning Lando's combat abilities. Quite the contrary. It was simply that the droid's most fundamental programming forbade him to take the life of a mechanical or organic sentient being. He was straining his cybernetic ethics severely even now, conning a fighting ship. Yet strain them he did.

In a long, graceful arc with a little flip on the end, the *Falcon* soared toward the pirate, taking her by surprise. A few guns warmed up feebly—too late—as their startled operators switched attention from remote-control panels to fire-control systems. The tiny flying weapons might be adequate against an unarmed freighter or a pleasure yacht that stumbled into the cloud, but they hadn't been conceived or built for mortal engagement with a vessel like the *Falcon*, half pirate ship herself and bristling with more guns than her crew could handle all at once.

Trusting his ship's shields, Lando bore down upon the quad-gun, drilling its quadruple high-power beams at the reaction-drive outlet at the far end of the pirate's spherical section. Once again the *Falcon*'s interior lights dimmed, and for the first time, it occurred to Lando that his heavy trigger finger was costing something. However, the enemy's thrust tubes were beginning to glow. First red, they quickly became orange-yellow. They'd been molded to withstand heat and pressure right enough, but not from the outside in.

Suddenly, a starburst appeared in space between him and the pirate.

"Good shooting, Master. You got another one!"

"Nonsense, I didn't even—*Great Merciful Heavens!*"

All around them, balls of fiery gas stood out against the starry background. The drone fleet was destroying itself! The pirate swiveled on her center of gravity, glowed savagely from her own internal fires, and streaked away.

At the extreme end of her flight line, toward the edge of the nebulosity, Lando could make out the flash as she shifted into faster-than-light. It was a deadly risk even so; they must be frightened badly.

"Well, well! Stand down from Battle Stations," he informed his mechanical partner, "I'll be up to the cockpit in a minute. Put some coffeine on, will you? And by the way, Vuffi Raa..."

He unstrapped himself from the gun-chair webbing, turning his captain's hat—the one with all the golden braid—around the right way, and zipped his shipsuit up a couple of inches.

"Yes, Master?"

"Don't call me Master!"

Stepping into the broadly curving main corridor, Lando passed the sublight-drive area of the *Millennium Falcon*. As if sprouting from the floor, there stood a tapered chromium snakelike entity, about a meter long, tending the control panel. At its slenderest end, it branched into five slim, delicate "fingers" that twisted knobs and adjusted slide-switches. In the center of the "palm," Lando knew, was a small glassy red eye-spot.

Farther along, where a cluster of instruments comprised the radar and other detection devices, another metallic serpent stood watch. There were three more like it elsewhere in the ship, giving attention to sensitive areas that could not be handled from the cockpit monitors.

Up front, Lando flopped into the left-hand seat, a pride-preserving concession tacitly made between himself and the real pilot of the vessel. *It* lay in the other seat, a pentagon-shaped slab of bright silvery-colored metal and electronics. A large lens pulsed redly at the top. The object was strapped down firmly to the seat. One of the "snakes" hovered over an instrument panel, half a meter away.

"Vuffi Raa, you've got to pull yourself together," Lando chuckled, fumbling under the panel. He brought out a slim cigar and lit it, eyeing the armless, legless contraption next to him and waiting for a reaction. Outside, the fog began to disperse as their own reaction drives brought them to the margin of the nebulosity. Was he imagining things, or was the plastic window transparency slightly pitted? More dust in the region than he'd calculated—and another expensive repair.

The snake floated downward, attached itself to one flat side of the pentagon, and waggled at the gambler. "Master, that wasn't funny the *first* hundred times you said it." Vuffi Raa began unstrapping his torso from the copilot's seat, one-tentacled.

From the passageway outside, another snake drifted in, settled in the chair, and linked itself, becoming the second of Vuffi Raa's limbs to rejoin his body. Lando looked over the ship's instrumentation, and his glow of combative satisfaction evaporated completely.

"By the Edge! Look at those power-consumption gauges! Those quad-guns are expensive to shoot! We would have used less power going the long way around!"

It was a hell of a note, Lando thought, when even defeating a band of pirates had to be calculated on the balance sheet. And at a loss.

"We'll be lucky to break even on this load, do you realize that?"

Regaining yet a third tentacle, the robot refrained diplomatically from pointing out that he'd opposed the shortcut in the first place. He hadn't known exactly why. The big, regularly scheduled companies avoided the route although it took parsecs and whole days off the run, exactly as Lando had insisted. On the other hand, big, regularly scheduled companies seldom attempted anything new or daring—which was what always made the future so bright for newer, smaller companies.

Now, between the star-fog and the pirates it concealed, both of the partners knew what was wrong with the nebulosity.

Fourth and fifth manipulators in place, Vuffi Raa cautiously punched up the interstellar drive. The stars stretched into attenuated blurs and vanished.

Yet, none of that explained what was wrong with Dilonexa XXIII.

THREE

"*Fishing poles?*"

The customs agent was a small man with wiry arms and legs, knobbly knuckles. He was dressed, like everybody else on that self-consciously agrarian planet, in bib overalls. In his case, they were made of a deep green satyn, heavily creased. His shiny pink scalp shone through a field of close-cropped gray stubble.

"You gotta be kidding, Mac! In the first place, there ain't a body of water on the planet bigger'n a bathtub; we don't like to spare the land. In the second place, nobody here has any time for fishing. An' in the third place, the native fish taste *terrible*—lacka trace metals or something."

The sun of the Dilonexa System (a catalog number

Lando didn't remember and hadn't bothered asking Vuffi Raa about as they'd made their approach) was a gigantic blue-white furnace. The twenty-two planets nearest it were great places to get a suntan. In a couple of micro-seconds.

The outer seventeen were iceboxes.

But the planet in the middle, at least in the view of its early colonists, made it all worthwhile. It was large, nearly twenty-five thousand kilometers in diameter, composed mostly of the lighter elements, which gave it a surface gravity not too unreasonable. Nearly everything of metal had to be shipped in.

But Dilonexa XXIII was rich, an agricultural world whose fields stretched unimaginable distances around its surface, providing foodstuffs, plastics, combustible fuels—everything with an organic base. Its inhabitants, fat farmers and their fatter families, had acquired a taste for some of the finer things in life.

Which was why Lando had brought his valuable, somewhat perishable cargo there.

He shook his head ruefully as he watched the Dilo-nexan ground crew put fuel elements into the *Falcon* where it rested on the ferrocrete apron—and gaping wounds in his credit account.

"Well, then, how about the jelly and the hides? Surely—"

"Had a second cousin once named Shirley," the little man explained, scratching a mole under his chin and squinting up at the cloudless sky as if in aid to memory. "Tried that wintenberry stuff you're haulin'. Broke down with the gallopin' gosharooties. Too many trace minerals for a fourth-generation colonist. We gotta watch what we eat, us Dilonexicans, that's a fact."

Lando shook his head again; it was getting to be a habit. "But look here, Inspector, I—"

"Call me Bernie. You wouldn't happen t'have a cigar on you?"

The gambler visualized the big chest of cigars in his safe aboard the *Falcon*. "Even if I did, they'd be from Rafa IV, a place just *lousy* with heavy metals. Probably kill you. What about the leather, then? I have a hold full of beautifully fur-tanned hides, and—"

The wizened customs officer interrupted Lando again, this time with an upraised hand. He pointed toward the prairie that surrounded them. Lando knew that virtually the entire globe was plains just like the scenery he saw now. He also knew that city-sized tornados swept, un-impeded, around the planet's circumference—that is, they had until gigantic weather-control satellites had been in-stalled. Their potent, tornado-destroying energy-weap-onry also made it impossible to smuggle on or off the planet—or to get away with unpaid bills.

"Whaddya see out there, Mac? A zillion acres of grain crop, that's what. We can't eat it, but the native bovines can, an' we can eat them. Lookie here! when's the last time you saw a genuine leather awning? You got it— over on that building right there. We got leather comin' out our ears. There's a sixty-five percent import duty on hides, seventy-five percent on fishin' poles an' other recreational goodies, a hundred an' five on poisonous substances like that jelly you're pushin'."

Lando groaned. First the expensive battle with the pirates, now this—plus he was out his landing fees, permits, and refueling costs.

"But say, you're Cap'n Calrissian, ain'tya, from the *Millennium Falcon*? Gotta message for you somewhere

here." He fumbled in his overall pockets until he pulled out a chip with a keyboard displayed on its face, punched numbers and letters into it.

"Right! From the Oseon, it says. That's quite a ways away, ain't it? You want it now?"

"Oh, very well," Lando answered despondently. He didn't really care. All he really wanted was a nice quiet place to lie down for a century or two.

"Okay, that'll be thirteen-fifty, Mac."

Lando blinked. So it wasn't a paid message. Odd, and thirteen and a half credits seemed a little cheap for interstellar communication, but... He pulled a few bills out of his pocket.

"You don't unnerstand, Mac. There's an import fee on interstellar messages here. We figure a fella oughta be content with what's on just one planet, an' not go sashayin' off... Anyway, that'll be thirteen *hundred* an' fifty credits."

"Forget it, then," said Lando in disgust. "It's probably just an—"

The little man grinned up at him. "There's a two-thousand-credit penalty for *not* pickin' up interstellar messages. Ain't neat t'leave 'em lyin' around."

In the comparative quiet and sanity of what passed for a lounge aboard the *Millennium Falcon*, Lando inserted the coded chip into a playback machine. An overstuffed, cheerful face materialized above the instrument.

"To Captain Lando Calrissian of the Millennium Falcon: *greetings and salutations! I am Lob Doluff, Administrator Senior of the Oseon System. You haven't heard of me, I'll wager, but, my dear boy, I have heard of you!"*

The recording continued: *"Your reputation as a player of sabacc is perhaps wider spread and more salubrious than you know. My associates and I, a small group of fanciers of the game, would like to invite you here at your convenience, to play with us. If you are interested, please name the time and stakes. Every courtesy will be extended to you during your stay with us. My very warm-est and anticipatory regards to you. Lob Doluff, signing off."*

A grin began to spread itself across Lando's face. In that context, he could cut his losses. All he needed was a small stake when he got to the Oseon. He thumbed a communicator switch.

"Vuffi Raa?"

The robot was below, out on the concrete, supervising the last of the fueling operation. *"Yes, Master?"* came his voice.

"Don't call me Master." He'd sell the fishing rods to *somebody*—there wouldn't be a scheduled import duty if there wasn't *some* market, no matter how small. Too bad no one needed tinklewood radio antennas. Not sur-prisingly, he'd learned the agricultural planet would pay top credit for the contents of his ship's waste-cycling system. "Get up here and give me a hand, will you? We've got a thousand hides to chop up and several hundred crates of jelly to put down the disposal."

He'd used his own communications equipment, once they were out of the atmosphere of Dilonexa XXIII, saving several hundred credits in the process. Doluff was delighted that Lando was on the way, and promised a high-stakes game in the most luxurious of surroundings. Lando shaved and showered, dressed himself in civilian clothing, though they were still several days' transit from the Oseon. He simply wanted to get the feeling back of doing what he was properly cut out to do. As Vuffi Raa droided the controls, Lando sat in the lounge practicing with the cards.

There were seventy-eight of these, in five suits: Sabres, Staves, Flasks, and Coins, plus the special suit of face cards with negative values. The object was to build a two- or three-card hand adding up to twenty-three, no more. What made it especially difficult was that the cards were "smart"—each was, in fact, a sophisticated electronic chip capable of changing randomly to another value, while the card it replaced changed to something else. This made for a fast-paced, nerve-wracking game combining elements of skill and fortune.

Lando thought of it as relaxing.

He held up a card, watched it blur and shift and refocus, from Commander of Staves to Three of Coins. In the surface field of a gaming table, the cards would retain their identities. This was necessary for scoring: imagine tossing down a perfect twenty-three, only to have it transmute itself into a losing hand.

Another card, the Seven of Sabres. It stayed its old familiar self for rather a longish time, finally changed into Endurance, one of the negative cards. Lando shuffled it back into the deck.

The Oseon, he thought: I should know a great deal more about it and its people. Principally, what the traffic will bear. He turned from the cards to a datalink, punched a few buttons. There it was: oh, yes! While it might be remarkable for its rich inhabitants, it was downright famous for its seasonally spectacular scenery.

Oseon was the home of the Flamewind.

Many stellar systems have asteroid belts, where whole

planets have come unglued or never quite managed to coalesce. Circular zones occupied by rocks rather than worlds, their constituents could range in size from sand grains to objects hundreds—even thousands—of kilometers in extent. Some few systems had more than one such belt.

The Oseon had nothing else.

In the Oseon there were no planets at all in the proper sense of the word. Not even the Core knew what disaster had taken place there, perhaps billions of years before the advent of humankind. Maybe a rogue star had passed too close, its gravity well disrupting the planet-forming process. Maybe some unique element in the makeup of the system had caused the planets to blow themselves up.

Perhaps there had been an ancient, alien war.

Whatever the cause, the Oseon sun was now surrounded by seven broad bands of floating debris, billions upon billions of subplanetary bodies. The largest of these worldlets, Oseon 6845, was an artificially honeycombed mountain seven hundred kilometers in diameter, filled with luxury hotels, nightspots, and palatial residences. Other rocks in other belts had been converted into estates for the rich and superrich. There was plenty of room.

All of this, while quite extraordinary, was not in itself sufficient to turn the place into a five-star tourist attraction. But once a year (by what reckoning Lando forgot even as he read it), the Oseon System's sun flared in a peculiar manner (giving rise to the theory about a unique element blowing up the planets). As the flares tore streamers of excited vapor from the nearest of the asteroids, the entire system fluoresced, pulsed, resonated, generating enormous bands of shifting color, fairy brilliance, millions of kilometers long and wide, like the spokes of an enormous wheel. Colors ranged across the humanly visible spectrum, exceeding it broadly at both ends.

There was, very possibly, nothing else quite so impressively beautiful in the known universe as the Flamewind of Oseon.

Lando did a rapid calculation: yes, if his luck ran well for long enough, he and Vuffi Raa would be there at the right time. Perhaps that had been intended by Lob Doluff as an incentive of sorts. How nice: a kind of bonus they could both—

KABLOMMMMM!

The *Millennium Falcon* pitched end over end with sudden violence.

Through the ports, stars whirled crazily about them in a meaningless pattern. Alarms went off, filling the cabin with an ear-splitting wail. Smoke began seeping into the room as random bits and pieces—Lando's cards, his cigars, an old pair of socks—clung in odd, unpredictable places, responding to the primitive artificial gravity imposed on the ship by its wild head-over-heels spin.

"Vuffi Raa!"

Grasping the nearest bolted-down furniture, Lando shouted at the intercom. "What in the name of the Eternal was that?"

There was no response.

Pulling himself hand over hand against the nonsensically vectored drag, Lando made slow, unsteady progress to the bridge. Klaxons beat upon his head, their noise a tangible thing. The final turn of corridor was like crawling up a vertical sewer pipe, each rung of the emergency ladder coming with greater difficulty as he climbed above the ship's new center of gravity.

Once in the cockpit, he climbed exhaustedly into his

seat and strapped himself in, trying without much success to catch his breath.

Rendered virtually invisible by their speed, Vuffi Raa's tentacles were flying over the controls. It must be some emergency, thought Lando, if even the multitalented robot was too busy now to talk. To the continued tune of shrilling alarms, Lando began assisting him, newly acquired knowledge coming sure and true to his fingertips. First, they stabilized the ship's insane changes of attitude. Up became up once again, down, down.

Next, they located the source of the explosion. It was in the bottommost level of the *Falcon*, seemingly just under the belly skin. They triggered cannisters of firefoam, then jettisoned the resultant mess into open space. Temperature indicators relaxed, a few red lights winked to green. The alarms shut off; a deafening silence reigned.

Finally, Vuffi Raa laid the proper course back in, and they were on their way to the Oseon once again, although at something less than normal interstellar cruising speed.

"How bad is the damage?" Lando was already unstrapping himself. He wiped a shaking hand over his dampened forehead.

Vuffi Raa looked over the control panel, several sections of which were still ablaze with red and yellow lights. "It would appear, Master, to be superficial. The difficulty began when I shifted into faster-than-light drive. We shall have to inspect it close up, however. I don't trust the remote sensors."

"Very well," the gambler answered, "let's get below. I'll put on a pressure suit and—"

"Master, it is standard procedure in such instances for one crew member to remain at the controls, while the other—"

"All right, then," Lando said, a trifle irritated, "*you* stay here. I'll suit up and—"

"Master, I can operate perfectly well in a hard vacuum without a suit. Explosive decompression doesn't bother me. And I know how to weld. Do you?"

The little droid, of course, showed no expression, but Lando felt as if there were a pair of human arms somewhere inside his shiny chassis, folded across an imaginary chest, beneath an unbearably smug grimace.

"Have it your own way, then! I'll *still* suit up. It seems a sensible safety precaution, just in case you open the wrong door somewhere. Keep me informed, will you— *and don't call me Master!*"

Vuffi Raa unstrapped himself from the copilot's seat, rose, and strode to the back of the control area. "I'll do better than keep you informed, Master. Observe that monitor nearest your left elbow."

Swiveling his neck, Lando was suddenly seeing himself, quite plainly if somewhat distortedly, as if by a wide-angle lens held too close to its subject. The colors seemed a bit off, and the gambler realized he was seeing a translation of infrared and ultraviolet information in addition to the usual spectrum.

"I get it: I see what you see. You know, this could come in very handy: like, say, the next time I'm in a game, and—"

"But Master, that would be unethical!"

"Wouldn't it just? All right, we'll talk about it later. Meanwhile, let's get to work on the damage."

They both shuffled out of the cockpit, headed toward separate destinations.

Ten minutes later, Lando was again seated in his pilot's recliner, watching the monitor through the transparent faceplate of a spacesuit helmet. He thought about opening the visor to smoke a cigar, remembered the magic words "explosive decompression," and desisted. After all, they didn't know yet how badly hurt the *Falcon* was. A footfall, no matter how light, in the wrong place might blow a hull panel, which—

On the screen, Vuffi Raa had made it to the site of the explosion. His viewpoint approached a heavily damaged piece of machinery.

"Why, that's just one of the hydraulic jacks for the boarding ramp," Lando exclaimed, almost indignantly. "There's nothing flammable or explosive in that section—and what does it have to do at all with the ultralightspeed drive?"

The camera angle tilted downward. A tentacle reached for something wedged between two heavy springs. The object had to be sawed and twisted out of its place, then the tentacle lifted it nearer the robot's eye.

"What the devil is *that*?" Lando asked the intercom.

The thing looked like a spring itself, a section of thick-gauge wire coiled and then twisted around into an evasively familiar shape, rather like a doughnut, but with an extra turn, pretzel-wise.

"It's a Möbius coil of some kind, Master," Vuffi Raa answered at last, "They're used as tuners and—my word, it's an *antenna*. Master, someone placed a device here to detect the shift into ultralightspeed. You see, there's a hyperwave generated by the—"

"Yes, yes," Lando interrupted impatiently. "But what's the point of all that?"

"There would be a considerable point, Master, if the antenna was connected to a controller that, in turn, was connected to a bomb."

The gambler pondered that. "You mean, someone just walked up and attached it back on Dilonexa, while we were refueling, and when we buttoned up for takeoff, we effectively brought it inside the ship ourselves?"

"Something like that, Master."

"A bomb. Do you suppose they found out about the wintenberry jelly?"

FOUR

DEEP SPACE.

The officially decommissioned Imperial Cruiser *Wennis* bored through the blackness like a thing alive, a hungry thing, a thing with the need to kill. It had been built for that, nearly three-quarters of a century ago. Now it was an obsolete machine, displaced by more efficient killers.

Still, it served its purpose.

On the bridge, a uniformed crew quietly attended to their duties. They were a mixed lot, officially—again, *officially*—civilians. Many were the worst of the worst, the scum and misfits of a million-system civilization. Others were the best that could be had, the cream of the elite.

Like the *Wennis*, this, too, served a purpose.

All were military personnel, now indefinitely detached to serve aboard the decommissioned cruiser. In this, they served their Emperor (although not without an occasional—extremely discreet—grumble) and hoped for early promotion and other rewards.

In practicality, all served an entity who, although somewhat less elevated than His Imperial Majesty, was nevertheless quite as frighteningly impressive. This figure stalked the bridge as well, draped from crown to heel in the heavy dark swathings people had come to associate with the mysterious and sinister Sorcerers of Tund.

Rokur Gepta, all features save his burning eyes concealed behind the final windings of his turbanlike headgear, barely suppressed a scream.

"Do you have the temerity to tell me you have failed again?"

The officer he addressed was not happy with his present assignment. In the first place, his uniform had been stripped of all rank and unit markings. It made him feel naked. In the second place, he could not understand why a battle-ready cruiser and its full crew were pursuing a single tiny tramp freighter.

The officer gulped. "I only mean to say, sir, that the device our agent planted seems to have gone off prematurely. It was supposed to explode, on your orders, just before atmospheric entry at their next port of call."

"So you have failed twice! You idiot, they're en route to the Oseon—there will *be* no atmospheric entry! I have had enough of this!"

The sorcerer made a gesture with his gloved fist. The officer groaned, sweat sprang out on his forehead, and he sank to his knees.

"You see how much more effective it is than mere pain, don't you? Everyone has memories, little items

from their past best left buried: humiliations, embarrass-
ments, mistakes . . . sometimes fatal ones. All the ways
we have failed those we have loved, the ways they have
failed us!"

Gepta made another gesture.

"No, you can think of nothing else! The ignobility
races round and round your mind, amplified, feeding on
itself!"

The officer's face went gray, he swayed on his knees,
his back bowed, his clenched fists began dripping blood
where the fingernails cut into the palms. A little froth
appeared at one corner of his mouth, followed by more
blood as he gnashed at his lips and tongue. Finally, he
lost all control, collapsed in a heap and lay there, twitch-
ing, moaning.

Gepta released him.

A pair of orderlies appeared, dragged the broken man
from the bridge. Oddly enough, he was far from destroyed. Gepta had noticed, in the past, a certain increase
in efficiency, perhaps even slightly enhanced intelligence
after one of these crises. So why not make a good tool
better? The tool was not in any position to complain of
the stresses involved, Did it hurt a knife to grind it to
razor sharpness? Who cared?

Slightly invigorated himself, the sorcerer turned, strode
back to the control chair he usually occupied on the bridge.
He was not captain of the *Wennis*, but he liked to stay
on top of things.

He sat. Beside the chair was a pair of cages, each
perhaps half a meter cubed. In the first, he kept his pet.

It was scarcely visible in its bed of gray-green muck,
simply three stalky black legs thrusting upward crook-
edly, curving inward with a certain hungry, greedy en-

ergy perhaps only Gepta could see and sympathize with. The legs were sparsely hairy.

In the second cage, Gepta kept another type of creature. There were half a dozen of the things; soon he'd need a new supply. They were about the size of mice, very like mice, in fact, but with curly golden pelts and impossibly large blue eyes. Each creature was sleek and clean, seemed to radiate warmth. Each had a bushy tail, rather like that of a miniature squirrel.

Suppressing a shudder, Gepta reached into the cage of the furry creatures. Using a large pair of plastic tongs, he seized one—it squeaked with surprise and pain—and transferred it from its cage. He opened the top of the other cage, dropped it into the center of the upraised hairy legs.

There was a squelch!, another terrified squeak, which was cut off sharply, then a crunch! Gepta let the lid drop, a warm glow inside him as his pet preened itself, one dark, many-jointed leg grooming another until all three were clean of the blood and fur of its meal.

It did him good to imagine that the small, furry, helpless creature he had just destroyed was Lando Calrissian. It did him a great deal of good. Others had attempted to interfere with Gepta's plans before. Only one had managed to survive. Why, of all people, this insignificant vagabond, this itinerant gambler and charlatan should so frequently come between the sorcerer and his plans was a mystery. Yet it had happened.

Very few individuals understood how much—and how little—the Sorcerers of Tund believed in magic. Even fewer were those who lived to pass the knowledge on to others. Calling up the *Wennis*'s captain's ugly memories, for example, amplifying them, driving out everything else—there was nothing to it, nothing that couldn't be done by anyone, given the proper electronics.

Yet those of Tund had their own beliefs about things that transcended science, and Rokur Gepta was a superstitious soul. He believed that some perverse kind of luck, some fate, karma, kismet, or destiny kept throwing Calrissian in his face. Sometimes it appeared the young gambler wasn't even aware that it was happening.

Now the sorcerer would have an end to it.

He pressed a button set in the arm of his chair. An officer materialized, one a little younger than the captain.

"You are the second in command?" Gepta hissed.

The officer saluted uncertainly. He'd seen his superior dragged from the bridge. "Y-yes . . . yes, sir, I am. I, er . . . shall we maintain our course for the Oseon, sir?"

Rokur Gepta waited a while to reply, knowing that the prolonged silence would further ravel the young officer's nerves. In a military hierarchy there was *always* something to feel guilty about. It was designed that way, so that an individual couldn't go through a single day without having to stretch, bend, or break a rule. This, of course, worked to the advantage of those at the top of the pyramid.

Just as it was working now.

When a fine sweat sprinkled the officer's brow, Gepta finally spoke.

"No, no. We shall digress for a short time. I'll give you the heading. Your captain will be indisposed for several hours, and I want to be well on my way by the time of his . . . recovery."

Many parsecs away, in space equally as deep as that which enveloped the cruiser *Wennis*, a strange apparition manifested itself.

At its center lay the naked core of a dreadnaught-class ultralightspeed drive engine, pulsing, glowing, seeming to writhe with unholy energies as it twisted space around itself to deny the basic laws of reality. A closer examination would have disclosed that it was old, very old, patched and welded together out of many such drive engines, long past obsolescence, verging on dangerous fatigue.

Surrounding it were at least two dozen equally weary and obsolete fighters of nearly as many separate pedigrees, some constructed by inhuman races and sloppily converted. They were connected to the drive core with gleaming cables that glowed and sparked and writhed in time to its fundamental frequency. The fighters appeared to be towing the engine. In fact, the reverse was true. These small craft were incapable of making the translation to faster-than-light velocities themselves. They let the core field do it for them.

Militia Leader Klyn Shanga sat before the controls of his aged spacecraft, his eyes unseeing, his mind turned inward. It had been thus for over eleven days—this was the most excruciatingly dull voyage he had ever endured. Yet it was necessary: honor demanded it.

Though alive with lights, his controls were, for practical purposes, inert, locked into the controls of all the other fighters, each of them in turn slaved to a cobbled-together navigational computer on the drive engine.

There was nothing to do, and all the time in the universe to do it.

He had long since stopped thinking of his home, a little-known backwater planet, settled long generations before the present wave of Imperial colonization—settled even before the Old Republic had sent its own explorers outward. He had long since ceased thinking about his family. There was little point: it was highly unlikely he would ever see them again.

He had devoted even less time to thinking about his present task, the mission of this motley group of militiamen, retired policemen, adventurers, and professional soldiers as ancient and obsolete as the craft they flew. They were their culture's expendables. The task was simple and straightforward: find someone and kill him. It didn't matter that their target, their enemy, had damaged their civilization severely, exposed it to a galaxy-wide culture more potent and wealthy, stripping away its hidden safety. It mattered less that the life they sought to take was the very embodiment of evil. Evil or not, it would pass out of existence if they did their work right.

If they didn't, their fates were academic. Evil abounded in the universe, and one life more or less wouldn't make much difference. The damage was done; this was for revenge, pure and simple—and perhaps to protect other helpless, defenseless worlds.

Klyn Shanga glanced through the canopy of his fighter at the rest of the group clustered around the battleship engine. All together, they looked laughable—the same way, no doubt, their world had looked to the intruder. They resembled nothing more than a grotesque, dessicated plant, an interstellar tumbleweed being blown wherever the fates would have it. Shanga tried to take comfort in the notion that nothing could be further from the truth, that they were a spare and deadly force who would take their adversary completely by surprise.

At that moment, his communications console sprang into life.

There were no greetings, no salutations. The beam was tight, intended only for the cluster of fighters. It boomed and faded with the galactic drift.

On the screen, a young military figure was visible, his gray uniform unadorned by rank or unit markings. Shanga knew him to be the second officer of the decommissioned Imperial Cruiser *Wennis*.

The figure did not speak, but only nodded.

Keying his transmitter, Shanga asked, "He is on his way, then?"

The figure nodded again, but hatred and fear burned in his eyes, just as it burned in the heart of Klyn Shanga and all his men.

"He will be there when we arrive?" asked Shanga.

For the first time, the officer spoke. "There is the possibility of some delay—of a detour, apparently—but I believe the original course will be resumed in a short time."

Klyn Shanga rubbed his calloused hands together. In the many decades since his world's last war, he had been a farmer, living peaceably and contentedly among animals and plants and children. Now that could be no more, because of the person they were discussing. He knew his men were listening to the confirmation that the prey was at last near to hand. They had come a long, long way to hear that news.

"You take considerable risk," Shanga said, some sympathy seeping into his weathered expression.

"It is unnecessary to discuss that. It is well worth it. I must signal off; the chance of detection grows by the second."

Shanga nodded. "Be well, then, and good luck."

"The same to you."

Many parsecs away, an impatient Rokur Gepta closed a switch and sat back, to ponder. His first, most immediate inclination was to choke the life—better yet, the sanity—from the young pup who was betraying him. Not for the first time was he grateful to himself for having installed the secondary system of surveillance devices in the personal quarters of his underlings. The second officer had easily fooled the official bugs.

Well, Gepta would have his revenge at the appropriate

time. Now it was important to let this complication re-solve itself. He did not recognize the individual with whom the officer had spoken, but then Gepta was very old, so old that the truth would have frightened most ordinary beings. He had seen and done a lot in the many centuries he had lived. He had made many enemies, most of them now long dead.

So should it always be.

One thing he could do: hasten the process. He shelved his earlier plans; they had had a certain hesitancy to them anyway. He keyed a switch on the table beside the bed in his living quarters.

"Bridge? Gepta. Cancel previous orders. Reinstate the course I previously gave you. We will proceed directly to the Oseon."

FIVE

LOB DOLUFF WAS A PEAR-SHAPED MAN WHO LOOKED larger on the televisor than he was in fact. He had what Lando found himself thinking of as a skin-tight dark beard and a naked scalp that looked as though it had been waxed and polished.

His manner was ingratiating, he was an enthusiastic *sabacc* player, and a good loser. This was something of a necessity, it appeared, since enthusiasm and skill do not always go together.

Sitting across the table from Lando, Doluff managed to hold his cards up while resting his elbows on his protuberant stomach. Fate had presented him with a Six of Flasks and a Mistress of Staves on the initial deal, yielding a value of nineteen. Courage and enthusiasm do not always go together, either. He stood pat, somehow failing to take into account the fact that the longer he held the cards, the likelier it was they would alter themselves before his very eyes.

Lando, with a Seven of Coins and the negative card, Demise, needed something better than minus six to win this hand. He dealt himself an Ace of Sabres, bringing the score to nine—still insufficient. The next player also took a card; the Administrator Senior had already decided to refuse; the player to his left took a card; the one to Lando's right stood pat.

Lando dealt himself another card, the betting proceeding with each turn around the table. They had anted at a thousand credits that night, Lando's fourth in the Oseon, and after three rounds of betting, an impressive amount of money lay on the table.

Mistress of Coins. Lando was one point short of a pure *sabacc*. He held his peace. The cards seemed slow tonight, reluctant to perform their transmutations. He could feel his luck glowing warm within him. He was relaxed.

The player to his left took a card. The Administrator Senior still stood pat. The next player took a card—and immediately slammed her hand down on the table.

"Zero!" she grumbled in disgust. There were three ways of going out in the game: exceeding twenty-three, falling below minus twenty-three, or hitting zero. The player to Lando's right stood pat.

A flicker of movement in his hand caught Lando's eye. One of the cards was changing.

"*Sabacc!*" he said with satisfaction. Demise had made itself into Moderation. The odds against such consecutivity were high, and so was the value of the pot the young gambler raked in.

The others tossed their cards on the table. The deal would stay with Lando for another hand.

Shuffling the cards, he considered those playing with him. There was, of course, Lob Doluff, too conservative a player to make any real gains—no threat, but a reliable source of income. He should stick with managing a bureaucracy. He wasn't cut out to be a gambler.

That night they were at Doluff's estate. The game shifted to a new place each night it was played. A few kilometers outside what passed for a city, it was a rather large dome on the surface, filled with moist air and tropical plants. The cold stars rose clearer and sharper than they had any natural right to do above the thick jungle that surrounded the players.

The table had been placed on a broad, tiled walkway in the very center of the giant decorative greenhouse. A fountain burbled agreeably nearby. It was practically the only noise: the Administrator Senior had not seen fit to populate his garden with animals. From time to time, a mechanical servant would emerge from between the heavy plantings to offer the players a drink. Lando stuck with *snillik*, a thick liqueur from somewhere near the galactic Center, one he actively detested and therefore drank slowly and judiciously.

Having shuffled the deck a fifth and final time, he offered it to the player on his right for a cut. That worthy accepted, divided the deck into three stacks, and reassembled it in a different order. Lando kept an eye on him; he had the look of yet another professional, although he'd claimed to be a retired businessman. Perhaps he was both.

Approximately of middle age, Del Cycer was extraordinarily tall for a human being, well over two meters. He was also extraordinarily thin. He was dressed in a bright green caftan and wore a great many rings on his fingers.

"You have been recently to the Rafa, I heard it said,

Captain Calrissian. Is it true they've found the legendary lost civilization that was supposed to be there?" Cycer's tone was conversational, friendly, interested.

Lando reclaimed the cards, dealt them around the table in a practiced, leisurely manner.

"It might be more accurate to say the lost civilization found *us*. I was there when it happened. The ancient Sharu are back and setting up in business."

"How dweadfuw!" the creature to Lando's left responded. It was something nasty looking, with a small trunk dangling beneath its bloodshot eyes. Even more unfortunate, its blood was green. The veins clashed with the deep blue of the irises. "Does that mean theah won't be any mowe wife-cwystals?"

The creature had a large Rafa orchard-crystal pendant from a chain around its thick, wrinkled neck. It wasn't the only one here to sport the expensive gems. Lando had learned that they collected a sort of ambient life force given off by all living things, collected and refocused it on the wearer. He shunned them himself; they made him feel like a vampire.

"No", he answered, handing the creature its second card. "I think the new management will eventually start shipping them again. Probably at substantially higher prices."

Lob Doluff took his second card without comment. It was obvious to Lando that he had a winning hand—and that he'd manage to lose the advantage somehow before the play was over with.

The player to the Administrator Senior's left was a female human being, younger than Lando, blond and not unattractive. She had been introduced to him as Bassi Vobah, and some vague reference made to her being an administrative officer. The young gambler wondered where she got her money. He was unimpressed with her playing so far, and more than a little bothered by the fact that she seemed to be watching him closely.

And not in a friendly way.

He handed her a card, dealt to Del Cycer and himself, then, without looking at his cards, took a tiny sip of *snillik*. "Cards?" he inquired.

The trunk-being nodded, its proboscis flopping obscenely, then threw all three down in disgust. "Thirty-seven!" it exclaimed. "Amazing!"

Lob Doluff stood pat.

Bassi Vobah took another card, said nothing.

Del Cycer accepted a card, laid his hand down gently. "Out, confound it."

"Anybody again?" Lando asked. Bassi Vobah responded, took the card, stared grimly at her hand. This time the centerpiece was not as rich. Lando finally looked at his cards: Nines, of Flasks and Staves. "Dealer takes one."

Sweat began forming on Lob Doluff's shiny pate, his fingers seemed to tremble a little. Finally, in an explosive gesture, he threw his cards on the table, face up. "Twenty-two! Can you beat that?"

Lando glanced at Bassi Vobah.

"Fourteen," she said. "Forget it."

With the Four of Sabres Lando had drawn, he, too, had twenty-two. He displayed the hand, picked up the deck to deal again. "Sudden Demise."

Doluff received the Three of Staves, breaking his hand. Lando could have stopped there, but flipped the next card over. The Idiot, worth exactly zero. The pot was his again.

"Let's take a break."

Since it was his winning streak, he could recommend a rest without engendering resentment. That was easy: he didn't believe in winning streaks, and wasn't afraid of interrupting them. He did need to consider, though, whether to begin losing a few hands deliberately. His livelihood, well-being, ultimately his survival depended on maintaining goodwill—which meant losing on the small bets and winning quietly on the big ones. He'd believed such a ploy to be unnecessary in a rich-man's playground, but was discovering that it wasn't any different from playing in a hard-rock miner's bar. Psychology, human and otherwise, remained the same.

He'd made enemies in the past.

"Five minutes to breakout, Master."

Once again, Lando sat in the lounge of the *Millennium Falcon*, riffling through the cards and thinking odd-shaped thoughts to himself. He and Vuffi Raa had repaired the damage to the ship as best they could. Luckily they carried a good many replacement parts in stores, and the boarding ramp seemed to be something that needed fairly constant upkeep in any event. Moving parts.

Then, they'd gone over the interior of the *Falcon* centimeter by centimeter, being the untrusting types that they were, looking for additional sabotage. They had found nothing. Vuffi Raa had wanted to climb outside and check the hull, but had been severely vetoed: the fields around a ship in ultralightspeed drive were not only physically dangerous, but the distortions of reality they created could drive even a droid insane. Besides, he'd studied the manuals enough to know that the defense shields flowed along the surface of the ship, in the first few molecules of her skin. A bomb attached outside could only do less than minimal damage.

They'd take their chances. He wasn't a gambler for nothing, and he had a friend's concern for the continued health of his mechanical sidekick.

He realized suddenly that he hadn't replied to the intercom.

"All right, old can-opener, I'll be up in a moment."

This was to be Lando's first planetary landing under the tutelage of the talented robot. His previous attempts, before he'd acquired Vuffi Raa, had been fiascoes. Perhaps setting down on the surface ("*next* to the surface" might be a more accurate description) of an asteroid wasn't a very spectacular exercise, but he needed the practice.

This time he'd made it to the cockpit *before* the explosion occurred.

Afterward, they spent some time untangling arms and legs from tentacles. Lando hadn't had the time to strap in, and Vuffi Raa had momentarily unstrapped himself to check a gauge at the rear of the control deck. They both wound up between the pilot's seats, stuffed under the control panels.

The *Millennium Falcon* turned lazily, end over end.

"Master, I hate to point this out, but that explosion was on the *outside* of the ship, in the outboard phase-shift adaptor."

Lando studied the boards, while rubbing several bruises. "Yes, but I think it may have been spontaneous. Look at the readings on the phase-shift controls—they aren't very far away from where that bomb went off the other day, are they?"

It was the droid's turn to ponder. "I believe you are right. Nonetheless, had we been making a genuine planetary reentry, into a full atmosphere and full gravity, this accident would have destroyed us, Master. Observe the remote cameras: the cowling's been torn and lifted. It would have ablated away, leaving us with—"

"Uh, I think that will do, my friend. I can well imagine us tumbling and burning out of control. How long to fix it?"

"Not more than a few hours, nor will it interfere with our landing now."

Lando dealt the cards again, not quite as honestly as before.

Of course it had turned out to be a second bomb. Whoever had planted it apparently hadn't known their ultimate destination was to be an airless worldlet too small to suck them in and burn them up. Vuffi Raa had found part of the control module, like that in the first bomb, a device built to detect a change in their velocity relative to the speed of light. This one had been set to go off when they dropped below lightspeed.

Somebody really meant to kill him.

He tried to remember all the really big coups he had made at the gaming table. Had he unknowingly pushed someone with enough resources and anger to carry out a vendetta? Well, it appeared that caution might be in order, now. And a little sleight of hand.

He dealt the trunk-creature a Two of Staves, Lob Doluff a Ten of Staves, Bassi Vobah the Queen of Air and Darkness, valued at a minus two. Cycer got a Master of Coins; the young gambler dealt himself a Commander of Coins.

Going around a second time, he handed the alien the Star, a negative card worth seventeen; Doluff took a Nine of Sabres; Bassi Vobah got a second negative, the Evil One, which brought her count to minus-seventeen. He dealt to Cycer and had scarcely given himself the Nine of Coins for a respectable but unspectacular twenty-one, when the tall, thin retiree shouted *Sabacc!* excitedly and slapped his original Master on the table, along with the Nine of Staves.

Lando breathed a secret sign of relief and passed the deck over to Cycer for the deal. Sometimes winning included knowing when to lose.

Cycer had the deal for exactly one hand, which Doluff, barely able to contain himself, won. Then the deal passed to the trunk-thing (Lando was beginning to feel a little guilty about not remembering the creature's name—which was humanly unpronounceable in any case), where it stayed for two hands, then back to Del Cycer.

Bassi Vobah didn't seem to be having much luck.

Cycer was dealing the cards when a small spherical droid rolled up beside Lob Doluff and whistled imperatively, then split into a pair of hemispheres.

Doluff looked up from the screen and keyboard thus revealed, all color drained from his face.

"Captain Calrissian, I believe you'd better hurry to the spaceport. I have a message here that your ship, the *Millennium Falcon*, is on fire."

SIX

THE ASTEROID OSEON 6845 HAD BEEN ARTIFICIALLY AC-
celerated to complete a rotation every twenty-five hours,
giving its inhabitants a comforting sense of day and
night—and those whose task it was to land spaceships
there a severe headache. Touching down upon a surface
moving at eighty-eight kilometers an hour in the tight
and tiny circle that was the planetoid's circumference
doesn't seem a difficult job until one tries it.

Consequently, from the Administrator Senior's equa-
torial garden home, Lando took a pneumatic tubeway to
the north pole of Oseon 6845. There a small and relatively
stationary spaceport had been leveled out of the barren
rock.

Unfortunately, the tube car had no communicator of

its own, nor did Lando make a habit of carrying one. Momentarily, he regretted it: he could learn no more in transit about the fate of the *Millennium Falcon*. All he had with him was the forty-seven-odd thousand credits he'd acquired that evening, and a tiny, unobtrusive five-shot stingbeam pistol tucked into his velvoid cummerbund.

It was all the personal weapon he allowed himself in a dark and perilous universe; he preferred to rely on his brains for the heavy firepower.

The tubeway shot him northward through a chord beneath the curvature of the asteroid's surface at several thousand kilometers an hour. Lando fidgeted every second, every centimeter. He'd sent Vuffi Raa to the space terminal to continue repairs on the *Falcon*. And to keep a big red glassy eye on her.

What had gone wrong?

The little robot was a pacifist by nature, it was ineradicably programmed into him. Could some saboteur have taken advantage of this handicap, overpowered him, and set fire to the ship?

With a plastic-gasketed wheeze, the tubeway lurched to a halt. Its transparent doors opened to let Lando out into a maze of service corridors underneath the landing field. He ran down seemingly endless crossing and countercrossing passageways until he reached one numbered 17-W. A temporary holosign in a bracket on the wall displayed in six languages the legend:

MILLENNIUM FALCON

LANDO CALRISSIAN, CAPT. & PROP.

Overhead, a large circular pressure door hung open, connected by a short, accordion-pleated tube to the underside of the *Falcon*. A metal ladder led upward through it. Oddly, there was no one else about in the harshly lit cylinder of the service corridor. The only sounds Lando could hear were those of small mechanical things going about their business.

Shaking his head, Lando climbed the ladder.

He emerged in the curving companionway of the *Falcon*, the somewhat dimmer light and familiar clutter something of a comfort after the stark, brightly lit port corridor. Everything was perfectly quiet. He stalked along the passage until he came to the first intertalkie panel he found set in a bulkhead.

Nervously, he pressed a button. "Vuffi Raa?"

"Yes, Master?" a cheerful voice replied. *"I'm out on the hull, finishing up with the phase-shift adaptor."*

"Oh. Well, I'm aboard, very confused. You didn't happen to have a fire here tonight, did you?"

"Master? Why, no, aside from some welding—and that was vacuum-synergetic, no open flame of any kind. Why do you ask?"

Suspicions of several and various distinct flavors began to fill Lando's mind. "Er, this may sound silly, but how do I know it's really *you* I'm talking to?"

"Master, what's wrong? Of course it is really I. Please come to the starboard gun-blister and I'll show you."

That could be an altogether different kind of invitation than it sounded. Lando drew his stingbeam, every nerve on edge. He crept into the short tunnel leading to the gun-blister, his back tight against the low, curving wall, and slid sideways until he could see out past the quad-guns through the hemispheric plastic.

Outside, the Oseon sun shone garishly on a stark and rocky scene.

The spaceport had begun as a huge natural crater many kilometers in diameter. The *Falcon* sat in its approximate center. Here and there a ship lay, positioned over its own assigned service hatchway. Pleasure yachts, company vessels, those of traders, distributors, and caterers. Halfway across the crater to the rim, Lando could make out the impressive bulk of an elderly but well-maintained battle cruiser. Well, everyone to his own taste. Stars beat feebly downward, making a miniscule contribution to the solar brilliance.

A flicker of movement at the corner of his eye sent Lando into a tense crouch, both hands wrapped professionally around the small grip of his pocketgun, its muzzle seeking, sniffing after something to bite.

A chromium tentacle rasped across the plastic before him. Lando found himself staring into Vuffi Raa's eye as the robot swung down in front of the blister and hung on one manipulator.

The gambler punched the intercom button beside the gun chair.

"Sorry, old boltcutter, I'm a touch paranoid tonight. Some thoughtful individual interrupted my game—and quite a profitable one, I might add—with a fire alarm. Anything at all exciting happening at your end of the planet?"

Through the plastic, the droid gave as much shrug as it was capable of. *"I've simply been tidying up here, Master. There have been no communications, visitors, nor have I so much as seen anybody within a hundred meters of the ship except a few of the spaceport automata. Shall I come in and—"*

"Don't trouble yourself. Perhaps I still have time to return to my game."

The robot waggled a free tentacle in farewell. *"Very good, Master, I'll see you at the hotel."*

"Good night, Vuffi Raa."

The light flickered momentarily, as if a ship had flown between the *Falcon* and the sun.

Out of the blister and around the passageway, Lando went directly to the hatch he'd entered through. He clambered down the ladder, more careful this time not to get his semiformals greasy. On the next-to-last rung, he heard the sharp grit of a footstep behind him, twisted to see who it—

CRUMMMP!

Something hard and traveling fast smashed savagely across his lower back. Grunting with shock and pain, he released his hold on the ladder, fell rapidly in the artificial gradient, scraping his face on the ladder.

A second swipe missed him, zipping over his head to clang noisily on the metal rungs.

Hitting the floor with a gasp, Lando rolled over in desperate haste, clawing at his middle. A pair of dirty boots tromped toward him. They were all he had time to see before something came swooshing downward toward his head.

He fired the stingbeam upward.

There was a high-pitched piercing whistle from the weapon, a high-pitched scream of agony from the target. The club—whatever it was—clattered noisily to the surface. Lando's adversary fell backward, the chest area of his jacket bursting into flame. Smoke and the nauseating stench of flaming synthetic fabric began to fill the corridor.

Lando rose stiffly, millimeter by tortured millimeter, pulling on the rungs of the ladder. There were tears in his eyes from smoke and pain. Leaning hard against the ladder, he reached around behind himself, felt his back where he'd been struck. His life had probably been saved by the forty-seven thousand credits distributed in his compartmented cummerbund.

Stingbeam hanging limply along his thigh, he staggered over to see who had attacked him. The figure lay still, the brief-lived flames—accidental byproduct of a close-range discharge—had died.

So had the assailant.

A soldier of some kind. That's how he appeared to Lando. The gambler tugged a soft leather helmet off the fellow's unresisting head, the kind of headgear customarily worn under the larger bubble of a spacesuit during extended periods in hard vacuum. The club, a two-meter section of titanium pipe, was the only weapon visible, although Lando detected wear across the dead man's trousers where a gunbelt had abraded the fabric.

The uniform, if that's what it was (hard to tell with only one of the things around) was patched and faded, many times mended. It seemed to match the wearer's condition. He was a large man, gray and weathered, his face deeply furrowed with age. Lando didn't recognize the insignia. In a million-system civilization, chances were he wouldn't.

What to do now?

In the big cities of many a civilized planet, one was far wiser, having disposed of a mugger or burglar, simply to pass on, leaving a small mystery behind for the authorities. Such was Lando's inclination. They were accustomed to it, as they had every right to be. They were the ones who had made the act of self-defense a worse offense than the crime that had provoked it.

In the Oseon, would that be the case? Lando didn't know. He couldn't very well afford simply to walk away. A dead body, at the docking entrance of his ship, plenty of other physical evidence scattered around, and a partially discharged energy-weapon in his hand. Embarrassing, to say the least.

Well, down the corridor there was a public communicator.

He climbed back up the ladder.

Vuffi Raa, back now from the hull, met him at the top of the ladder. In the dimly lit corridor, his eye glowed like the coal of a cigar.

"Master, what is going on? I heard shouting, and—"

"I've just killed a man, old thing. Be a good sort and com Lob Doluff. We may have a bit of pull in this system; I suspect we're going to need it." He sat down suddenly on the decking, leaned against the wall, and collapsed, sliding over sideways.

It wasn't bad, as jails go.

The life of a gambler was somewhat checkered. Often people took offense when they lost money. Sometimes they were in a position to do something about it *outside* the rules of whatever game they'd lost money at.

The suite was semitastefully decorated in cheery plastic colors that did not quite make up for the colorless music drifting blandly from a speaker in the ceiling. A separate bathroom offered modest privacy—as long as one overlooked the large mirror over the sink that was undoubtedly a window from another point of view. There was a genuine skylight, heavily barred and shielded, that served to reduce claustrophobia and gave a fine, undistorted picture of the stars overhead. There had even been a band of plastic around one of the ceramic facilities stating that it had been sanitized for Lando's protection.

Somehow, he couldn't quite summon up the appropriate gratitude.

His injuries had been properly attended to. They weren't many: a couple of cracked (or at least severely bent) ribs, some abrasions. The tape was supposed to fall off of its own accord sometime in the next fifty hours.

They'd confiscated his clothing and personal papers, his cummerbund with the forty-seven thousand credits, and, of course, his stingbeam, leaving him a set of shapeless drab pajamas with a number on the back and front in six languages and a pair of step-in slippers that threatened to deposit him on his head every time he took more than three paces.

There was only the one bed, and it wouldn't turn itself down when Lando told it to. Technically, he was in solitary confinement. That was all right with him, the acquaintances one makes in jail are seldom broadening, nor was he enamored of any sort of company at the moment. There was nothing to read, nothing to watch, nothing to do—but think. Lando was good at that.

Lob Doluff had answered the call himself.

The Administrator Senior expressed gratification that Lando's ship hadn't actually been on fire. He couldn't understand the false alarm, however. Such criminal offenses were prosecuted harshly in the Oseon.

"There is one small complication," Lando added, "however."

"However? And what is it, Captain?"

In the background, Lando could make out the figure of Bassi Vobah, drink in hand. They were still in the starlit garden dome. He wondered whether the other players were still there as well, and if not, what else might be going on in the upper echelons of Oseon Administration.

"Well, sir, the false alarm seems to have been intended as a trap. Someone ambushed me as I was preparing to return to the *sabacc* game—a stranger.

"I'm rather afraid I've killed him, Administrator Senior."

The older man's eyebrows danced up a fraction of an

inch and he leaned into the video pickup. "You aren't joking, are you, Captain Calrissian?"

Lando sighed. "I don't believe I'd joke about something like this. He surprised me, attacked me with a piece of pipe, and I was forced to shoot him."

The Administrator Senior's eyes widened and his eyebrows soared impossibly close to the crown of his naked scalp. "*Shoot* him? Did you say—"

"That's what I said. I—"

"Hold on a moment, Captain . . ."

Bassi Vobah leaned over and whispered something. Doluff looked puzzled a moment, then nodded.

"Captain Calrissian—Lando, my boy, stay right where you are. I'm going to send Miss Vobah directly over to you. I believe she can be of help to both of us in this affair. In the meantime, leave everything exactly as it is; I'll order access to your service corridor closed off. We'll get this over with as quickly and discreetly as possible."

Another whispered conference.

"Yes, and by the way, it is perhaps better that you tell Miss Vobah and myself nothing further about what happened. We are duty-bound to testify in court about it, being administrative personnel, the both of us. You understand."

Lando understood. He nodded, signaled off, slouched back in his pilot's chair disconsolately. Outside, the light seemed unnaturally harsh, even for an airless asteroid, and flickered now and again as if a fleet of ships were passing overhead. The colors all seemed a bit off, as well, but that may have been explainable by the mood of the observer. Finally he turned to Vuffi Raa.

"Well, old vegetable-slicer, it looks as though we're in for it again. I must be losing my touch."

"Now, Master," the robot replied, patting the gambler on the shoulder with a gentle tentacle, "I'm sure everything will work out. You would not have done what you did, had you not been forced to."

He extracted a cigar from beneath the control panel, trimmed it, handed it to Lando, and lit it with a glowing tentacle tip.

"I didn't know you could do that. Do you suppose he was the party behind the bombings, the fellow I shot?"

"The idea had crossed my mind, Master. I do not know."

A glum silence settled over the pair.

The control panel beeped. Lando flipped a switch. "Yes?"

"It's Bassi Vobah here, Lando. I'm in the service accessway beneath you. Come down and meet me, will you?"

"Very well. Shall I bring a toothbrush?"

Her voice was apologetic. "It might be a good idea."

Lando gave the robot a few instructions, then turned and retraced his steps to the bottom of the ladder. When he turned around, she was bending down, dispassionately examining the body.

She was wearing the uniform of the Oseon police.

In his cell a few hours later, Lando once again resisted the urge to get up and pace. He'd never taken very well to confinement. It was well past local midnight, there on a different spot on the equator, closer to the small city of which the Esplanade formed the core. Yet the lights had been left on—more or less standard practice in jails everywhere. Worse yet, the syrupy music still dribbled from the overhead. Resentfully, he looked up—

—and was nearly blinded by a flash of overwhelming brilliance in the sky. As his eyes began to readjust, he saw that long streamers of color had begun to creep across the zenith, deepening every second in hue, like mutant fingers closing over the transparent bowl of the heavens.

Crimson flared. Yellow seethed. Blue and green pulsed steadily against a syncopated counterpoint of violet.

The Flamewind had begun.

SEVEN

A POLICEPERSON'S LOT IS NOT A HAPPY ONE.

Sometimes, it was downright discouraging, thought Peacekeeper Bassi Vobah as she wrote up her report on the *Millennium Falcon* killing. What a time for something like this to happen!

Flamewind had begun, and she was going to miss it.

Born in the Oseon System, she was one of the many who served the few, her function—not terribly different from that of the countless robots that populated the asteroids—spare her masters a possible inconvenience. That has been the essential task of police officers everywhere in time and space, she was unaware. Her education had been specific and to a point. It had not been noticeably cosmopolitan or analytical.

Her parents, even less well off than she was, had originally immigrated as merchants after passing batteries of examinations, probes into their backgrounds and intentions, studies of their attitudes and goals. Nevertheless, they had not been terribly successful. In the end, she had worked to support them, and by the time it was no longer necessary, what she did for a living had become a habit with her, although not a particularly comfortable one.

Her one relief, her one vacation every year, was Flamewind.

It was a deadly and spectacular time. Brightly colored streamers of gaseous ionization filled the open spaces— a thousand kilometers on average—between floating mountains. Fantastic lightnings blasted from rock to rock. The seven belts of the Oseon fluoresced madly.

Radiation, static discharges, and swirling, colored fogs distorted navigational references, drove instruments and men alike insane. All interasteroidal commerce was grounded by law for the duration, averaging three weeks, to protect would-be sojourners from their own folly. The sleet of particles that lashed the system was only one opportunity for misadventure and destruction. Communications of any sort between the asteroids or with the rest of the galaxy were physically impossible, blotted out by wailing electrons.

No one went anywhere. Or wanted to.

And there were spooky stories of a less scientifically verifiable nature that circulated every year during Flamewind. Legendary disappearances, ominous apparitions, phenomena of the oddest, ghastliest, most relishably gossipable sort.

Yet—or consequently—tourists flocked to the Oseon just before the cataclysmic display. It had become a carnival of continuous parties, public and private, unceasing gaiety. Hundreds of different intelligent species inter-mingled from a million systems, giving some meaning and adventure to the otherwise humdrum life of a small-town girl.

Like Bassi Vobah.

And now this. Aside from the arrest itself and the keyboardwork it engendered, there were the impound-ment documents, to be completed in nanolicate, it seemed. This Lando Calrissian, a wandering tramp who hadn't filled out so much as a single visa form, had so far collected one hundred seventy-three thousand credits from his betters (and hers) without lifting a finger to do any honest work. That had been confiscated, of course, and, whether he was ultimately found innocent or guilty, would go to pay the expenses he'd imposed on the administrative services of the Oseon.

That much money would have supported half a hundred families like Bassi Vobah's for a year. It was simply indecent for an individual to gain so much so easily. At least justice reached a long arm out to punish evil-doers *sometimes*. This was one occasion when her job generated a great deal of satisfaction.

And then there was the broken-down smuggling vessel he claimed was a freighter. That was worth fifteen or twenty thousand. If she could think of additional appro-priate charges, the ship would go on auction to pay for them. Also that pilot/repair droid. It was worth consid-erably more than the ship and would have a much more enthusiastic market in the Oseon. Mark it down at fifty thousand credits.

Incidental personal items of property, worthless—and, of course, the murder weapon. *No*, she wasn't legally justified calling it that. Yet. The confiscated stingbeam, then. It would make a nice addition to her tiny depart-ment's "museum." Such killings didn't happen often in the fat, complacent community she served. It would make an interesting story to tell.

But that scarcely made up for the trouble Calrissian was causing, and if possible, she'd see him fried for that. The other complication was his fault, indirectly, as well. She'd argued with her superior, Lob Doluff, about it, but pressure was being put on him, and the pressure worked its way down onto her shoulders. Calrissian would pay for that, as well.

Flamewind had begun, and she was going to miss it.

Vuffi Raa paced the curved companionways of the *Millennium Falcon*. He was a most unhappy machine. Below, the hatchway to service corridor 17-W was closed, clamped with an impound seal, and it had been all he could do to persuade the authorities not to stencil a seizure notice on his body—or take him away and lock him up in some warehouse.

Maintaining a modest silence about his manifold additional capabilities, he'd convinced them that, as a pilot, navigator, and repairbot, he was essentially part of the ship. As a consequence, they had affixed to his torso a restraining bolt—a bit of electronic mischief that was supposed to inflict enormous pain on his nervous system should he attempt to leave the *Falcon*.

It had taken him all of thirty seconds to disable it, once the police had departed. Nonetheless, prudence dictated that he stay there unless he could think of something useful to do for himself and his master.

Outside, huge sheets of polychrome gas filled the sky, punctuated every few minutes by terrifying displays of lightning. Flamewind was barely underway and yet, for most observers, the phenomenon was overwhelming.

Vuffi Raa didn't even notice it.

He supposed that Lando had offered at least a hundred

times to set him legally free. For some reason it bothered the gambler deeply to own another sentient being, even a mechanical one. Vuffi Raa had always turned him down, preferring to stay with his adventurous master. Now he wondered — very briefly — whether it mightn't have been a better idea to accept. As a manumitted droid, he would have been at liberty to deal with the situation.

Although what, specifically, he would have done remained a mystery.

As an article of property, he was told nothing by the authorities about Lando's fate or that of himself and the *Falcon*. However, from long, long experience with human culture, the robot could make a fairly accurate guess. Somehow all of that must be prevented, some bargain struck that would at least leave them even, leave them in the condition in which they'd arrived.

Vuffi Raa had very little experience making deals.

Outside, the sky writhed with the seven colors of the spectrum — and with every possible mixture in between. For Vuffi Raa, there were more than a hundred basic colors, from lowest infrared to highest ultraviolet, and the permutations and combinations possible had to be expressed in exponentials.

Yet the spectacle was lost on him, and not from any lack of aesthetic sensitivity.

He *liked* Lando Calrissian. The little droid had a deceptive appearance; he always looked brand-new, and his mere meter of height made people think diminutive thoughts about him. In reality, he had a powerful mind and a lifetime that stretched back centuries, even further than he could remember.

Apparently, that was the result of a pirate attack on a freighter in whose hold he'd occupied a commercial shipping crate. It was his first clear memory, the jarring, shouting, screaming. The groaning of the fabric of the victimized ship. He hadn't been supposed to awaken until arrival at his destination. The premature activation was a survival mechanism, but it had cost him something. He could remember nothing of his origins; had only the vaguest impression that the race who had created him looked something like him.

In all the time since, through hundreds of owners, hundreds of systems, planets, cultures, he'd never grown so fond of a human being. He couldn't exactly say why Lando Calrissian affected him so, but affection was the truth. They laughed together: Vuffi Raa's separating tentacles (once the robot had disclosed this capability) had become the basis for a number of Lando's rare but elaborate practical jokes. They prospered together, and in financial extremes, Lando had divided his small fortunes between buying food for himself and whatever small electronic items the robot's maintenance required.

They were friends.

And now, Vuffi Raa was helpless to aid his master.

Outside, a braid of raspberry red, lemon yellow, and orange orange twisted through the heavens, across a constellation locals called the Silly Rabbit.

No sentient sighted being could have cared less than Vuffi Raa.

Rokur Gepta floated in an utter blackness not half so dark as the secret contemplations of his soul.

Deep underground, where the final traces of the minuscule natural gravity of the asteroid were canceled, he hung suspended in the center of an artificial cavern, momentarily free of all sensation, free of the annoyances attendant upon suffering the incompetence of his underlings, free of the steady, grinding presence of the warmth and bustle of life.

His plans were well in motion. The *Wennis* was some

distance away, its crew performing drill after endless drill, not so much to sharpen their abilities—they were, after all, only the best of a hopeless lot—as to keep them out of the kind of trouble that uncontrolled individuality never fails to generate. Gepta smugly affirmed to himself that chance favors the prepared mind: a happy turn of fate had placed his enemy, Lando Calrissian, in the custody of Oseon officialdom. Since that officialdom was a government, and he was who he was, Calrissian was already three-quarters of the way into his hands.

They would be cruel hands, once they received their prey.

And deservedly so. Who had kept the sorcerer from obtaining and using the Mindharp of Sharu, an instrument of total mental control over others? Lando Calrissian. Who now owned the ancient enigmatic robot that seemed the key to yet another sheaf of tantalizing unanswered questions—and limitless power? Lando Calrissian. Who had evaded trap after trap, including that prepared for him on Dilonexa XXIII and the device planted aboard that cursed wreck, the *Millennium Falcon*? Lando Calrissian.

How he hated that name! How he would make its owner squirm and writhe until he learned the secret of his weird luck, or the other, hidden powers for which he was a front! How he would crush the life—slowly, very slowly—out of Lando Calrissian's frail body, after first destroying most of the mind (but not enough so that its owner couldn't appreciate the final moments).

Gepta thought back to an earlier, a happier time, to his first years as an adept among the ancient Sorcerers of Tund. How he had deceived the doddering fools, even while stealing their esoteric and sequestered learnings. As intended, they had mistaken him for a young apprentice and had been unable to penetrate his disguise.

Already, he had been, even those thousands of years ago, far older than the most ancient of the sorcerers, and *they* knew how to stretch a life-span!

Ah, yes. The galaxy still believed that somewhere the hidden planet Tund was home to the mysterious Order. Only Gepta knew it was a sterile ball. Not so much as a tiny fingerbone was left. The thought—the memory of what he had done on that final day—filled him with delight and satisfaction.

Someday he'd do it to the entire universe!

Meanwhile, that universe wasn't big enough for Rokur Gepta and Lando Calrissian. As Lando Calrissian was going to discover very soon.

Slowly, with elaborate precision, the sorcerer everted his body—turned inside-out on the axis of his digestive system as a form of meditative relaxation—and resumed a true appearance only slightly less disgusting than the one he had given a few seconds before. No human being had ever seen him thus, none ever would—and live to relate the horror of it. He relaxed his numberless alien appendages, stretched them, and relaxed, then spun about himself the appearance of the gray-swathed presumably humanoid sorcerer the world knew.

Summoning a power of which the universe was equally ignorant, he drifted slowly, deliberately, toward the floor of the cavern. There was work to do, and he must be about it.

And yes . . . he must feed his pet.

Klyn Shanga concealed his grief. Year after year, it never got any easier to bear. Now, Colonel Kenow, his old and valued companion, was dead. Dead and gone. Forevermore.

They had fought in the battle of the Rood together as boys. It had been an insignificant sideshow in a vastly greater war, but to them, it had been a lifepath-altering cusp. They had survived, toughened by the ghastly experience, transformed from callow farmboys into soldiers.

And friends.

And now, Colonel Kenow was dead.

The worst of it was that it had been a senseless, purposeless death spurred by an impetuosity Shanga wouldn't have believed possible in a man of Kenow's age and battle experience. The stringent rich-man's laws of the Oseon had forced the veteran to abandon the weapon he was used to in favor of a crude length of pipe. Then he had been shot down by a stranger only tangentially involved with the enemy they sought, an accidental, not altogether innocent bystander. If only Kenow had listened . . .

Lightning flared, shaking the entire fabric of the odd assembly of fighters. Keeping station off the asteroid was growing more difficult by the minute. He could scarcely see across the few hundred meters that separated him from the farthest ship in his tiny fleet, thanks to the colored vapor that smoked and roiled around them. The radiation-counter needles climbed inexorably, despite the fact that they were in the shadow of a billion tons of iron-based rock. How much longer they could keep it up . . .

Well, in the end, it wouldn't matter. The giant engine still pulsed reliably, the cables connecting it to the fighters were sound. They'd had to rebalance to make up for Kenow's missing ship, but that had been simple, really. If they could just hold on long enough to do their work, it wouldn't make a bit of difference whether they survived the fury of the Flamewind, whether their skin flaked off and they lost their hair and vomited up the last drop of their lives. Those lives would have been well accounted for, the loss well worth it.

Shanga, like the rest of his companions, bided his time, hid his grief. The sleet of energy around them was making even line-bound communication impossible. The cables acted like a huge antenna, gathering up a howling cacophony that ground on the nerves, eroded morale and resolve. It was as if all the dead the universe had ever seen gathered in an unholy chorus once a year in the Oseon.

And now there was a new voice, that of Colonel Kenow, Klyn Shanga's old friend.

Well, soon there would be other voices, Shanga thought. His among them.

Lob Doluff wasn't any happier than anyone else that carnival season. He regarded the whole Flamewind foo-foraw as an enormous, unnecessary pain in the neck. He had never liked it, never understood why anybody else did.

Lob Doluff was color-blind.

He was also worried—half to death. Dressed as he was in lightweight indoor clothing, his head uncovered, his plump arms bare to the chill of the special section of his garden, standing in the middle of half a hectare of snow, his hands were sweating.

The Administrator Senior's visual disability did not affect his appreciation for flowering plants although his reasons for collecting them may have been a bit different from those others might have. He loved their perfume and their persistence. To him a weed that cracked a ferroconcrete walkway was something of a miracle, and here, where tiny, almost microscopic flowers poked their small, courageous heads up through snow and ice, there was something especially miraculous.

It did little to cheer him now, however. He was in a bind.

Unlike his subordinate, Bassi Vobah, he was one of the *few* who served the few, while making an unusually honest effort to serve the many. He was quite as wealthy as anyone in the Oseon, and yet a sense of civic duty, personal pride, drove him to sit in the Administrator Senior's office and attempt to govern the essentially ungovernable millions upon millions of falling worldlets that comprised the system. He kept the peace. He maintained minimal social services. He acted as a buffer between the Oseon's inhabitants and a galaxy that often clamored for their attention, either in response to their great wealth, their enormous fame—or their criminal reputation.

At all of this he was very good, and his independent wealth allowed him a certain latitude denied the average civil servant. He might not *quite* be able to tell his superiors to take a flaming jump into the Core, but he had *thought* about it more than once and made the recommendation to many of their representatives.

Unfortunately, he was unable to indulge himself on this occasion. Pressure—greater pressure than he had known existed—was being placed on him to betray many of the things he stood for. If he complied, it was distinctly possible that no one would ever learn of it. But he, Lob Doluff, would know, and it would remove a great deal of the satisfaction from his life.

At the other end of the proposition, he stood to lose his position, his wealth, his reputation, even his life if he insisted pushing things to their extreme. In addition, many, many others would suffer. It was ugly, and he hadn't thought such things could happen in a civilized universe.

Now he knew different.

He turned from his absent contemplation of the snow-flowers of a hundred systems, walked through an invisible air curtain into a semitropical wedge of the dome, strode to a tree stump, and flipped the top upward. Reaching in, he seized a communicator and brought it to his lips.

"This is the Administrator Senior," he said after asking for the correct extension number. "Have Captain Calrissian brought to my office in an hour."

His hands were sweating again. He'd never sent a man to certain death before.

EIGHT

IT WAS TWO AND A HALF METERS TALL, HAD AN ORANGE
beak and scaly three-toed feet, was covered with bright
yellow feathers, spoke in an annoying high-pitched ef-
feminate voice despite its repulsively obvious masculin-
ity, and answered to the name of Waywa Fybot.

It was also an undercover narcotics agent.

Lando hadn't learned any of this yet as a pair of robots,
spray-painted the same color as Bassi Vobah's uniform,
dragged him from his comfortable cell to confront the
Administrator Senior.

"The charge is carrying a deadly weapon, Captain
Calrissian, and the customary sentence, upon conviction,
is death by exposure."

Lob Doluff paced back and forth before the floor-to-ceiling window in his office. Outside, the Flamewind filled the sky with racing garishness, but most of it was obscured by the dozens of hanging plants that turned the window into a vertical carpet of shaggy greenery. Other plants were scattered about in pots, in long narrow planters, in aquaria, even drifted in the air on lacy pale wings. A gentle frond brushed Lando's cheek as a flying plant passed over his head.

Lob Doluff didn't have a desk. He didn't need one. Tucked away in an alcove was a datalink with its screen and keyboard; a pair of secretaries awaited his summons in an anteroom. What he had were several comfortable chairs, none of which had been offered to Lando, and the enormous bird-thing that none of the mobile plant life would even approach.

And Bassi Vobah herself, looking prim and starched and heavily armed.

Lando reached downward to thrust his hands in his pants pockets, discovered once again he hadn't any, and folded his arms across his chest. He looked from Bassi to the Administrator Senior, spent a moment on the weird creature in the corner, then back to the humans.

"I take it, then, that you're not charging me with murder."

Bassi Vobah nodded. "That would be irrelevant. In the first place, there's ample evidence that you killed him in self-defense. In the second place, we have no record of him having entered the Oseon by legal channels and therefore, at least in legal terms, he doesn't—never did— exist."

Lando shook his head. "Nice government you have here. Why is carrying a weapon a capital offense, and what have I got to do to get out of it? I take it that I wouldn't be here if you weren't going to offer me some nasty alternative to being shoved out an airlock."

The gambler had been in the position before, on more than one occasion. Odd, how government people needed extragovernmental people to manage their dirty work on occasion. The things that he'd been asked to do, however, could scarcely be classified under civil service job descriptions.

Bassi Vobah had stiffened at Lando's reply, and only steely nerves and training had kept her hand away from the gigantic military blaster hanging at her hip.

Lob Doluff, however, seemed relieved. He nodded toward the nonhuman observer, introduced the creature to Lando. Waywa Fybot flapped his short arms as if in greeting, ruffled his feathers, and settled back into silence.

"In one sense, Captain, you are mistaken. You have been arrested and are soon to be tried and duly convicted of the offense." The Administrator Senior made a gesture. The robots on each side of Lando stepped back, Lando was signaled to a chair facing those in which Lob Doluff was seated and Bassi Vobah stood behind at a sort of parade rest.

"As I said, the punishment as prescribed by law is exposure to the heat, cold, and vacuum of interplanetary space. There is, however, no provision for the precise method to be employed, and I am moved, my boy, to suggest a means by which the law may be obeyed and yet spare you from the unpleasantness such an experience ordinarily brings."

"I get it. You're going to shoot me before you stuff me out the airlock. By the way, Administrator Senior, have you ever *seen* somebody after they were spaced?"

(Lando hadn't either, but he had a good imagination and hoped that Doluff did as well.) "Pretty messy."

He made a face, eyes bulging out, tongue lolling at the corner of his mouth.

Lob Doluff grimaced painfully, gulped, and placed a protective hand on his large stomach. "That's exactly what we're trying to prevent, my boy. To my knowledge, there has never been a formal execution in the Oseon, and I have no desire to be the first—"

"Nor I," Lando agreed, "I suppose this is where our avian friend comes in, isn't it?" He indicated Waywa Fybot, taking up a great deal of room in the corner.

Fybot stepped forward. "Tell me, Captain,"—the creature squeaked ridiculously, especially considering its size—"have you ever heard the name Bohhuah Mutdah?"

"Sounds like somebody bawling for his mommy." Lando was sick of being the eternal patsy. He knew by then that they needed him, and had become determined to make things as difficult as he could for them.

The humor of the response—what little there was of it—was lost on everybody present. Lando even detected a little shudder from Lob Doluff. The Administrator Senior shut his eyes, wiped sweaty palms on the creases of his trousers.

The big bird took another step forward, towering over Lando.

"Bohhuah Mutdah is a retired industrialist, a trillionaire. His holdings in the Oseon are the largest in the system by a single individual, and it is possible that he is the wealthiest person in the civilized galaxy.

"He is also thoroughly addicted to *lesai*."

Lesai. Lando shut the bird-being out of his mind for a moment, summoning up what he knew of the rare and extremely illegal drug.

The product of a mold that grew only on the backs of a single species of lizard in the Zebitrope System, *lesai* had many desirable qualities. In the first place, it eliminated the necessity for sleep, thus effectively lengthening the human life-span by a third. Unlike other stimulants which consumed something vital in the human brain, *lesai* provided that something vital itself, meaning it could be taken indefinitely.

Yet, it was not without its cost. It turned the user into an emotionless, amoral calculating machine. In the end, family and friends, the lives of thousands or millions of other individuals—at least so the authorities claimed—counted as nothing, compared to whatever goals the addicted mind had set itself. One had to be careful; those in power often lied about things like the effect of drugs, and even Lando, who was strongly predisposed against any mind-altering substances, took what the government said with a very large grain of salt.

Nonetheless, some of this made sense. He could understand how *lesai* and the richest individual in the known universe might be associated. There wasn't any particular trick to becoming rich—as long as one devoted his whole life to it to the exclusion of everything else. Lando wasn't capable of it; to him, money was a means to an end. It became meaningless when it was an end in itself.

But not everybody felt that way. Perhaps Bohhuah Mutdah was a person like that.

"Okay," he interrupted the avian creature, "so we have a fabulously wealthy *lesai* addict, and you're a drug cop. What's the matter, didn't he pay his protection money on time?"

Waywa Fybot stood up even straighter than before, his feathers fluffed straight outward as if in shock. "Captain Calrissian, you forget yourself! I, after all, am a—"

"—An agent of a government fully as corrupt as any government that ever existed. Don't kid me, worm-breath. Vice laws are always written to be selectively enforced, to serve other purposes. What have you people got against this Mutdah character—or is it simply that you don't like the size of his bank account?"

The bird-creature blinked, began to tremble with rage. It opened its beak to reply, shut it again, opened it again, and subsided into the corner, speechless. Lando grinned at the Administrator Senior and his Peacekeeper, spread a hand that was half a shrug.

Bassi Vobah was nearly as scandalized as her professional colleague.

Lob Doluff, however, chuckled and appeared to relax for the first time since the interview had started. His smile became a grin to match the gambler's, then became outright laughter. He glanced, guiltily at first, at the feathered VIP, then shook his head and laughed again, this time without qualms.

"By the Core, Captain Calrissian—Lando, if I may— I *do* admire you! You're a gambler through and through, not just at the table. Please allow me to make this unpleasantness more comfortable. Have you had anything to eat?"

Lando nodded. "Best food I've ever had in jail. I could use some coffeine, though, and maybe a cigar."

"And by Core, Edge, and Disc, so shall you have them! Bassi, see to it immediately!"

The police officer stared at her boss indignantly, decided he was serious, and stalked out of the room to attend to the chore. Doluff snapped a finger at one of the guard-robots who had retired to the corners of the room behind Lando.

"Bring this gentleman his clothing, this very minute! By the Eternal, if I have to go through with this charade, I'll bloody well go through with it in my own way!"

Lando had sat quietly through it all. Now he sat up a little straighter as the Administrator Senior settled back, fully relaxed. Coffeine and tobacco arrived in due course, delivered by a seething Bassi Vobah. A police-robot brought Lando's personal property, which the gambler ignored for the time being as more interesting matters occupied his attention.

"Now," Lob Doluff said, when everyone was settled in again. At his insistence, a strange-looking rack the size and shape of a pair of sawhorses had been brought in by a robot, and Waywa Fybot encouraged—at the Administrator Senior's insistence—to perch on it. The bird got a dreamy look on its face, its feathers smoothed once again, and it was quiet.

"Now, sir, I will tell you the plain truth—as much as I have been told, in any case—and we will *all* understand. You're quite right, of course. Bohhuah Mutdah's corporate enemies and business rivals are preparing to overthrow his commercial empire. But they fear him greatly, sir, as I would in their place, and, accordingly, are seeking to put him personally and physically out of the way.

"I rather guess they hope he will resist arrest, providing them with an excuse to make things permanent. But that is only a surmise. The point is, Lando, I must ask you to help make all of this possible, and there is no way I can refuse to do so. I have what amount to direct orders— by Gadfrey, it feels good to tell the truth!

"Were it simply my position, I would tell them—well,

I hold this office quite voluntarily—quite unnecessarily if the truth were told. I like it, but not so much that I'd betray a fellow *sabacc* enthusiast and gentleman adventurer I admire."

Bassi Vobah squirmed uncomfortably in the chair she'd been ordered to take.

"Why do I have the feeling you're going to find another reason to betray me, then, old bureaucrat?" Lando asked. "That's what you're leading up to, isn't it?"

The Administrator Senior sighed. "I'm afraid so, my dear fellow. I offer no excuse. Means have been found to exert leverage upon me which my scruples cannot withstand. I do not ask you even to understand my position. I am attempting to arrange things so as to minimize the damage the situation inflicts on us both. I'll thank you to believe that much, at least."

Lando shrugged again, noncommittally. "How much does a hangman's apology count for, Administrator Senior?"

Doluff grimaced uncomfortably, then nodded. "You're quite right, sir. But look here, this is how I am prepared to hold up my end of a bad bargain." He turned to Waywa Fybot.

"Listen to me, you ridiculous creature, and listen well—"

"Adminis—" interrupted a shocked and outraged Bassi Vobah.

"Hush, child, I'll get to you in a moment. Are you listening to me, you absurd collection of flightless feathers?"

The Imperial narcotics agent blinked stupidly. Apparently the position it had been forced to assume triggered some reflexive sleep reaction. It shook its head, peered at the Administrator Senior, but said nothing.

"Very well, then, and you can inform your mercantile-class sponsors that I gave you this direct order: you may arrest Bohhuah Mutdah, I haven't the power to stop you. But you will return him to *me*, alive and in condition to stand trial in the Oseon, or I'll have you plucked, dressed, and roasted for Founder's Day. Am I making myself clear?"

The bird-creature nodded, a look of hatred latent in its large blue eyes.

Doluff turned to Bassi Vobah. "And as for you, my dear, remember who it is you work for. Your orders are to see that my orders are carried out. And you are to use that oversized chicken-roaster of yours"—he indicated her energypistol—"if the occasion calls for it, on whomsoever merits it."

He nodded significantly toward Waywa Fybot.

"Now, Captain Calrissian—Lando—this is what you are to do. As you probably are aware, it is perilous in the extreme, and also illegal, for ships to travel from asteroid to asteroid in the Oseon during Flamewind."

As if to underline the Administrator Senior's words, lightning flared briefly outside the window, washing the colors from every object in the room. The flash subsided.

"Nonetheless, I am required to instruct you to take this pair of law-enforcement officers to Oseon 5792, the home and estate of Bohhuah Mutdah, so that they may make their arrest."

Lando shook his head. "I don't get it. Why not just—"

"Because, my dear Captain, it seems he must be caught in the act. His enemies lack sufficient evidence at the moment, and even they dare not move without it. You are the goat because of your avocation as captain of a tramp freighter. It must appear that you are taking him his regular shipment of the drug; apparently he supplies himself every year under the cover of the Flamewind, and—"

Lando stood up suddenly. "Now wait just a minute, Admin—"

The bureaucrat slammed his large hands down on the arms of his chair. "*You* wait a minute, Captain! I have no latitude in this; my instructions are clear, detailed, and unavoidable. We will provide you with a large amount of *lesai*, which has been seized from Mutdah's regular connection. You will make transit to the next Belt inward, to the particular rock owned by Bohhuah Mutdah, and sell him the drug. You will be observed doing so by Officer Waywa Fybot and Oseon Peacekeeper Bassi Vobah, who will then seize both drug shipment and payment and take Mutdah into custody. That is how it has been ordained; that is how it shall be done." Doluff subsided once again and took two or three deep breaths.

Lando sat quietly for a moment, thinking, then asked a question. "All right, so we're boxed in, if I'm to believe your word. But—well, I've won rather a deal of money here in the Oseon in the last few days, nearly two hundred thousand creds. I can anticipate that it would suit certain interests if *I'm* arrested in the same illegal exchange, wouldn't it?"

A predatory gleam became visible in Bassi Vobah's eyes.

Lob Doluff, on the other hand, simply smiled sadly. "Lando, we already have you on the weapons charge; I repeat, a capital offense. Those whose interests I serve desire that no one besides themselves possess the means of deadly self-defense, and they enforce the rule—or expect me to, which amounts to the same thing—quite severely.

"Besides, although you have been quite fortunate—

no, let us acknowledge your skill—at the gaming table, I assure you that no one you played with, excepting Miss Vobah here, who was appropriately subsidized, will miss so much as a micro of your winnings. We are a wealthy people.

"However, if it will make you feel more comfortable, you'll recall I offered you an additional assurance of my goodwill in this awkward matter. This is what I had in mind: transport these two individuals and help them make the arrest. In return, I shall see that you take your winnings with you, along with every other item of your property, and you may depart the system directly from Bohhuah Mutdah's estate. He owns a large number of small interasteroidal craft, and I believe that the Flamewind may have quieted enough that Bassi, here, and Officer Fybot can make their way with evidence and prisoner back to this place unassisted. Is that fair enough?"

Lando thought it over, nodded reluctantly.

"And you, my dear, have I made myself sufficiently clear to you? Should you oppose my will in this, inconvenience Captain Calrissian in any way, I shall expect you to leave the system directly from Mutdah's asteroid, in his place."

The policewoman gulped visibly and nodded fully as reluctantly as Lando.

Once more Lob Doluff frowned at Waywa Fybot. "And as for you, you hyperthyroid whooping crane, should you interfere in my wishes concerning the good captain here, after you have been plucked and roasted, I shall stuff a cushion with your feathers and rest my fundament upon it for the rest of my life. Do you understand?"

The bird nodded, adding a third portion to the general grudging atmosphere in the room.

Doluff folded his hands across his paunch, a satisfied expression on his face. "Very well, then, we are agreed, and everything is settled. By the Center, it is good doing business with a group as straightforward and understanding as you all are. I am feeling extremely fond of the three of you. Shall we see about having lunch, then?"

NINE

In the Oseon System during Flamewind, the inhabitants and their guests have little to do but party and watch the fireworks. But even the most spectacular display in the known universe begins to pall after sufficient time, and attending parties has its limits—and its consequences.

Thus it is an interesting fact of demographics that, although the majority of Oseoni, owing to what is required of them to achieve their high place in the general scale of galactic society, are long beyond childbearing age, yet the human birthrate in the system inevitably jumps every year nine months after Flamewind.

One reason for the increase is the peril of traveling during Flamewind. The deadly rain of radiation accompanying the display vastly accelerates the decay of electronics that control navigation and life-support equipment.

Even travel on the surface of an asteroid is dangerous.

And yet, Lando Calrissian, once resigned to the journey, was anxious to be underway. Freedom in the Oseon, he was discovering rapidly, had its severe drawbacks. There would be no more *sabacc* games for a variety of reasons: he had effectively cleaned out the available talent, not so much depriving them of their discretionary funds as convincing them that it was pointless to oppose him at the gaming table. In this he had been, if not directly careless, then overly enthusiastic. It was not a mistake he would have made in less opulent surroundings; he had yet fully to appreciate how much more tenaciously the rich hold on to what they have.

Had he been a waitress or a bell-bot, no one would have needed to tell him. The wealthy are notoriously lousy tippers.

What was worse, given the local standard of living, the fact that there were so many wealthy inhabitants and that the commercial overhead was so high, he was once again watching his money—his winnings—being eaten up. Everything was expensive, from a simple meal in the humblest eatery to the equipment and supplies his ship required for the journey ahead.

As usual, Lando's luck, both good and bad, was operating at full blast.

The day after his revealing conference in the Administrator Senior's office, he and Vuffi Raa were bolting down the weirdly shaped seating rack that had been sent over for Waywa Fybot.

"One more turn ought to do it!" Lando grunted. "I wish there was room for an autowrench in this corner—unh!"

The head of the bolt had twisted and torn off. This

meant they had to undo all the other bolts and move the rack while Vuffi Raa drilled out the broken hardware and removed it for a second try.

"Master, why is the installation necessary? We could override the gravfield in this part of the ship and let Officer Fybot spend the trip in free-fall. It would be much more comfortable." Having drilled a hole through the soft metal of the bolt, he inserted a broken-screw remover, the twist of its threads being opposite those of the bolt, and tightened it, turning the offending artifact neatly out of the deck.

"What, and have his birdseed floating everywhere? Not a chance. Besides, his physiology is supposed to be delicate or something, like a canary's. Don't ask me why they made somebody like that a cop—that would require an assumption that logic functions at some level of government."

Together, they moved the distorted chair back into place over the boltholes drilled for it in the decking. Somehow, thought Lando, the parties responsible for this—the final straw of messing up his nice, neat spaceship—would be brought to a reckoning.

The first three bolts went in perfectly. Again. Lando and Vuffi Raa looked at each other with resigned expressions (Lando reading the little droid's body posture since it had no face), placed the fourth bolt in its hole, and locked the wrench around its hexagonal head.

"If it doesn't work this time, old power-tool, we're going to send for a big wire cage!"

Deep within the honeycombed recesses of Oseon 6845, down where enormous pipes the diameter of a man's height conveyed air and water and other vital substances from fission-powered machinery to hotels and offices and stores and other places habituated by human beings, down where no one but an occasional robot made its perfunctory rounds, a meeting was being held.

"So you came," a gray-clad figure whispered. The clothing had the look of a uniform, although it was barren of the insignia of rank or unit markings. The face above the stiff collar, below the cap, was young. It was the first officer of the *Wennis*, lurking in the shadows of a ship-sized power transformer, his voice drowned within a meter or two by its titanic humming.

The other figure was even less conspicuous, hidden more deeply in shadows, cloaked for anonymity in many yards of billowy fabric. It was taller than the *Wennis* second-in-command, and stood there silently, acknowledging the greeting with a nod.

"Good," the officer hissed. "And do you understand what you are supposed to do when you get to 5792? There must be no mistake, no hesitation. The Administrator Senior has found a legal means of circumventing our intentions in this matter, and it must not work! The orders come from very nearly as high as they can."

Once again, the tall disguised figure nodded.

"All right, then. In return, you will be richly rewarded. Our, er...principal understands the pragmatic value of gratitude. Be sure *you* understand the consequences of failure."

The cloaked form shuddered slightly, but that may have been the cold. Even with the machinery in full operation, there was a chill in the air that converted both their breaths into clouds of barely visible vapor.

It shuddered again. And it may not have been the cold.

The gray-uniformed officer departed without further conversation. He was in a hurry. Before he returned to the *Wennis*, he had another meeting, even deeper in the planetoid's core, and it was not one he was looking forward to particularly.

Behind him the tall, cloaked figure departed as well, leaving a single, downy yellow feather that trembled in the cold draft along the floor, then was still.

With understandably mixed feelings, Lando tucked his freshly recharged stingbeam into the waistband of his shipsuit. Mere possession of the thing inside the Oseon System was a capital offense, and the manner of execution made hanging, gassing, perhaps even the nerve rack seem desirable ways to end it all.

On the other hand, he was operating under the direct verbal orders of Administrator Senior Lob Doluff, whose concern for Lando's continued existence, it appeared, was sincere and rivaled only by his desire that Bassi Vobah and Waywa Fybot carry out the mission precisely as the administrator had instructed. Lando's pistol was a small but additional guarantee he had insisted upon.

On the third hand (Lando looked at Vuffi Raa, whose capable tentacles were flicking switches, turning knobs, and doing other things mandated by the preflight checklist), the Administrator Senior had adamantly refused to issue the young gambler a written permit to carry the weapon, fearing, perhaps, that his original leverage on Lando would be weakened thereby.

Ah, well, Lando thought, if things went according to plan (he had no great confidence that they would, being a cynic by inclination and having lived long enough to see his natural suspicions confirmed more often than not), he and Vuffi Raa would be out of the confounded system in a few days, and the whole issue would be irrelevant.

He had taken some pains of his own to assure this.

He intended to take even more.

As Lando and his mechanical partner warmed things up in the cockpit of the *Millennium Falcon*—illuminated through the forward canopy by the multicolored glare and flash of the Flamewind—their passengers were in the lounge area, each keeping his or her trepidations about the coming voyage to him- or herself. Bassi Vobah, having reluctantly abandoned the psychological protection of her police uniform, sat in a sort of semicircular booth with an electronic table in its center, glumly watching an entertainment tape from the *Falcon*'s meager library. It was the saga of some early star travelers, marooned on a harsh and barren world through the failure of their spacecraft during a magnetic storm. At present, the characters were casting lots to determine which of them would eat the others.

Somehow it failed to elevate her mood.

Waywa Fybot was essentially a bird in his anatomy and physiology, although no more bound by the characteristics of such creatures than are men by their fundamental origins. While he was nervous, he could remind himself that what he was about to endure was in the line of duty, what Emperor and Empire expected of him, and consistent with future promotion and increases in salary. While he felt murderously angry at the local administrator who had verbally savaged him (Fybot's own people had plenty of snappy remarks applicable to mammalian species in general and simian ones in particular, but Doluff's office hadn't seemed the place to trot them out), the prospect of bigger game and future rewards helped him smooth his ruffled feathers.

Damn! He'd done it to *himself* that time.

Beneath the long thick plumage of his stubby left arm— a vestigial wing useless for flight long ages before his people had chipped their first crude stone tools—Fybot wore a small energy-projector that was something of an advance on Bassi Vobah's openly sported blaster. Half the military weapon's size, it had six times the power, coming close, in theory, to one of the modules of Lando's four-barreled quad-gun. The projector was a Service Special and a closely guarded secret, even from the regular military.

It didn't need to be drawn to be used, which was a blessing, as nature had not provided Fybot's people with the quickest or most adroit of manipulators.

He looked over at Bassi Vobah as she tried hard to keep her attention on the entertainment tape. It wasn't easy. Calrissian and his robot were running the *Falcon*'s engines through a series of tests that shook the vessel like a leaf at irregular intervals and left stunning silences between. Their caution in assuring themselves of the ship's operating condition only served as a grim reminder of what risks they were all about to take.

Which brought Waywa Fybot around again to his nervousness. He settled deeper into his resting rack, enjoying the reflexive drowsiness that came with the action, and wished his species still had sufficient flexibility to tuck their heads under their wings.

Come to think of it, he'd only bruise himself on the weapon he carried.

A gentle snoring sound began to issue from the small round nostrils pierced through the narcotics officer's beak.

"Item one ninety-six," Lando quoted from the manual, "navigational receivers on standby. Well, old can-opener, we can skip that one. How'd that dead-reckoning program of yours turn out, or do you want to say?"

Vuffi Raa paused, a tentacle tip over a switch on the panel before them. "I wish, Master, that there was another name for it. It sounds awfully final, doesn't it?" He flipped the switch, watched the panel indicators go crazy as the Flamewind's ionization attacked the navigation beam receivers.

He flipped the switch to off again. Both partners felt relieved.

"Item one ninety-seven," Lando said, ignoring Vuffi Raa's rhetorical sqeamishness. "This begins a subseries of thirteen intermediate items before we get to one ninety-eight. First item: check main reactor core-temperature, which should be up to optimum by now. Check. Second item: make sure that moderator fluid is circulating freely in the heat exchangers. Check—at least according to the instruments. Third item . . ."

Administrator Senior Lob Doluff had stoically suffered the indignity of ordering the datalink, normally tucked inoffensively away in an alcove and concealed by a hanging fern, rolled out into the center of what was supposed to be his office and what was, in reality, a miniature of his greenhouse home.

By landline he was having a view transmitted to him of the north polar spaceport, specifically, the central area where the *Millennium Falcon* vibrated in readiness.

Maybe, he thought to himself, he hadn't the intestinal fortitude to be a first-rank administrator. He found it difficult in the extreme to order those beings, Lando Calrissian and his doughty little Class Two droid, into the fury of the Flamewind at its most colorful and dangerous moment. His heart would be traveling with them, he knew, and might not ever return to its proper location.

He wished them well.

However, he sighed, he did know a cure for the anxiety and guilt he was experiencing. In another alcove, across the room from that in which the datalink normally was exiled, he kept a terrarium filled with odd spongy growths from a planet a quarter of a galaxy away. Even to him, the great lover of green, growing things, they were utterly repulsive. But they were necessary to nurture and conceal an even more repulsive specimen of lizard that lived in symbiosis with them and shared the planet Zebitrope IV.

On the back of the lizard, another symbiont, there grew a rather disgusting purple mold.

Lob Doluff locked his office doors, extracted a small plastic spatula from beneath the datalink, trod over to the terrarium, seized the lizard, and scraped a bit of mold from its back. This he rubbed with thumb and forefinger into the hollow at the base of his throat, covering the resulting stain, which looked rather like a bruise, with some flesh-colored powder he kept for just that purpose.

He settled back in his chair.

They were wrong, thought the governor, those "experts." He watched the *Falcon* detach itself from the accordion tube beneath it and seal up its belly hatch. *Lesai* didn't stop you from caring.

Lob Doluff wished it did.

Several thousand kilometers away, a missile streaked past an odd conglomeration of battered and obsolete fighting craft attached with long and brightly pulsing cables to the core of a starship engine.

It was a signal, the only means of conveying information across space during the Flamewind of Oseon. Klyn Shanga watched it sizzle past his canopy, began punching buttons to place himself in wire-communications with his companions.

"That's it, men," he said in a grim, determined voice. "Now it begins, and it will not end until *we* have ended it. Call off your status when I say your name. We have to get this damned mess synchronized just right or we'll wind up slamming into a rock somewhere between here and there.

"Den Sait Glass!"

"On the tick," came the reply.

"Glee Jun!"
"Hot and ready!"
"Stec Eddis!"
"On the mark!"
"Mors Eth!"

"Item two twenty-three," Lando read. "At long last. Landing tractors out, prepare to lift."

"Landing tractors offline," Vuffi Raa answered. "Zero weight on the landingjacks, negative weight, we're clear! Ease forward on the throttle, sublight drives engaged at three percent power. Altitude—if that's the word for it—twelve thousand meters and rising."

"Good!" the gambler/spaceship captain replied. He hit a button, spoke toward a small grill in the arm of his acceleration chair.

"This is Captain Calrissian speaking. Hope you two are comfortable over there. We're off the ground and headed toward the Fifth Belt. If we arrive in one piece, it won't be any fault of yours!"

TEN

VIOLET FRINGES LASHED AT THE *MILLENNIUM FALCON*, purple flames licked at her hull as lavender-colored lightning flashed in a sky that was infinitely mauve.

"Vuffi Raa, according to these instruments, we're spinning like a top and following a course that's essentially a giant figure eight!" Lando shook his head. The plum-colored glare through the cockpit's canopy was souring his stomach, and the hard vacuum of space, which supposedly was incapable of conveying sound waves, rocked as if with the laughter of malicious giants.

He could scarcely hear the droid's reply.

"I'm sorry, Master, there isn't any help for it. We must trust the program I fed into the engines and attitude controls. I can't see a single instrument on the panel that's reliable." Even the robot's voice had the faintest hint of an hysterical edge. Or perhaps it was Lando's ears, battered by the screaming of a universe tearing itself into bits.

In the passenger lounge, Waywa Fybot was aroused from a sleep unusually deep even for his deep-dreaming species. He stirred, felt the feathers on his long neck ruffling themselves, and tried to close his eyes again. A glimpse through a small round port across the room caught his attention. His gaze became involuntarily fixed upon it, as, one by one, his feathers lifted, stood perpendicular to his body.

Bassi Vobah's hands covered her eyes.

Had she been capable of a single linear thought, she would have wished for a second pair to cover up her ears. It seemed to her that the very Core of the galaxy was shrieking at her for some terrible thing she'd done and somehow forgotten. With a sob, she collapsed sideways on the curving couch, squeezed herself into a huddled ball, knees up to her chin, eyes shut so tightly that they were slowly blackening under the self-inflicted pressure.

Her hands were on her ears, now, so that the titanic bellowing of a sun gone mad and its resonating orbital companions transmitted itself through her very bones.

Beneath her face, the cushion of the couch was soaked with tears.

What end was there to madness?

Starboard, in the cockpit, Vuffi Raa switched off another bank of useless instruments. They were distracting and therefore worse than useless. In a similiar disgruntled humor and for identical reasons, he had shut off his hearing, but it hadn't done quite as much good. Where humans had a small cluster of senses, seven or eight at most, he had nearly a hundred, and at the moment, every one of them seemed to be his enemy.

Unlike Lando, who could suffer the effects but never feel the machine-gun sputter of ionizing particles through his body, part of Vuffi Raa's sensorium was a sophisticated scintillation counter. He could *experience* the density and frequency with which a dozen distinct kinds of particle drilled through him. For the first time in his long existence, he wished sincerely that he had the same limits to his awareness as his master. For the first time in a very long existence indeed, he entertained the notion that what he didn't know mightn't hurt him.

Lando had finished being sick—or at least with having something to be sick with. Fortunately the cockpit sanitation unit was still functioning. Of course it wasn't electronic and had almost no moving parts. Lando, wishing for the impossible like everybody else, was wishing *he* didn't have any moving parts, because, every time he moved something, it sent waves of nausea up whatever limb it happened to be, waves that zeroed in on his solar plexus and waggled it back and forth until he had to inspect the sanitation unit again.

Closely.

He didn't think he ever wanted to see anything purple again as long as he lived. If he lived. Or wanted to.

A blueness that was more than blue seeped in through every port, window, blister, bubble, and televisor on the ship. With the same delightful irony that determines every other day-to-day event in a malicious universe, the only electronic devices on the ship that worked perfectly were the outside visual pickups and their repeaters inside the hull.

Navy blue, robin's-egg blue, sky blue (the sky of a million different planets, all mixed together indiscriminately in agate whirls), powder blue, denym blue, velvet blue, true blue.

Lando blew his nose.

His stomach seemed to have subsided a little. He glanced at Vuffi Raa, who bristled with alertness, tentacles on the controls and his big red eye fastened on the cockpit transparency.

"How are you feeling, Master? Better?"

"Don't call me master. Yes, I'm feeling better. How are you feeling, old trash-compacter?" Lando thought about lighting a cigar—and immediately had to lean over to the sanitation unit again. False alarm, but it very nearly made him stop smoking for the rest of his life.

"I don't know, Master. I'm afraid I had to shut my feelings off in order to function. Please forgive me if I don't seem quite myself for the duration of this journey."

Lando laughed. "I'm never going to be myself again! What can I do to help? You look like you have your tentacles pretty full."

"There is really nothing either of us can do, Master. The course is logged in and—one trusts—being followed. I am merely monitoring life-support and other housekeeping functions. And wondering how reliable even *those* indicators are."

"We could always go back and look—you *or* I, I mean, whichever you think best." He tightened his chair harness a little, straightened up. He'd always wondered why sadness was described as being "blue." Now he knew: much more of this, and he'd be looking around for something sharp to cut his wrists with.

He'd never known there were so many shades of blue, all of them ugly.

"I think not, Master. If something goes wrong up here, I believe it will require the attention of both of us to correct it. You might try asking one of our passengers how things are elsewhere in the ship, though."

"Good idea." He pushed an intertalkie button. "Hello, over there! Anybody listening? We just want to know if the air and lighting and heat are all working. Hello? Can you hear me? Bassi? Fybot?"

Nothing could be heard over the roar of static in the system. Lando looked at Vuffi Raa and shrugged. The instruments said everything was all right in the lounge and elsewhere in the ship. Other instruments, however, said that they were traveling in a spiral now, looping the loop as if riding down the coils of a cosmic corkscrew.

Everything was blue outside. Lando felt a tear creep down his cheek and, for the first time, in a long, long time, thought about a dog he'd had once. It had been run over by a hovercraft.

Bassi Vobah felt green inside.

As a matter of fact, she felt green outside, as well. The leaf-colored radiation then battering at the *Falcon*'s viewports seemed to penetrate to her very marrow, turning it and the blood it produced green, as well.

It didn't make sense. Nothing made sense, and that alarmed her far worse than the light or radiation. She was a person of certain bounds, of linearity, of rationality, of rules. She was a person—an upholder, a maintainer—of law and order.

Now see what had become of her. The penetrating green light let her do exactly that. She could see her own heart beating, deep green muscle fibers pumping bright green blood to medium green tissues and organs—all of which she could watch functioning—and returning, gray-green, to be reoxygenated in her spongy green lungs.

With transparent green oxygen.

* * *

Vuffi Raa examined his tentacles one by one. Reflecting bright yellow light from the cockpit canopy, they gleamed back at him as if made of gold. He had been silver-colored all his life. Now he was a golden droid, glittering at every joint. He rather liked it.

A beeping on the control panel indicated another set of instruments gone mad. Irritably, he shut them off, then returned to a pleased and fascinated contemplation of his highly polished self. Perhaps when it was over, he'd have himself gold plated. Tastefully, mind you, nothing ostentatious. How would gold and the red of his eye look together? Rather nice, he thought.

A yellow light began blinking on the console. It clashed with the yellow streaming in the windows, so he flicked a tentacle down and squashed it. There was a *pop!*, a fizzle, and—blast it all, he had soot on his tentacle tip! He searched around for something to clean it with, found a tissue beneath the panel, and began tidying up. Must be perfectly clean, unless I want the plating to peel on me, and that would be atrocious!

Absently, he reached down to turn off another half-dozen switches, and suddenly became aware of a sallow pinkish starfish of a being sitting right on the dash in front of him. Vermin! How in the name of—

"Vuffi Raa! What are you doing, old cybernaut?"

"What did you call me, you—"

"Vuffi Raa, listen to me! You've busted up the intercom, and you were starting to turn off the life-support monitors. Get hold of yourself, droid! What's the matter?"

With considerable effort, Vuffi Raa forced himself back into something resembling a normal frame of reference. "My word, I'm sorry, Master, I must be taking radiation damage! I don't know what to do about it, though; it's so hard to think. Would you like me better if I had myself gold plated, or would it be too garish?"

Lando stared in blank amazement at his friend. "Can you turn yourself off temporarily? If you removed your tentacles, I could put you in the safe—the one under the panel where I keep my cigars. Would that work?"

"...Er, *what?* You want me to *what*, you organic slug, you blind, groping grub, you sniveling, hydrocarbonated—*yawp!*"

Lando snatched the robot from the pilot's chair and, tentacles trailing, crammed his pentagonal body into the safe.

"I hope you appreciate what I'm doing, old geiger counter. I've ruined my entire supply of cigars—crushed them to a... Vuffi Raa, are you all right?"

The robot responded groggily. "I think so, Master. Did I really call you all those things?" The heavy genuine steel antique safe—left by a previous owner of the *Falcon*—surrounded him on all sides but one and seemed fairly effective at shielding him from the radiation. Lando swung the door as far shut as the robot's tentacles would allow, and chuckled.

"I believe that's the most gumption you've shown since I met you. I rather liked it—but don't make a habit of it. And don't call me master!"

"Master, I'm still feeling the effects of the radiation. Can you get by without me for a while? I'm going to disconnect my manipulators, and ask you to close the door. I'm terribly sorry, but—"

"Don't have another thought about it. That's right, I'll take care of your legs. I'm closing the door now. Have a nice nap. I'll wake you when it's over."

He shut the door, suddenly feeling very lonely, and carefully placed the little robot's tentacles on the pilot's seat, strapping them down. He took a look at the instruments, decided there wasn't very much he could do about them, and sat for a while, wishing he had a cigar.

Waywa Fybot awoke suddenly with the oddest feeling that he was home.

Familiar orange light poured in from somewhere, and suddenly the world felt better, looked better than it had since he'd left his native planet decades ago to join the police.

Why, yes! There was his hometown, a lovely place, not too large yet not so small it didn't have all the conveniences a being could want. He could see it now, wavering a little on the horizon as the sun beat down upon it. He kept walking...

Egad, it had been a long, lonely time out among all those weird alien races. Everywhere he went, they made bird jokes. Could he help it if his people were evolved— and proudly so—from avians?

He only wished that somewhere along the track of time they hadn't lost the knack of—

—but what was this? He was *flying*! A glance to either side assured him that his arms had somehow lengthened, broadened, strengthened. Well, it was all in the genes somewhere, he supposed. Recapitulation, he recalled, recapitulation. He banked steeply, enjoying the sensation, banked the other way to get himself headed right, and passed over the rooftops of the town to the house that he'd been hatched in, a large place of cement and steel beams with a thatched roof. He saw now that the place had been reroofed with genuine straw. His folks were nothing if not stylish. Those checks he was sending home were going to a good cause, then!

He hopped over the fence, stirring the lawn lice with the power of his wings and making them complain in their mewling tones. There were thousands of them, of course. It was a well-kept lawn of a lovely shade of magenta, alive with crawling, rustling legs.

He went inside the house.

The *Falcon* seemed to be flying in right triangles as the Flamewind shifted from orange to red. Lando caught it in the act that time, blinked as many-branched lightning bolts blasted all around the ship.

He fought the urge to seize the controls as the apparent geometry of the *Falcon*'s flight path shifted with the colors from triangles to something indescribable that would nauseate a pretzel-bender. Well, I'll be damned, he thought, we're traveling on the inside surface of a Klein bottle.

Or so it felt.

Satisfied that the ship was flying true to course (or at least resigned to trusting its computer), he bent down and put his head next to the safe.

"Vuffi Raa?"

"Yes, Master?" the robot answered meekly, its voice severely muffled by the metal door and barely audible over the Flamewind's titanic howling.

"Are you all right?"

"I'm all right," the box said. "How are things with you?"

"I'm having a wonderful time, wish you were here. I—*by the Galaxy Itself*! Hold on, I'll get back to you if we live!"

Directly ahead of the *Millennium Falcon* was a vision out of a nightmare. But it was no illusion. Half a kilometer wide, the thing loomed up out of the glowing starfog and ominous red glow like an impossible spider with too many legs.

It seemed to be a starship engine attached to a great number of obsolete one-man fighters. Even as he watched, the smaller craft detached themselves, leaped toward the freighter, their energy-guns spewing destruction.

These were no remote-control pirate drones. These were the real thing.

And they were ready and eager to kill.

ELEVEN

STEADILY THE MOTLEY FIGHTER SQUADRON BORE DOWN on the *Millennium Falcon*. Its instruments unreliable, bound to a predetermined course, the converted freighter was a helpless target. Lando reached to the panel without hesitation, flipped a bank of switches, cutting off the artificial gravity and inertia buffers. Loose items in the cockpit swirled and floated as he punched the override and took control of the ship from the computer.

He couldn't see—not with the dials and gauges acting the way they were—but he could feel. He could con her by the seat of his pants. Whether or not they reached their destination was of secondary importance; survival came first.

A pair of fighters streaked by, spitting fire. The *Fal-*

con's shields glowed and pulsed, absorbing the energy, feeding it into the reactors. There were limits to the amount that could be absorbed that way—in which case the reactor would come apart, taking the ship and everything within a thousand kilometers with it—but for now, each unsuccessful pass fed the *Millennium Falcon*'s engines.

And her guns.

Rolling to defeat another run by the fighters, he slapped the intercom switch. "Bassi Vobah, try and reach the starboard gun-blister! I need some help with the shooting!"

Silence.

Diving steeply, finishing up with a flip that left four fighters soaring helplessly past the freighter, Lando realized that Vuffi Raa, in a moment of demented frustration, had wrecked the intertalkie. He was on his own, for the first time since acquiring the little robot.

He wasn't liking it much.

A pair of smaller weapons on the upper hull was controllable from the cockpit. Lando started keyboarding until he had established fire control through a pair of auxiliary pedals beneath the console. Then, turning sharply—and feeling for the first time the stresses of acceleration as it piled his blood up in odd parts of his body—he trod on the pedals, blasting away at three of the enemy as they passed.

They kept on passing. Either Lando had missed, distracted by maneuvering the ship, or he didn't have the firepower to do the job. It was like a nightmare where you shoot the bad guy and he doesn't fall down.

Half a dozen fighters overtook the *Falcon* from behind, their energy-cannon raking her. She shuddered, staggered. Lando brought her back under control, rode the shock waves out, and continued to pour fire at an enemy he saw—to no effect at all. He slewed the ship around, getting angry, and found he faced at least a dozen of the fast, vicious little craft, coming head on.

He picked out the leader, got it in the canopy cross-hairs, and stamped on both pedals. Every move the fellow made, he matched, keeping the fighter centered, keeping the guns going. The enemy's nose cowling suddenly disintegrated, the small craft burst into flames, showering debris over the *Falcon* and his squadronmates. One of the companion vessels staggered suddenly and veered off, trailing sparks and rapidly dispersing smoke. Two with one—rather prolonged, Lando admitted to himself—shot.

The *Falcon* lurched, as if lifted suddenly from behind, then stabilized as Lando applied counterthrust. Something solid had smacked her in the underside vicinity of the boarding ramp, always a weak point. He skated her in a broad horizontal loop, gave her half a roll as she came around, and there it was: another fighter, its fuselage accordioned, its engines spouting flames.

Ramming? In this century? They must be pretty desperate.

And certainly not pirates, Lando thought as he fought the ship into a better attitude to fire from. No profit in ramming. The bombers, then? The man he'd killed on 6845 could have been a fighter pilot. What had he done to get an entire squadron of fighter pilots that angry with him?

The *Falcon* jumped again. This time the instruments—if they could be relied upon—showed heavy fire being poured into the hull about where the fighter had rammed her. Sure enough, the shields, never at their strongest there, were steadily deteriorating. He rolled the ship, only to be attacked in the same place by another group of fighters. The battle was getting serious.

All right, then: he hadn't anyone to help him, and a battle by attrition was a losing proposition. He only had one ship to lose. He'd taken the measure of the fighters. They were maneuverable and fast—more maneuverable than the freighter, that was only natural. But not as fast, either, not on a straight course. Trusting his feel for direction, he ironed out the circle he'd been making, rolled through three-quarters of a turn to bring him parallel to the Oseon ecliptic, and shoved all throttles to the ends of their tracks.

Behind him, the sublight thrusters outshone the Flamewind for a moment. Then, from the viewpoint of the fighters, they were gone, lost in the multicolored mist.

Lando knew his enemies—whoever they were, confound it!—would not be long in following. They'd had that gigantic antique battleship engine they were using as a collective booster. He had to think of something clever, and he had to do it *fast*.

Momentarily, the Flamewind paled. They were out of the Sixth Belt where they'd begun, and crossing the narrow space between it and the Fifth Belt, their destination.

Either that or they were headed from Six to Seven—Lando didn't trust his navigational capacities at the best of times, let alone now.

No, they were headed toward the Oseon's fractious primary. His hand swept instrument switches. The screens still showed an indecipherable hash, but coming up a little to the starboard was a small cluster of asteroids, irregulars, following their own course through the belt.

He modified his course to meet them.

As he switched the instruments back off, he could see the tiny fleet of fighter craft behind him.

The screen had shown him half a hundred asteroids. His naked eyes showed him half a hundred more, all small—none greater than a few kilometers—all very tightly bunched together. Taking a great chance, Lando cut straight through them until he saw a sort of miracle ahead.

Whether it had been a single rock, struck and not quite split in half, or a pair of floating worldlets that upon colliding had not quite wholly fused, there was a deep crack around its circumference, seventy or eighty kilometers long, no more than twenty meters wide.

Using everything he had to stand her on her nose—without smearing everybody aboard into roseberry jam in the absence of inertial buffering—he steered for the crack, orienting himself correctly and establishing a tangent course to the double asteroid. At the last moment he killed everything but the attitude controls and the docking jets, brought her to a gentle stop deep within the crevasse.

The portside windows showed a half a dozen fighters streaking past without noticing where he'd hidden. Puffing little bursts of attitude reactant, he ground the *Falcon* gently into place. The guns he could control he aimed at open sky. The Flamewind pulsed luridly, looking like a far-off fireworks display.

Which is when he noticed the instruments.

One by one, as he checked them, most of his instrumentation seemed to turn reliable again. He guessed his hidey-hole was an iron-nickel asteroid that acted as a shield against the storm of radiation. The protection wasn't perfect, but it was within the abilities of the ship's electronics to correct.

He ducked his head beneath the panel, spoke loudly and distinctly.

"Vuffi Raa, come out of there! Coffeine break's over!"

Reconnecting the little robot's tentacles was not as easy as it was under ordinary circumstances. They themselves were sophisticated mechanisms, the equal of the fully equipped droids that drove buses and typed stories in newsrooms everywhere in the galaxy. Even deactivated, they had taken a lot of radiation, and their self-repair circuits, set in motion once they were attached to their owner, would require some hours to bring them to full efficiency.

Lando left Vuffi Raa in the cockpit to watch for enemy strays, and wended his way around the corridor to the passenger lounge.

Where he was greeted by utter chaos.

It looked as though a herd of house-sized animals had stomped through. Freed of the restraint of artificial gravity, impelled by sudden changes of direction without inertial damping, everything loose in the room had collided with everything stationary at least once. Perhaps more than once.

And that included Waywa Fybot and Bassi Vobah.

Wires hung loose from ceiling and walls. Small articles of furniture had ended up in extremely strange places. The female police officer was beginning to stir. She moaned heartily, lifted herself up on an elbow, and shook her head.

"What happened? Where are we?"

"Two very good questions," the captain responded. "We were attacked—I don't know by whom—and we escaped. But I don't know to where. Are you all right?" He stopped beside her, assisted her in righting herself. She breathed deeply, made a sketchy self-examination.

"I don't think anything is broken—although to look at this room, that would require a small miracle. Ohhh, my head!"

"Take it easy, you're not expected anywhere very soon. That's me: Lando Calrissian, miracles made to order. You stay there, I'm going to look at our fine feathered fuzz."

He rose and stepped over the debris toward Waywa Fybot's sleeping rack. In the bird-being's case, there had been somewhat less of a miracle. Both the creature's legs were broken, in exactly the same place, apparently where a bar of the rack crossed them. The arrangement had never been intended for free-fall *and* high acceleration.

Nonetheless, the avian officer seemed to have a blissful expression on his face, if Lando could rely on his interpretation of it. The gambler felt a presence at his elbow. Bassi Vobah had made it to her feet and across the room. She stood a bit unsteadily, but she wasn't leaning on anything or anybody.

Lando liked her a little bit more for that, but not much.

"What's wrong with Officer Fybot, and why in the name of the Eternal is he smiling in that idiotic way?"

"Shock, perhaps," Lando answered her. "He's broken both his legs—rather, I've broken both his legs. I'm having a bit of trouble regretting it very much, considering the circumstances. Although I wish I knew how to examine him for further damage. I don't know where he's *supposed* to bend, let alone where he isn't."

Bassi seemed a bit hysterical all of a sudden, and Lando subtracted a few of the points he'd given her. "Well, can't you do something? We can't just leave him lying there!"

He shook his head. "That's exactly what we're going

to do, after I splint those legs. I don't think we'd better move him."

The birdlike creature sat up suddenly, opened his great blue eyes, and said delightedly, "Yes, I'll have another centipede, Mother, if you don't mind!"

TWELVE

" . . . And this one is worth a *NEGATIVE* eighteen—am I clear, so far?" the robot asked. The gigantic yellow avian towering over him at the lounge table nodded, trying to shift to a more comfortable position.

Lando looked up from the covered free-fall dish that contained his long-overdue meal and chuckled, wondering who was going to take whom to the laundry when the bird and the droid had the rules of *sabacc* straight between them. Vuffi Raa's literal-mindedness could be a handicap; on the other hand, Waywa Fybot was a bit preoccupied at present, between his injuries and whatever it was he'd seen during the onslaught of the Flamewind.

They'd gotten the narcotics officer splinted up all right: tinklewood fishing rods had turned out to be good for something, after all. Lando had never been able to sell the blasted things back in the Dilonexa. He still had a bundle of them stacked in one of the auxiliary holds.

Ah, well. Things could be worse.

They could all be dead.

Looking up again, he winked and smiled at Bassi Vobah, likewise feeding herself from a covered tray. It had taken them the better part of an hour to manhandle the bird into a position where his broken legs could be treated, even in free-fall. Then, all at once, it seemed they had a million things to attend to, and it hadn't been until later that they could think of food.

The first order of business had been the *Falcon* herself.

She'd been pretty badly battered by the desperate flight through the Flamewind and the battle with those tramp fighters—Lando still didn't know who the Core they were or why they had attacked him. She'd never been constructed for astrobatics with her inertial dampers shut down. The stresses to her hull and frame must have been titanic.

In addition, she'd been shot at and even rammed, albeit by a tiny, lightweight single-seater with insufficient mass to do very much except momentarily overload her dynamic shielding. That was the key, of course: her force fields had held her together through everything; she was basically a loose pile of nuts and bolts kept in one place by electromagnetogravitic gimcrackery.

But—like his girlfriend the bootlegger's daughter—he loved her still.

"*Master, that should be another centimeter to starboard, I believe.*"

Vuffi Raa had been on the other side of the hull—the inside—measuring the effects of Lando's exhausting labor on the outside. There was a huge ugly dent—but no more than that—in the underside of the boarding ramp where the fighter had smacked it. Lando laughed to himself. You shoulda seen the other guy!

There was nothing he could do right now about the purely mechanical battering. Her seals were intact, the ramp would work perfectly (although there'd be a slight bulge to stumble over, exiting the ship), and what really counted was the shielding.

He moved the micropole another centimeter to the right, waited for the robot's confirmation, and riveted it in place. He didn't understand why the *Falcon*'s previous operators hadn't done this long ago. They had the parts in stores. Just lazy, perhaps. When he was done, the effective density of her defenses would be doubled—of course with a correlative increase in what the shields pulled out of the power plant. Maybe that explained things.

It was hot and sweaty in the vacuum suit, and he was hungry again. Worse, it was extremely claustrophobic working in the skinny wedge of space between the *Falcon*'s belly and the face of the asteroidal crevasse. Well, he had no one but himself to blame for that: he'd sheared half a dozen communications and sensory antennae wiggling her in there, items that by their very nature had to protrude through the defenses in order to operate.

The fact that they hadn't been operating at all, on account of the Flamewind, had helped to guide his instantaneous decision. That and the twenty-odd hostile spacecraft determined to blow the *Falcon* to smithereens.

He began to back from the cramped enclosure. "Let's see about those soft spots on the upper hull, now. Then I'm going to have to quit for a while. This is rather tiring, I'm afraid."

The little droid's response was laden with apologetic overtones. *"Master, if it were possible, I would be doing that for you right now. I—"*

"Vuffi Raa, for once shut up and let somebody else do the donkeywork. You come out here and the blasted sun will start frying your brains again. It's like that safe in the cockpit: we're shielded by the asteroid, but not perfectly. You need the extra protection of the hull."

"Yes, Master. How lucky it was that this crevice runs perpendicular to the direction of the Flamewind. Were it a few degrees the other way, it would function as a funnel or a wave guide and concentrate the—"

"Yes," said Lando with a shudder, "how well I know!" He hadn't been thinking about all that when he'd ducked the *Falcon* in there. He'd simply been trying to get away from the fighters. He'd been flying and fighting by the seat of his pants. Even now it gave him a chill to contemplate.

"All right, I'm out from under. Start the lock cycling. I'll rest for five minutes and then get out on the upper hull." This may be hard work, Lando thought, but when I'm finished, my ship and passengers—and *I*!—will be as well protected from the Flamewind as we are now. *Without* having to hide inside an asteroid and go wherever it feels like taking us.

"Sabacc!" Vuffi Raa cried, displaying his cards to the bewildered bird. "You see, this comes under a special rule: whenever you have the Idiot—that's worth zero, you know—then a Two of anything and a Three of anything are considered an automatic twenty-three."

Dejectedly, Waywa Fybot handed over a few credits. "But that's ridiculous," he said in his ridiculous voice. "It doesn't make sense. Two and three are five, not twenty-three, and besides, the addition of a zero—"

"That's why it's called the Idiot's Array, old passenger pigeon," Lando supplied. If things kept going that way, he was going to fly the ship and let Vuffi Raa do the gambling. Lando opened a flap in his tray, took a final bite of whatever it was, and slid the container into the mass recycler. "Why don't you play with them, Bassi? A three-handed game's more interesting."

"Not on your life!" She shook her head ruefully. "I've played enough *sabacc* to last me a lifetime, thank you."

"Master, would it be presumptuous of me to say that your piloting of the ship earlier today was highly proficient?"

"Only if you don't call me master when you're doing it." Lando could not have been more pleased by this modest praise. He had been a perfectly terrible flyer when Vuffi Raa had taken him in hand—rather, in tentacle. Now, at least sometimes, it was as if he were *wearing* the *Millennium Falcon* instead of riding in her. The little droid had been mortified about his own failure to stand up to the sleet of radiation, at his momentary irrational irresponsibility. But Lando had pointed out that even a diamond, subjected to the proper stress at the proper angle, would shatter.

He tightened down another micropole, this time on the upper surface of the *Falcon*, and went on to the next designated location. No bloody wonder the vessel was so vulnerable; there were a dozen spots where the fields failed to overlap properly.

Carefully he pulled his arm out of the suit sleeve, pulling at the glove with his other hand, snaked his fingers up through the collar into the helmet, and wiped perspiration off his nose. You'd think that after all the centuries people had been wearing pressure suits that someone would have invented—

A red light lit up on the surface just below his chin.

Now what the devil did that mean? Great Edge! It meant a heat-sink overload! He was cooking himself to death! He examined the readouts on his left arm; everything looked nominal there. What was the matter, then? He keyed the suit's transmitter.

"Vuffi Raa, you'd better start the lock going. I've got to get out of this suit. There's something—"

No response.

"Vuffi Raa, do you copy?"

Still no response.

Again he checked the indicators on the panel inset in his sleeve. The communicator pilot was burning steadily. He hoped that his little friend was all right. The difficulty there lay in the fact that the high point of the *Falcon*'s hull was precisely at the upper airlock. He'd had to crawl out from below, climb around the edge of the ship, to get to where he was. Now, with an apparently malfunctioning suit, he was going to have to repeat the procedure in reverse, with no guarantee he could do it in time to keep from being poached in the shell.

Vuffi Raa could save him a critical few minutes—if only he'd answer!

"Captain to *Millennium Falcon*, do you read?"

Nothing.

He sat as still as possible, thinking as hard as he could. It seemed to be getting hotter inside the suit by the second.

Suddenly, he glanced at the riveting gun in his hand and at the airlock wheel wedged against the rock that formed a roof over his head. Crawling slowly forward a meter, he rapped against the shank of the wheel. The *clank!*, transmitted by the hull, reverberated in his suit. He tried it again. And again.

A few moments later, there was another kind of reverberation in his suit.

"Master, is that you making that noise? I can't raise you on the comlink."

Uncertain whether Vuffi Raa could hear him, he bashed the riveter against the wheel again, once.

"Are you in some kind of trouble other than communication's being down?"

Good guess, Vuffi Raa. *Clank!*

"I'll come and get you, right—"

Clank! Clank!

"But, Master . . . !"

Clank! Clank!

A few sweaty minutes later, another suited figure clambered toward Lando over the edge of the ship. Bassi Vobah—her pistol strapped to the outside of her borrowed vacuum-wear—crawled beside him, placed her helmet in contact with his.

"Once a cop, always a cop," Lando said before she got a chance to open her mouth.

"Don't be an idiot. What's wrong with your suit?"

He shook the sweat out of his eyes. It floated in tiny droplets inside the helmet, distracting him. "Coolant failure of some kind. I was worried about getting dinner; now it looks like I'm going to *be* din—"

"Oh, shut up! You relax and lie still. I'll pull you out of here. Your little five-armed friend and Officer Fybot are at the downside lock right now, waiting for us."

"Not the bird, he's accident prone!"

"You should talk!"

Lando was approaching unconsciousness when they cycled through the lock. Vuffi Raa practically tore the helmet off his master—and his ears with it. The resultant blast of fresh air in Lando's face was like an arctic gale.

"Well, another small adventure," the gambler observed as the three of them stripped him down to his underwear and handed him a plastic bag of water, "when what I really needed was a few days in a sensory-deprivation tank. That's the universe for you. Anybody think of slapping something in the food-fixer?"

Bassi Vobah huffed and stomped her way out of the lock area, not an easy thing to do in the absence of gravity. "You're welcome!" she said over her shoulder.

The alien officer followed her, limping awkwardly on his splinted and bandaged legs.

Vuffi Raa looked up at Lando from where he was minutely examining the vacuum suit. "Master," he said cautiously, and in a very quiet voice, "did you remove this suit between the time you were working down below and when you went topside?"

Lando floated on his back beside the airlock hatch, thinking—but only thinking—about getting up and going forward. The cold metal felt extremely good to him at the moment.

"Had to," he replied, hoping the robot wasn't headed where he thought he was headed. "Call of nature."

"So that's when it was done. Master, somebody—"

"Sabotaged the suit when I wasn't looking, is that it?"

"I'm afraid so. They crossprogrammed the communicator with the cooling system. Oddly enough, if you'd continued trying to call me on the radio, it would have saved you from being roasted."

Lando shook his head, grabbed a stanchion, and sat up stiffly. "That's a little obscure, even as practical jokes go. Which one of them do you suppose it is?"

"Bassi Vobah helped to save your life."

"When she couldn't avoid it. Come on, I want a smoke. Do you suppose I could roll a cigarette out of one of those crushed cigars in the safe?"

"Why would you want to, Master?"

"Because it's there."

* * *

The next order of business—after getting something to eat—was figuring out where they were. Lando's running battle with the fighter squadron had taken him through many turns and twists, and across what distances he couldn't guess. He and Vuffi Raa spent a good deal of time pondering all that over the navigational computer.

"The device is useless, Master. The radiation's finished it off. That gives me an eerie feeling, I must confess. However, the catalog has some information: this asteroid is uninhabited, but it isn't uncharted."

In the seat beside the robot in the cockpit, Lando's shoulders jerked in surprise. "What? You mean you know where we are?"

"I know the catalog number and some other characteristics of the asteroid we're on—or in, if you prefer. Its configuration is unique, and has been noticed in the past. On the other hand, I can't say precisely where the *asteroid* is at the moment. I have its orbital elements, but everything in this system is subject to everything else, gravitywise—"

"'Gravitywise?'"

"Yes, Master, and predicting where anything will be at any given moment amounts to a billion-body geometry problem. At any other time than Flamewind, there are continuous long-range sensor inventories, and the system's databanks are updated hourly, but you see—"

"I see." Lando turned a knob, activating the deck plates at their lowest intensity so he'd have just enough gravity to roll a cigarette. He lit it, kicked them off again, and reclined in his chair, mind working furiously.

"Once we get out in that mess again, we won't be able to navigate," he said, more to himself than to the robot.

Vuffi Raa agreed, adding, "However, I shall be of more assistance, now that you have increased the shield-

◆ 118 ◆

ing, Master. The trouble is that we don't know where to go."

"We still have that dead-reckoning program of yours?" Reflexively, he flicked ash off his cigarette. It drifted in the cabin, finally settling on Vuffi Raa's carapace. The droid, equally absently, flicked it off. It broke up and they both lost sight of it.

"Yes, Master—with what amounts to a big ball of unknown squiggles at the end of it where you evaded those fighters."

"Can you estimate how big a ball?"

"Yes, certainly. From the power consumption, if nothing else."

"Then that's our margin for error. We simply follow the course as if we'd never deviated and hunt through a sphere of space the same size for Bohhuah Mutdah's estate."

"I'm afraid not, Master, if for no other reason than that the sphere doesn't stay the same size. It increases as a function of probable error as we travel sunward. During Flamewind, there's no way of accurately estimating drift, and—"

"Does that catalog of yours give details on Mutdah's asteroid?"

"Fifty-seven ninety-two? Yes, Master, I—"

"Then it should give us some hints about the other asteroids around there; it's interested in the weird shape of this one. Let's get as close as we can, then pick our way, rock by rock, until we find the right one."

"Very well, Master, I see no other alternative."

"Neither do I. Now, while we're still up here and have some privacy, we're going to talk about who it is *this* time that's trying to kill me."

"We're nearly a day behind schedule!" Bassi Vobah

protested. They were sitting in the lounge again. Lando had powered up the gravity, assuring himself beforehand that his passenger with the broken legs was settled comfortably, and asked Vuffi Raa to prepare another meal before they started.

"Do you realize," the female officer continued to an unappreciative audience in general and an increasingly irritated Lando in particular, "that, under ordinary conditions, this trip would have required a little over two hours?"

"As an inhabitant of the Oseon System, my dear hired gun, you should appreciate better than anyone else the inapplicability of the expression 'ordinary conditions.' There's a storm going on out there, and although I'm not altogether unwilling to venture out in it again, some preparation is essential."

"Captain, may I remind you that the discretion in this matter isn't wholly yours to—"

"Officer, may I remind you that I am the captain, and that, if you continue nagging me, I'm going to take that blaster away from you and stuff it up your nose?"

The policewoman blinked, sat back in stunned outrage. Even her superiors had never spoken to her like that! Lando grinned—not altogether unironically, and laid down the law:

"Now see here: one of you attempted to murder me when I was outside the ship. I'm going to be rather busy when we quit this refuge, both Vuffi Raa and I are, and I don't want to have to watch my back. Therefore, until we can arrive at an agreement concerning arrangements, we will sit right here. My inclination—and if you think I'm joking, you're woefully deceived—is to handcuff the pair of you together until we get to 5792. Unless you can think of an alternative that suits you better—and will satisfy me—that is what we'll do.

"Or we'll park here until the Core freezes over."

Bassi Vobah sat in angry silence, her arms folded across her chest, a sour expression on her face. Waywa Fybot blinked his huge blue eyes, looked thoughtful, but in the end said no more than did his colleague.

Finally: "Now look, you two, I'm not kidding! I haven't figured out who's doing what to whom and why, yet, but there's something—possibly *several* some-things—going on. I make it a practice to avoid getting killed. One of you get out your handcuffs and lock your-self to the other immediately, or—"

"*Master!*" came a shout over the intercom. "*We've got trouble—big trouble! I need you on the flight deck!*"

Rising quickly, Lando glanced from one cop to the other, smashed a frustrated fist into the palm of his other hand, turned, and hurried to the cockpit.

"What is it, Vuffi Raa? Just now I've got—"

"Look forward, Master, to the edge of the crevasse."

Lando settled in his chair, strapped himself in, and, as a happy afterthought, turned the local gravity in the lounge up to approximately three times the normal pull. "*That* ought to keep them in one place! I—*oh, no!*"

"Oh, yes, Master. You can make out the reflections from their hulls. The fighter squadron has found us. They'll be firing into this canyon—without any chance of missing—in a very few seconds!"

THIRTEEN

"MASTER, I HAVE FAILED YOU AGAIN! WE CANNOT ES-cape, my pilot skills are therefore useless. Nor can I man the guns—my programming forbids it!"

Lando waggled back and forth at the controls, loos-ening the *Falcon* in its rocky nest. He was wishing he could bring the starboard quad-guns to bear, but that was asking too much.

Aside: "We all have our limits, Vuffi Raa, remember what I told you about diamonds. Just—"

Diamonds? That gave the gambler an idea—a *gam-bler's* idea, to be sure, but it was all he had at the moment.

"Get out of there, old automaton, strap yourself in the jumpseat behind us, and warn me if anybody comes up the tunnel to the cockpit. I may be able to get us out of this mess, but I want my back safe and my elbows un-jogged."

As soon as the droid had restationed himself, Lando began hitting switches. He had some time: the crevasse was deep, composed mostly of metal-bearing rock. It would take the enemy a while to find the *Falcon*, especially since they were out in that impossible...

Taking his first risk, he cut the gravity in the lounge. A needle on a power-consumption gauge dropped slightly to the left. Next, he began robbing power from every other system. Out went every light in the ship. Off went the life-support—they'd all be fine for a few minutes without it, and, if his plan didn't work, they wouldn't need it. He'd never reactivated the inertial damping; he placed it on standby, contingent on what happened next. When he was finished, only the panel lights were glowing, that and Vuffi Raa's great eye behind him. The ship was deadly silent.

With enormous reluctance, he cut the standby power to every gun on the ship. It made him feel naked, but they were useless for what he had in mind.

"All right, Vuffi Raa, everything quiet back there?"

"I can hear the pair of them wondering what's going on, Master."

"Let them wonder."

He reached across the instrument array and flipped the shields on. Lights sprang into bright existence, making him feel better. Then he unlatched a metal cover over a graduated knob. Normally it was set at a tiny minus value, placing the main strength of the shields just under the first few molecules of the ship's skin. There were sound reasons for this, but Lando didn't care about them now.

He turned the knob, slowly, very carefully.

The ship's structure groaned as the shields expanded, first a millimeter, then a centimeter away from the surface of the hull. Stresses were transmitted through the hull members to the heavily buttressed casing of the field generator. Lando turned the knob a little more.

The *Falcon* had been tightly wedged within the rock, the wheel of her upper airlock hatch scraping one side of the crevice, the bottom of her hull abraded by the other. There hadn't been a millimeter to spare.

Now Lando was demanding more room, expanding the shields against the asteroid's substance. He turned the knob again; something groaned like a living—dying—thing aft of the cockpit, but the panel lights still showed everything intact.

Half a dozen fighters shot by the lip of the crevasse, seeking, searching, probing. One of them fired an experimental shot. It penetrated and rebounded half a dozen times within the walls before it faded.

Another group of fighters swooped past.

And another.

They were circling the asteroid, searching the long canyon, hundreds of kilometers in extent, for the hidden freighter that had burned at least two of their number out of the polychrome skies of the Oseon.

Their flybys were becoming more frequent as they narrowed the search.

Lando turned the knob a little more, a little more.

A brilliant beam of energy cascaded across the forward shields. By accident or design, the enemy had found its prey. The power needle jumped. Lando slammed the knob to the right as far as it would go.

There was a deafening exploding sound. Multicolored light showered in on Lando and the robot as the asteroid burst under the stresses of the shields and the Flamewind swept around them again.

Secondary explosions punctuated the space around them: one, three, five—Lando lost count as the hurtling rock fragments smashed and scattered the fighter squadron—seven, eight. Perhaps more, he wasn't sure. No one turned to fight. He diverted a little power to the inertial dampers, cut the shields back to normal, fired up the drives and kicked in the dead-reckoner.

They were on their way again.

He turned up the gravity in the lounge. Even he could hear the thump and a curse from Bassi Vobah. He grinned and shook his head.

The improved shields seemed to help considerably. Vuffi Raa retained his reason, Bassi Vobah was as rational as she ever was. Waywa Fybot dozed in his rack, recovering from his injuries with the aid of an electronic bone-knitter from the *Falcon*'s medical bag of tricks. He ought to be completely well in a few more hours, just in time to arrest the trillionaire addict.

Swell.

Lando, for the most part, stayed up in the cockpit. He was tired of having police for company, preferred the company of Vuffi Raa. The little robot scurried around, tidying up and doing minor repairs. He reported that the hull was perfectly sound, despite the torture inflicted on it, and, in a spare hour, checked the mountings of the shield generator for stress crystallization.

There wasn't any.

Now that he had time to think about it again, Lando realized that his life had become very complicated.

He'd had many of the same thoughts in jail back on Oseon 6845, but things had been simpler, even as recently as then.

He was a simple man, he told himself, a relatively honest gambler who usually only cheated to avoid winning too conspicuously. Yet someone—several someones, it would appear—kept trying pretty hard to kill him. First with a bomb. Then with another bomb. Then, just to show a little versatility, with a big piece of titanium pipe. Finally, most recently, with a cleverly jimmied spacesuit. He didn't even count the pirate attack or the two encounters with the fighter squadron, although the latter seemed at least tangentially connected. He simply didn't know where it all fit in.

Everybody has enemies, especially a gambler who makes a habit of winning. But the vendetta was ridiculous. For the hundredth time, he reviewed his life over the past few years, trying to discover some person he'd known and hurt badly enough to merit such attention.

He was a skillful *and* fortunate man with the cards, and, despite his failings as a merchant captain, he was becoming a pretty good ship-handler, as well. If he did say so himself. Vuffi Raa said so, himself.

Unfortunately, when closely examined, his proficiency was a talent of no practical value. All it seemed to do was get him into trouble. He belonged on a luxury interstellar liner as a passenger, educating other passengers about the follies of trying to fill an inside straight. The soldier-of-fortune routine was beginning to pall.

Well, if by some slim chance he got out of this mess, he'd see about rearranging his life. He had come to love the *Falcon*, but it was a dangerous affair, one that threatened to get him killed at just about any moment. Vuffi Raa was quite another matter, a good friend and partner, an astute adviser. But this captain business...

With a sinking heart, Klyn Shanga inspected the remnants of his command. One lost at Oseon 6845. Two lost in the first engagement with that tramp freighter. And now, between the Flamewind and that exploding asteroid, a mere five fighters left. It was possible that more had survived, were even now trying to find their way back to the squadron through storm and radiation. Some of them might even live past the misadventure *because* they'd lost touch with their comrades.

Five tiny fighting craft, no two alike, except in general size, range, and firepower. They drew on the battle-cruiser engine, restoring their own power even as it pulled them through the nightmarish void.

Well, each of the men had known from the beginning what he faced: a cruel and cunning enemy; a being that took delight in human misery; a creature willing to sacrifice whole cultures, entire planets to satisfy whatever unknowably evil objectives it set for itself.

And each had understood, when he had assembled them in his home system from the ragtags of a dozen armies, how little chance there was of surviving the quest. To them, it had been worth it.

Five out of twenty-four.

It still was.

Bohhuah Mutdah lounged in a gel-filled recliner, watching a performance of surpassing obscenity. On the lawn before him, all manner of sentient beings mingled, progressing through every permutation of activity possible to them. He had hired them—over three hundred of them—for that express purpose. They were following his detailed instructions.

He found it boring.

Bohhuah Mutdah found very nearly everything boring. There was little he cared to participate in directly, owing either to security considerations—even now he was surrounded by an unobtrusive force field to protect him from potential assassins among his employees—or to his physical condition. He had seen too much of life, had too much of life. Still he clung to it, although he didn't know why.

To say that Bohhuah Mutdah was obese would be to engage in understatement. He had begun, a hundred years ago, with a large frame, a little over two meters tall, broad-shouldered, long-legged. That had been only the beginning, an armature on which he molded a grotesque parody of heroic sculpture. He was heroically obese, monumentally obese, cosmically . . .

On a genuine planet, with a real gravitic pull, he would have weighed three hundred kilos, perhaps three-fifty. He hadn't entered such a field for a quarter of a century. He was bigger around the waist than two large men could reach and working on three. His own arms looked stubby, his legs like cones turned over on the ends into absurdly tiny baby feet. His face was a bushel basket full of suet, dotted with impossibly tiny features: a pair of map-pin eyes, a pair of pinprick nostrils, a miniature blossom of a mouth.

He hadn't used his own hands for any purpose for five years.

He could afford to use the hands of others. He had no real notion of what he was worth. No truly rich man does. He'd heard it said he was the wealthiest human in the known galaxy. He wasn't sure about that, either, and didn't care.

He didn't care about anything at all—except, perhaps, *lesai*.

Maybe it was the drug that kept him going, maintained the mild interest he experienced in remaining alive. Everything else, the world, the entire universe, resembled a bleak gray plain to him. The Flamewind, lashing and snarling above his heavily shielded dome, seemed colorless to him, although the hirelings on the lawn paused long enough, now and again, to look up in awe at the display.

It wasn't being rich that had done this to him. As long as he could remember, since he was a child in rather ordinary circumstances, he'd puzzled over the phrase "will to live" and wondered what drove others to the bizarre extremes they sometimes reached while struggling merely to remain in existence. Mutdah's wealth had been the casual result of a decade's desultory application of his incredible intelligence, directing his modest substance toward a path of inevitable, automatic growth.

Nor did that intelligence provide him with an answer to his real problem. He knew submorons, many of them working for him, whose capacity to enjoy life was infinite compared to his. He simply lived on, whether he cared to or not, like a machine—no, even the machines who worked for him appeared to relish the mockery of life they possessed with greater fervor and satisfaction than their master.

It was a puzzle. Luckily, he didn't care enough about solving it to let it worry him unduly. He watched the sky, he watched his performers. He watched reflections of it all in the fist-sized Rafa life-crystal he wore upon a yard of silken cord about his neck, wondering why he'd bothered to obtain the thing in the first place.

That philosopher, whoever he had been, had been right: the greatest mystery of life was life itself. And the question that best stated it was: why bother?

A tear rolled down Bohhuah Mutdah's pillow of cheek, but he was far too numb to notice it.

In a hidden place, Rokur Gepta thought upon the art of deception. How ironic it was, and yet how fitting, that the surest way to lie to others is to lie to oneself first. If you can convince the single soul who *knows* the falsehood for what it is, then everyone else is an easy mark.

Salesmen had known this simple wisdom for ten thousand years, but Rokur Gepta had never known a salesman. Politicians knew it, too, but politicians were Gepta's natural prey, and while the spider knows the ways of the fly in many respects, she never asks him what he thinks of the weather.

Gepta, isolated by necessity now, from his cruiser, from his underlings, even from his beloved pet—they'd better be taking proper care of it, or they themselves would face a greater appetite!—did not regret the rigors which fulfillment of his plans required. Long centuries before an infant Bohhuah Mutdah moaned that life meant nothing, Gepta was consumed by an overwhelming lust for all the things life meant to him: power; hunger filled; power; humiliation of enemies; power.

He let himself be warmed, in his stifling concealment, by memories of triumphs past, by extrapolation to future victories. He saw himself astride the universe, whipping it on to exhaustion in his service. In a linear progression, he would make vassals of emperors, servants of gods. Nothing was beyond the scope of his ambition, nothing.

And his certain destruction of Lando Calrissian would be but a microscopic footnote, a token of good luck, a single four-leaf clover in an infinite field. It was an exercise in determination to Rokur Gepta, an example of taking minute pains to assure that everything, absolutely everything, was right.

The subject of a microscopic footnote to the future history of intergalactic space was pleased.

He rolled another cigarette and lit it while Vuffi Raa checked references against the Oseon ephemeris. Exactly as the gambler had anticipated, they'd wound up, at the end of the program, in a flock of asteroids which were well cataloged and identifiable.

And not too very far away from Oseon 5792.

A gambler's life had taught him to take satisfaction from success without being cocky or becoming careless. Well outside the range of the best-known ship-detection systems, and despite the fact that the Flamewind howling outside had blinded any such devices, he ordered Bassi Vobah and her feathered colleague into hiding. Examining the blueprints of the *Falcon*, it had occurred to him that there was space below the corridor decking that might be perfect for installing hidden lockers. Smuggling was merely an interest with him; it might someday rise high enough among his priorities to become a hobby. In the meantime, he had not as yet taken time or gone to the expense of building the lockers. He might never get around to it.

As a consequence, the two police officers were extremely uncomfortable just then, zipped into their spacesuits and stuffed beneath the decking. They clung to stanchions, cursing Lando and their jobs, wishing they had become clerk typists or shoe salespersons.

Which suited their chauffer right down to the ground.

"Fifty-seven ninety-two coming up, Master. I believe it's that big blob over there on the right."

"That's *starboard*, old binnacle; don't let's disillusion the tourists. Yo-ho-ho and a bottle of—You've got the package ready?"

The little robot turned from the controls, reached behind himself adroitly, and took a vacuum-wrapped parcel from the jumpseat. "I inspected it and analyzed it as you requested, although I don't quite understand why that was necessary. It's genuine *lesai*, all right, in its most potent form, enough for six months' use by even the most habituated addict, and worth more than—"

"Fine, fine. The reason why I wanted you to check it is that I didn't want to be caught delivering a shipment of phony goods. The recipients would likely find a way to reprimand me. Terminally. Also, I didn't want to be exposed to the stuff myself. I don't know how addictive it is, but it's potent applied to the skin."

Lando checked the lightweight vacuum suit he was wearing, made sure his stingbeam was handy in an outside pocket. The part of the mission that had always worried him was coming up. His gambler's wisdom told him it was a bad bet: when the owner of a big, well-defended estate found out he'd brought the law, there were bound to be some recriminations.

The *Falcon* drifted closer to Oseon 5792.

At approximately a hundred kilometers—farther than Lando would have expected under the current "weather" conditions—they were hailed by a cruising ship. It was small, like the fighters Lando had fought off, but brand-new and nearly as heavily armed as his own. Radio being out of the question, it was using a modulated laser to communicate. Unfortunately, Lando didn't have a *de-*modulator.

"They say we're supposed to stop here," Vuffi Raa supplied. "They say they'll fry us out of the firmament if we don't heave to for boarding. Good heavens, Master, they're listing the weaponry they carry! If they're only lying about ninety-five percent of it, we're done for."

"That's all right, old electrodiplomat. How do we tell them that we're stopping for inspection?" Lando had a password, but—with all the other details in his mind the past few days—it hadn't occurred to him that there might be a problem using it.

"I can tell them, Master." The robot leaned forward, directed his big red-faceted eye toward the security ship, and *blat!* a beam of scarlet coherency leaped through the canopy.

"Tell them the secret word is '*dubesor*'—I understand that's a native insult on Antipose XII." Lando took a final, not altogether relaxed, drag on his cigarette and put it out. Vuffi Raa's laser beam winked out almost at the same moment, and he turned to his master.

"They say we're late. I told them, who wouldn't be, considering the Flamewind and everything, and gave them a little edited version of our trouble with the fighters— presumed to be pirates. Did I act correctly, Master?"

"First *sabacc*, and now bluffing your way past the bouncers. I'm not sure whether to be proud of you or worried. I think I'm a bad influence. What did they say?"

"That we're expected and should set down on the small field opposite the surface mansion complex—but not to try any dirty tricks. They gave me another list of engines of destruction they can employ with pinpoint accuracy against a ground target."

"That guy must have been a drummer for an arms company. All right, let's set her down. You do it, won't you? I'm a little too nervous to risk it, considering my amateur status as a pilot."

"Very well, Master."

I wonder what the folks on Antipose XII are doing tonight, Lando thought, whooping it up in the local saloon and calling each other *dubesor*?

It beat hell out of what he was about to do.

FOURTEEN

O SEON 5792 WAS NOT PARTICULARLY LARGE AS ASTER-oids in the Oseon go.

It was perhaps fifteen kilometers across its widest span, a flattened disk-shaped accretion of many smaller bodies or a peculiar fragment from a shattered planet. To Lando it rather resembled an island, floating on a sea of impossible blue—that being the color the Flamewind was concentrating on at the moment.

Yet it was an island with two personalities.

The top side, as the gambler thought of it—perhaps because it was the first view that he had of it—was a mythological garden, dotted with small lakes, spread with rolling lawns, and punctuated here and there by groves of trees, all held down by high transparent domes and artificial gravity. As the *Falcon* approached, Lando could make out clumps of beings on the grass before a huge old-fashioned palace, doing something. He couldn't make out quite what it was.

The underside of 5792 was an impressive miniature spaceport, cluttered parking grounds to an enormous motley fleet of spacecraft, almost as if it were a hobbyist's collection, rather than a working landing field. The port was ringed, at the asteroid's edge, with heavy armament; Lando began taking the security picket's boasts more seriously. These folks believed in firepower and had the hardware to back up their belief.

Vuffi Raa settled the *Falcon* in a berth designated for him with a pulsing beacon. As the freighter's landing legs came into gentle contact with the surface, and the robot began slapping power-down switches, Lando slapped his safety-belt release.

"I'm going to finish suiting up. You understand what you're supposed to do?"

He pulled on a lightweight space glove, gave his stingbeam another check. It shouldn't look too obvious. No point making things easy for the opposition.

"Yes, Master, I'm to conceal myself in the main control-cable conduit between here and the engine area. I'll tap into the lines there and keep the *Falcon* ticking over for an instant getaway.

The little droid paused as if reluctant to continue. "I'm to stay here, no matter what, and blast off for deep space if you're not back within eight hours. Why do you ask me to repeat these things like a child? You know I have a perfect memory."

"Yeah? Well, I'd feel a lot better about that if you remembered not to call me master. Besides, you've been known to improvise."

The robot considered this gravely. "You could be right,

Master. I certainly won't depart as you've instructed me to. Not without looking for you first."

Though inwardly pleased at the response, Lando scowled. "To hell with you then," he snarled. "I've logged your manumission into the *Falcon*'s memories, just in case I don't get back. You'll be a free machine, my little friend, like it or not, with a fully operational commercial starship of your very own."

He was halfway through the rear door of the cabin when he turned and spoke again. "By the way, I've also made you my legal heir. I wish you better luck with this space-going collection of debris than I've had."

The droid said nothing, but his eye dimmed very slightly in a manner that indicated he'd been touched emotionally. Then: "Good luck to you, too, Master. I'll be waiting . . ."

But Lando was already gone.

He followed his master off the tiny bridge.

In the passageway, the robot loosened a ceiling panel, hoisted himself up inside, and drew the panel into place beneath himself. Within a few seconds, he was a part of the *Millennium Falcon*. A very expensive, highly unconventional, and sullenly (for the moment, anyway) independent one.

Carrying his helmet under one arm, the parcel of *lesai* under the other, Lando reached a certain point in the ship's main corridor where, transferring both burdens clumsily to one hand, he stooped down and rapped, not very gently, on the floor.

A section of roughly-sawn decking parted upward and an angry and uncomfortable-looking Bassi Vobah raised her helmeted head.

"I'll take my money now," Lando said. His own helmet began to slip from between his gloved fingers. He gave it an irritated hitch. He doubted he'd really need the thing anyway, but he was a man who took precautions. He was taking one now.

"You can whistle for it, low-life!" Bassi Vobah's spacesuit served a different and more certain purpose. It was a common quarantine practice to flood a visiting ship with poison gas. Hard on insects, germs, and furry creeping things of a million species, it also discouraged smuggling of certain types and illegal immigration where such phenomena were regarded as a problem by the authorities. "I don't keep bargains with criminals!"

"Then why do you work for politicians?" He thrust a determined hand out. "Give me my money, or I'll suddenly and to my innocent amazement discover a pair of stowaways. Just in time for Bohhuah Mutdah's security goons to take them into custody."

"You *wouldn't*!"

Lando smiled sweetly. "Try me."

Breathing heavily, and from more than exertion, Bassi Vobah struggled among the pipes and wires in the cramped, disorganized space beneath her. She fetched up a bundle, threw it at Lando's feet.

"Take it then, you mercenary anarchist!"

"That's me all over," he agreed charmingly, counting the credits. One hundred seventy-three thousand, four hundred eighty-seven of them. Well, at least Lob Doluff was an *honest* criminal. Better than that, by returning everything he'd won to Lando, the Administrator Senior had, in effect, underwritten the gambler's expenses on the mission.

"Thanks, fuzzikins. Try and understand it takes all kinds. *I* certainly do."

Bassi Vobah slumped back into the floor space, slammed the improvised lid down on top of herself. Lando took an angry step forward, stamping on the slab, ostensibly to seat it flush with the rest of the floor, but more as if afraid that some vindictive spirit would rise from its grave to haunt him.

Then he chuckled at his own annoyance with the lady cop, dismissed it, and continued along the passageway. A few meters farther, he bent again, tapped the beginning of shave-and-a-haircut on the deck, got the final two notes from Waywa Fybot, straightened, and went on.

Near the ship's main entrance, he used a screwdriver to good effect, stashing the wad of money behind an intercom panel. He let down the boarding ramp and stepped onto the "soil" of Oseon 5792.

Bohhuah Mutdah met him halfway.

The trillionaire's private planetoid, while more than a dozen kilometers in diameter, was less than three in thickness. Like nearly every other human-developed rock in the system, it had been steadily honeycombed over the decades of its occupation with storerooms, living quarters, utility areas, and spaces for every other conceivable use.

Two armed guards in stylish livery—and heavy body armor—met Lando at the foot of the boarding ramp, each stationing himself at one of the gambler's elbows. For what had appeared to be a bustling port facility from a few thousand meters overhead, the place seemed remarkably deserted just then. No one else was about, organic or mechanical, as far as the eye could see.

The guards bracketed Lando for a brisk walk across the ferroconcrete apron, into a corrugated plastic service building, through the door of an industrial-grade elevator, and down into the innards of the asteroid. He needn't have bothered with his helmet. There was enough artificial pull to hold a generous atmosphere. The helmet's transparent bubble made a not too terribly convenient receptacle and carrying case for the package of *lesai*.

"Well, fellows," Lando offered conversationally half-way through the elevator ride, "everybody here enjoying Flamewind? Where is everybody, by the way?"

A stony silence followed, during which the gambler spent a futile several moments attempting to peer through the mirror-reflective visor on the riot helmet of the guard at his left elbow. Instead, he saw the swollen and distorted image of a gambler with a mustache lamely trying to make conversation.

The elevator halted with knee-bending alacrity, its door whooshed open, the guards escorted Lando into what appeared to be a titanic library. The spherical chamber, half a klick from wall to wall, was lined with every known variety of book produced by any sentient race anywhere in the galaxy: chips, memory rods, cassettes and tapes of various compatibilities, bound and jacketed hard- and soft-cover publications, scrolls, folios, clay, wood, and bamboo tablets, stones, bones, hides stretched wide on wooden poles, clumps of knotted rope, and a good many other artifacts whose identity the young captain could only infer from their presence with those other objects he *did* recognize.

The only things missing were librarians and browsers. The place seemed utterly devoid of life.

Bohhuah Mutdah, Lando surmised, was addicted to the printed (written, punched-in, hieroglyphed) word as much as to *lesai*—either that or he had carried pretension to a new extreme. Perhaps it was a tax write-off.

The three, Lando and his personal bookends, were whisked by a length of fluorescent monofilament—one of hundreds drifting handily around the cavernous room—to the center, where an obese giant took his ease.

The trillionaire was being read to by a frail, elderly male servant in a long white robe. Mutdah himself wore nothing but a pair of purple velvoid shorts that would have made a three-piece suit for Lando with an extra pair of trousers.

"Ah, Captain Calrissian," hissed the enormous figure floating effortlessly in midair. His flesh billowed as he made a slight gesture. "I am given to understand you have a delivery for me and that you braved the perils of a solar storm to accomplish the swift completion of your appointed rounds, is that correct?"

Lando, angered by the condescension, cleared his throat, nodded in a way that someone foolish might have interpreted as a slight bow. He reached across his space-suited chest to extract the *lesai* from his helmet.

"Hold it! Freeze where you stand!"

That from a guy who wouldn't even discuss the weather with a fellow. He and his companion had their blasters drawn, pointed at the gambler's head. The first guard looked to Mutdah. His employer nodded miscroscopically. The guard took the drugs, helmet and all, examined them one-handed without reholstering his weapon, gave them back to Lando.

The second gunman thrust a palm out. "Okay, let's have it!"

Lando blinked. "What are you talking about?"

A wheezy chuckle emanated from the trillionaire. "Your pistol, Captain. Give him your pistol. You were thoroughly scanned in the elevator."

With a disgruntled expression, the gambler carefully extracted his stingbeam, handed it to the security man.

"The other one, as well, please, Captain."

Lando shrugged, grinned at Mutdah, bent over and removed an identical weapon from his boot. Straightening, he gave it to the guard on his right, who was having trouble handling three guns with two hands.

"What happens now?" the gambler asked mildly.

"That will be all, sergeant, thank you," Bohhuah Mutdah said cheerfully, then, turning to the servant, who had remained impassive, added, "You may go as well, Ekisp."

That left Lando and the trillionaire sitting all alone in thin air in the center of the cavern.

"I thank you sincerely for the trouble you have gone to on my behalf, Captain Calrissian. I ask you to forgive the concern for my continued health which my employees often demonstrate. It is personally gratifying, but sometimes a nuisance. Your property will be returned when you depart."

Not knowing what to say, Lando said nothing.

"On that table, beneath the book old Ekisp left behind, you will discover another package. Please open and examine it; assure yourself that it contains what it is supposed to. The package you have brought may then be left in its place. Will you do that now, please?"

Pulling lightly on part of the monofilament mesh surrounding them, Lando drifted to the table, the sort usually found at either end of a sofa, incongruous there in free-fall. The book, a heavy double roll of vellum written in an alphabet he didn't recognize, had been tucked beneath an elastic band that stretched across the tabletop from edge to edge.

Beneath band and book, as the trillionaire had said, was indeed a bundle. Lando stripped opaque brown plastic from it, attempting to control his eyebrows when he saw the stack of hundred-thousand-credit certificates it contained. With an experienced thumb, he riffled through the pile, estimated that there were at least two hundred of them. Twenty million credits—the gambler suppressed a whistle.

What price lizard mold?

He placed the package of *lesai* under the restraining band, replaced the scroll, and pushed himself back from the table. "Thank you, sir," the gambler said. "If that will be all, I'll be getting back to my—"

Mutdah had opened his mouth to reply, but whatever he had been going to say was muffled by a

BRAAAMM!

Beneath them, the elevator door bulged and split, impelled by a highly directional charge. Two mutilated bodies—the security men who'd stationed themselves on the wrong side of the door—spun end over end across the great library.

Through a cloud of smoke two figures swooped on suit jets, braked to an airborne halt in the center of the chamber, their weapons out and leveled at the trillionaire.

"Bohhuah Mutdah," Bassi Vobah stated formally, "you are under arrest on the authority of the Administrator Senior of the Oseon System, for trafficking and use of illegal substances!"

Mutdah smiled. The explosion hadn't startled him. Nothing seemed to take the obese trillionaire by surprise. He looked at Bassi, looked at Lando speculatively, then looked at Waywa Fybot, ridiculous in his outsize bird-shaped spacesuit.

Waywa Fybot looked back.

Mutdah nodded to the avian. Fybot changed the direction of his blaster, pulled the trigger, and neatly blew off Bassi Vobah's head.

FIFTEEN

Bᴀꜱꜱɪ Vᴏʙᴀʜ'ꜱ ʙᴏᴅʏ ꜱʟᴏᴡʟʏ ᴛɪʟᴛᴇᴅ ʙᴀᴄᴋᴡᴀʀᴅ, ɪᴛꜱ legs projecting rigidly. One arm caught briefly at a filament that turned the corpse as it moved. It drifted away to join those of the guards in the book-lined void.

Bohhuah Mutdah turned his mildly amused attention back to the feathered law enforcer. "Your report, Officer Fybot, if you please."

The creature gave him a salute.

"The order for your arrest, sir, originated in the highest possible echelons. The very highest possible echelons. In addition, shortly before I was dispatched to this system, I was given purely verbal instructions, sir, that you were not intended to survive the process. As insurance, pressure was applied to the local governor through his

family, his business interests, and by virtue of his...
er...his..."

The trillionaire's raisin eyes twinkled pleasantly. He
lifted a negligent hand, sending waves of obscene motion
through his bloated flesh. "Pray go on, my friend, you
may speak frankly. The truth does not offend a rational
being."

"Very good, sir: through his habituation to *lesai*.

"Somehow Lob Doluff knew or guessed about my
secret orders and sent *her*—" Fybot pointed in the approximate direction of the drifting body, now several
dozen meters away and dwindling rapidly—"to see that
they were not carried out."

The bird-being had been speaking more and more rapidly, an hysterical edge growing in his already high-
pitched voice. Now he paused, caught his breath before
continuing.

"Captain Calrissian was induced, under threat of pros-
ecution on a capital charge, to provide us transportation
and to assist in your entrapment. No one, however, not
the Administrator Senior, not his police chief, not Calrissian, and I most fervently hope not my superiors, seems
to have been aware of our...er, arrangement, sir."

Mutdah smiled. "An excellent report, Officer Fybot.
Most succinctly delivered. All in all, I am highly pleased
at the outcome.

"But tell me: you are very nearly twenty hours later
arriving than either of us anticipated at the outset. I appreciate the difficulties of negotiating the Flamewind,
but...twenty hours, Fybot? Really!"

The alien blinked, finally thought to reholster his blaster. He fastened down the flap. "In transit to this place,
sir, many queer events transpired. I myself suffered deep
hallucinations, although my Imperial conditioning is supposed to have rendered me resistant to most...Well,

that's as may be, sir. In any case, we were attacked, by a collection of odd military spacecraft. We took refuge. Some repairs were required."

Here, the alien hesitated, visibly nervous about the next part of his report. Lando thought he knew why, and doubled both his fists in anticipation.

"Sir, believing—on account of our pursuers—that Calrissian had become a liability, I took the initiative in attempting to dispose of him by sabotaging his vacuum suit. I also thought perhaps this would disrupt the plans of Bassi Vobah when it came time for your arrest. I was reasonably confident that I could get the *Millennium Falcon* here myself. Calrissian has a pilot droid that—"

"Yes, yes," Bohhuah Mutdah answered, for the first time betraying a touch of impatience. Lando relaxed, started breathing again. He'd hoped his little five-legged ace-in-the-hole wouldn't come up in casual conversation.

"But tell me more about these raiders," Mutdah continued. "Who were they? What did they want?"

"Sir, they made no demands, they simply—I have no idea, sir."

"Captain? Surely you must—"

Lando shrugged. "I've been trying to figure it out myself for days. There might be some connection with a pirate ship I fought off between Dilonexa and the Oseon. Then again, it might just be another sore loser."

Mutdah contemplated Lando's reply for a rather longer time than Lando could see any reason for, muttered, "Possibly . . . ," more to himself than anyone else, then ". . . and possibly not."

Finally he shook his massive head and turned very slightly to face Lando again. "I might explain that Officer Fybot has never been particularly happy in his line of work. He was, I ascertained when my intelligence sources informed me of this scheme, conscripted to pay tribute owed by treaty by his system to the central galactic government.

"A gentle being, our Waywa; at heart he nurtures no ambition greater than to become a gourmet chef. I suspect that you and I would find his culinary efforts quite resistible. Nonetheless, he possesses no small talent, in the view of his fellow avians, and fondly wishes to resume his education where he was forced to abandon it upon being drafted into service.

"Have I stated your case correctly, Waywa?"

The bird-being reached up, gave his helmet a quarter turn, detached it from its shoulder ring and tucked it under an arm. He wrinkled up the few mobile portions of his face in a grimace Lando had learned to recognize as representing happiness.

"Oh yes, quite correctly, sir!"

The trillionaire addressed Lando again. "In return for his cooperation, I have personally assured Waywa that he will no longer be required to suffer involuntary servitude at the behest of the government. I fully intend to make good upon that promise, keep my part of the bargain."

Abruptly, Mutdah raised a tiny pistol from where he'd concealed it in the deep folds of his corpulent body, drilled Waywa Fybot cleanly through the abdomen. The beam of energy pierced both suit and bird. A surprised expression froze on Fybot's face as his inert form wafted away slowly from the center of the room.

That made *four* corpses in the library. Things are getting pretty messy around here, the gambler thought.

"The anatomy," Bohhuah Mutdah said incongruously, "is somewhat differently arranged than one might anticipate. That was, believe it or not, a clean shot through the creature's heart."

His fat hand, which supposedly hadn't been used for

years, adroitly tucked the pistol into the waistband of its owner's shorts, then hovered there, ready to draw and use the gun again in a fraction of a second.

Lando had noticed that the fat man's reflexes were incredible.

Now he noticed something else: a glow of cruel satisfaction that suffused the trillionaire's decadent face. The man *liked* killing.

He looked at Lando appraisingly. "The question now, my dear Captain Calrissian, is what I ought to do with you. As you are aware, I have eliminated—have caused to be eliminated—two duly sworn officers of the law. They will doubtless be missed. I have illicitly purchased a substantial amount of a highly illegal substance. I have suborned an agent of the government. In short, nothing I couldn't easily pay to have taken care of."

The obese figure pointed toward the table once again. "There is a box of excellent cigars in the top drawer of the end table. Would you kindly remove two of them, light them with the lighter you will also discover there, give one of them to me, and enjoy the other yourself?"

The fat hand stayed near the gun.

Lando followed the instructions—with the exception of lighting the cigars. He handed one to Mutdah, offered to light it for him.

"Oh, come now, Captain. I suppose you are afraid of being poisoned or something silly like that. Here: If you don't mind, I'll puff on both cigars while you apply the flame—*no*, don't let the flame touch them. That's right, just hold it there until the ends begin to glow. That's the way to enjoy a fine cigar. Please choose either one you wish."

Lando was a gambler, a professional manipulator of cards. He knew how to "force" a draw, determine which card another person took while appearing to encourage a free choice. Mutdah wasn't doing it to him.

He took a cigar. It was very, very good.

"Well," he said after a couple of satisfying draws. He'd missed the cigars he'd accidentally crushed aboard the *Falcon*, and the crude cigarettes he'd rolled from their tobacco had been no substitute. "I don't suppose you can just let me go my own way. Believe me, I don't care *what* substances you find enjoyable, and these two"— he waved a hand broadly to indicate the room in which the remains of Vobah and Fybot were floating some- where—"were no friends of mine."

Bohhuah Mutdah slowly exhaled smoke. "I'd be a great deal more inclined to take that seriously, my boy, if I hadn't seen the expression on your face when they were killed. I suspect that you pretend to be a blasé Core- may-care, live-and-let-live sort of rogue, Captain. But you are a moralist at heart, and I would always have to be looking over my shoulder for you."

He waggled his massive, bloated shoulders. "As you can see, I would find that quite a burdensome task."

Lando's chest began to tighten. He hadn't any illusions about what was about to happen, not since he'd seen Waywa Fybot burned down, but here it was, unmistak- ably. Soon *five* corpses would drift on the air currents in the chamber, and the next few seconds would determine whether it was slim and uniformed or gross and nearly naked.

"So I guess we can't make a deal, then?" Lando asked rhetorically. The second pistol hadn't been his only cau- tious preparation, but he was damned if he could see what good his others would do now.

"I'm afraid not," Bohhuah Mutdah answered sadly. "And for more than one reason. In the second drawer of the end table, you will find a pair of manacles." He drew the gun, leveled it at the gambler. "I wish you to put them on. If you do not, then I will slowly roast you with this weapon, rather than kill you outright. The first shot will pierce your lower spine so that you will be helpless to resist the subsequent agony. Get the manacles and put them on, please."

Lando thought about it, looked at the muzzle of the pistol, looked into Mutdah's unwavering beady eyes, and got the manacles. They were force shackles, a pair of cuff bands connected by an adjustable miniature tractor beam. First class and very expensive. That figured.

"That's right," the trillionaire said encouragingly. "Now put them on."

Shrugging to himself, the gambler snapped the bands around his wrists. He wasn't altogether resigned; Mutdah had something in mind. After all, he hadn't handcuffed Bassi Vobah or her partner.

"Thank you very much, Captain. Now place the shackle beam in this loop of monofilament. Yes. You see, I mentioned that there was more than one reason why I cannot let you go? You recall that?"

An exasperated expression on his face, Lando asked, "Why do jerks like you always have to go into this thespian routine? If you're going to kill me, do it with the gun instead of boredom, there's a good fellow."

A flush spread itself across the vastness of Bohhuah Mutdah's face. With a gargantuan effort, he forced himself erect, pointed the weapon at Lando.

"The first reason I have explained. My enemies are hounding me and would see my power and fortune redistributed. Parenthetically, I must tell you that I do not care a whit about any of that. The continuation of the Bohhauh Mutdah 'empire' is of considerably less than no interest to me at all. I am constitutionally incapable of feeling any concern about it.

"The real reason, Captain, is that I don't *want* to let you go."

The obese trillionaire's body began to blur, its colors swirling together, its outline dissolving. It was replaced by the somewhat smaller form of an individual swathed in gray from top to toe. Only his insanely hungry eyes showed through the wrappings of his headpiece.

"For I am Rokur Gepta, and I'm going to torture you until you *beg* for death!"

SIXTEEN

"*SABACC!*"

Lando Calrissian slapped down the cards in triumph—
a triumph that turned to embarrassed agony when he saw
he'd hesitated too long between shouting out his victory
and sealing it in the stasis field of the gaming table.

In the brief interval between the acts, his perfect twenty-
three had transmuted itself into a losing hand.

The seventeen-year-old would-be professional gambler writhed inwardly. He'd practically begged for a
chance to join the game in the back room of the local
saloon. He'd lied to his family, ducked out on school,
broken or severely bent several ordinances about minors
and environments such as the one he found himself in
now.

He wished that he was home in bed. He wished that he was home *under* his bed. He wished he'd never seen a deck of card-chips in his life, never practiced with them, never imagined himself a dashing rogue and scoundrel.

It was all a dream, a foolish, idiotic dream.

"All is illusion, Captain Calrissian!"

Lando shook his head. The back room of the sleazy hometown saloon had vanished, and with it the embarrassed memory of humiliation and mistake. Actually, he'd gone on to win that game, taking home more money than he'd ever had together in one place before. Why hadn't he remembered that?

Replacing the saloon in his field of vision was a broad rich lawn, trees at the horizon, Flamewind spouting, roiling, and coruscating overhead. That was where he'd seen all those people on the approach to Oseon 5792. Where had they gone?

"The sights you see at this very moment are no more real, no more substantial than the memories you have just experienced so vividly, my boy! *That* is the fundamental truth the universe has to teach us, and like nearly everybody else, you have not managed to learn it until the uttermost end of your life!"

The hiss in that voice was unpleasantly familiar. Lando twisted his head around—he was tied up!—but couldn't find the source. The range of his vision was limited by the upended picnic table, a cold, synthetic marble of some kind, to which he had been bound. All he could see was the garden before him.

And the Flamewind.

The soft sound of slippered feet on grass. A shadow passed around the table—from the angle, Lando guessed it had been propped up on a bench—and turned to confront him.

"Rokur Gepta!"

The voice was filtered through a smile behind the turban windings. "And you thought I was dead, a victim of the uprising on Rafa IV. No, Captain, I have been quite thoroughly alive for a vastly longer time than you could guess. I am hard to kill and highly reluctant to let strangers terminate my existence."

Lando bit back a witty reply. In the first place, this was not the time for it, not when he was staked down and helpless. The tractor cuffs were anchored to the table, the beam of force between them lying in close and inseparable contact with the marble surface above his head. Likewise, another pair of manacles had been added to his spacesuited ankles. He and Gepta had moved from the bubblecavern in the asteroid's free-fall center to the surface, beneath the domes.

And he couldn't remember a moment of it.

"No remarks?" the sorcerer taunted. "I see that you have at least learned *some* discretion. This is not a moment for repartee, but a time for contemplation. You are about to experience an agony so excruciating, so unprecedented in the history of intelligent life, that being one of its first experimental subjects is a privilege and a signal honor.

"You have had a sample of it: *torture by chagrin*."

The sorcerer waved a leather-gloved hand.

A jail cell on Rafa IV at dawn. The open-fronted chamber looked out on a graveled yard. The noise was deafening: they were waking up the prisoners for a day of murderous labor in the life-orchards.

The guards beat on the bars. Lando had awoken with a start; now the fear of what was about to happen filled his being to the core. He backed into the cell, trying to escape the noise, his unsteady breathing slowly turning into a whimper.

BLAAASSSST!

The fire hose caught him unprepared. It dashed him against the wall, the icy water sluicing over him, blinding him, forcing itself into his mouth and nose. He fell to his knees, his head battered against the wall. He ducked it, trying to breathe, trying to stay alive against the killing force of—

"But, you protest, it wasn't like that at all?"

Gepta paced back and forth in front of Lando, relishing the gambler's agony. Despite the sweat on every centimeter of his skin, Lando was freezing, simply from the memory.

But Gepta was right: it hadn't been like that at all.

"It—it only lasted a few moments," Lando stuttered. Perhaps it was a surrender of some kind; he hated to give the madman any satisfaction at all. But he had to understand what was happening here.

"I wasn't nearly that frightened. I'd already worked out a way to escape. And it only lasted a few seconds—not the *hours* I just . . ." He tapered off, unable to continue because of his shaking. Shaking merely at the remembrance of something that hadn't bothered him all that much when it was actually happening.

"You're a brave man, Captain Calrissian. You don't like to think of it that way. What do you call it, 'creative cowardice'? You regard yourself a pragmatist, one not given to heroics."

The sorcerer had paused, stood now nearly motionless before the gambler. In the background, the Flamewind whorled around the demented sky, casting many-colored shadows. Lando shook his head to get the sweat out of his eyes, tried his bonds. As he'd expected, they were there to stay.

"And yet," Gepta continued, "what is bravery but the capacity to *reject* our fears, ignore and suppress them, then go on to do whatever it is we are afraid to do. What you are experiencing now, dear Captain, is the fear you *refused* to experience the first time. Now you have no choice!"

Surprise attack!

Wrestling the *Falcon* with one hand, Lando desperately tried to fire the cockpit guns with the other as the weird ragtaggle fighter-squadron bore down on him. It was a nightmare: they were too well shielded for his inconsequential guns to trouble, yet he couldn't operate the quad-guns without leaving the bridge.

Vuffi Raa, insane and helpless, couldn't assist him.

He fired again. He might as well have been shooting streams of pink lemonade as the pale, ineffectual fire that was all he could manage. The enemy fleet bore down on him, bore down, bore down . . .

Lando finished throwing up, coughed, choked, cleared his throat.

"Obviously," Gepta hissed cheerfully, "you survived the peril that you just reexperienced. Otherwise, you wouldn't be here now—it's only logical. It is a logic which enables us to live with our unpleasant memories, is it not? An integrative, healing contextualization which we all require to survive."

"Sure," the gambler gasped. "Sure, you rotten—anything you say!"

"Ahh! Resistance at last! As I was saying, however, the art of torture-by-chagrin lies in *denying* the mind that integration, that perspective. As you relive the minor horrors of your life, you don't recall that you survived, eventually triumphed. You see, even at moments of extreme peril, there are defenses, distractions, digressions which dilute the passions. What is more, my method does not allow its subject to experience anything *but* the fear. You can think of nothing else. The experience goes on and on, in circles, until the ego and the will are utterly crushed.

"Resistance," the lecturer trudged on relentlessly, "only adds the *brissance*, the, how shall I express it, the *snap!* which makes the quashing of the human personality possible. Get angry by all means, Captain. Insult me. Not only will it speed the process—without rendering your eventual agony any shorter in duration, I assure you— but I relish it, as you shall see to your dismay!"

Lando's breath was sour, the taste in his mouth bitter, but he managed a reply. "I'm betting that you're bluffing, Gepta. I'm betting that you're lying about that part. It would be like you. I think I'll continue hating your guts for a while, just as a matter of form. I think I'll imagine them pulled out through your navel and roasted over a slow—"

Lando's world was a forest of giant legs.

All around him, grown-ups on their private hurried errands jostled him, threatening to knock him down and trample him. There wasn't anything he could do. He was only three years old.

And he had lost his mommy.

The frightening alien city streets were crowded for the holidays, wet and dirty, dark with early evening. The lighted windows of the giant stores along the sidewalk didn't help. He stumbled in the slush and nearly fell, sagged instead against the wall below a window filled with toys, and fought back the tears rolling down his terrified little face.

"Mommy!" Where was she? Why didn't she come and get him? She'd left him at one of the windows—he'd wanted to watch the animated display—when he'd promised he wouldn't move. He was tired of the inside of the store; everything was up too high; there were too many people; and it hadn't been an interesting department anyway, where the lady had given mommy too much money back.

"Mommy?"

"Your mommy isn't here, Lando. You're all alone, and always will be."

"Who's that talking?"

"I'm your fear, little Lando, I'm your terror. I'm an eternity of anguish and I'm going to get you!"

"Mommy!"

Somehow the voice sounded familiar. Somehow he knew the voice hated him and wanted to hurt him. He didn't know what those big words were, terror, eternity, anguish, but they didn't sound very nice. He wanted his mommy.

But he was lost forever in the forest of legs.

"Ahhh, *that* was a deep and fundamentally traumatic one, wasn't it, little Lando? I could barely stand it myself."

Gasping, Lando shook the tears from his eyes, tried to catch his breath. It felt like he'd been crying for a thousand years. He remembered the incident very well. It had lasted, in reality, all of ten minutes, but somehow, he had never quite trusted the universe afterward.

"What do you mean *you* could barely stand it?" shouted Lando, then: "*You!* You were the voice! What are you doing to me?"

"Only beginning, my dear boy, only beginning. We've been at this, what? Half an hour? It will go on for days, Captain Calrissian, with any luck for weeks! I may attempt to prolong it for—But I see that you are puzzled, Lando."

Gepta had resumed pacing. Lando moved, tried to stretch, and discovered that he'd hurt himself. Where the force cuffs held him, where the marble table bore against his back, he was in pure, unadulterated physical agony.

It felt good by comparison.

"You see, the art of torture-by-chagrin requires that its practitioner experience what the subject experiences. He must guide the mind of the subject into always deeper, always more terrifying waters. He must suffer the experiences himself, in order to assure the quality, the depth, the texture of it.

"And in your case, Captain, and in mine, to make sure it is suitable as revenge!

"Yes, I have a way of living in your head, and yes, I am willing to suffer every bit of pain you suffer, so that I will know that I am torturing you enough!"

Overhead, the Flamewind sheeted the sky with a demented rainbow. Interplanetary lightning crackled across ionized paths. A hurricane of color whirled around the asteroid.

Gepta whispered, "The next little nostalgic digression will concern your business failures, Captain. But before we begin, I wish to tell you that they are not altogether the product of a malicious universe or your incompetence."

Gepta had been pacing back and forth a couple of meters in front of the tilted table where Lando was restrained. Now, for the first time, the sorcerer stepped forward until his eyes burned into those of the gambler.

"I hounded you!"

Lando shook his head, too groggy from pain of several kinds to comprehend fully what Rokur Gepta was telling him.

"I dogged your footsteps! Everywhere you went, I saw to it that the prices were a little higher, the rates you could resell at were a little lower! I warned the authorities anonymously that you were a smuggler, increasing the number of fees you had to pay, raising the amount in bribes! I devoured you by attrition—and then arranged for you to be invited to the Oseon!"

"What?" It didn't make sense. Hadn't the government wanted to destroy Bohhauh Mutdah? Hadn't—

"I anticipate the questions you are asking yourself, Captain. I and I alone arranged for that decadent leviathan to be harrassed by the government, then had him killed and took his place. All so I would be here when you arrived. I saw to it that more money was placed in your hands than you have ever had before—tens of millions!—money you will now never have the chance to spend."

Here, Gepta reached behind the table, took the thick sheaf of bills, and placed it on the ground at Lando's feet.

"Enjoy it, Captain Lando Calrissian, in the limited way that you are able. Enjoy it as you shall enjoy the memories of every sickening, humiliating, painful event in your life—including this one! I shall enjoy it all with you, purify it, help you to concentrate upon it to the exclusion of all else.

"And we shall see, as I have never had the opportunity to determine before, whether an individual can die of shame..."

He lifted a hand; Lando could feel something like drowsiness steal over him, just as he had in each instant before. He fought it, wrenching himself in the restraints, but his mind kept getting fuzzier, his eyes refused to focus on anything but his own terrifying inner realities. He fought it—

But he was losing.

SEVENTEEN

Magenta curtains shimmered against a stationary tapestry of pale stars as lightning exploded above
Bohhuah Mutdah's crystalline dome.

And exploded again.

Startled, Rokur Gepta whirled in mid-gesture as a flash
bleached his surroundings for a third time in as many
seconds. Somewhere, far away, there was a roar of
matching thunder—which should have been impossible—and a breeze began sifting toward its distant source.
The broad lawn rippled like the pelt of an angry predator.

The wind was fully as impossible as the thunder. Yet
it rose from an initial flutter to gale force in a twinkling,
whipping at the sorcerer's gray cloak, hurling dust and
loose papers along with it.

Lando squinted. The dead trillionaire's lofty architecture had been breached somewhere near the edge of the worldlet. The artificial pull of gravity this side of the asteroid was indolently kinder than at the spaceport, and consequently insufficient to maintain the present atmospheric pressure without help. That help was departing rapidly. The hurricane would roar until things equalized.

He hoped he'd be able to breathe by then.

Battered by the powerful current, Gepta lurched against its strength, trying to reach Lando. The gambler realized this was his only chance—and that perhaps the preparations he had made, however elaborate, might be worthwhile, after all.

Beneath his spacesuit, under the sleeves of his shipclothes, he was wearing his own set of tinklewood splints. In fact, it had been this idea that later served as inspiration when Waywa Fybot broke his legs.

In Lando's case the intention was to *prevent* injury. There were half a dozen twenty-centimeter rods, half a centimeter in diameter, running parallel to each of his forearms, tucked through small fabric loops in three neat circumferential rows, near the elbow, wrist, and in between. Vuffi Raa, thrilled at the chance to do some valeting at last, had sewn them on a heavy shirt for his master. Lando had speculated that they might be handy stopping a blow or parrying a blade. They were X-ray transparent, nonmetallic, indetectible by the usual run of security scanners.

Unlike his pistols.

He wore similar crude armor around his lower legs, knee to ankle.

Wriggling an elbow, he finagled one of the rod ends until it was free of the force cuff on that wrist. This would have been a futile effort while Gepta had the upper hand. Now, fighting the incredible wind blowing into space through the broken dome, the sorcerer was too busy to interfere.

The rods had added enough girth to Lando's wrist that he was able—very painfully—to tear his hand through the manacle just as Gepta reached him. Quickly, he slipped one of the rods out of his sleeve, *jammed* it through the turban slit into the sorcerer's eye.

Gepta screamed, clapped a hand to his shrouded face, and stumbled backward. The wind caught his voluminous cloak and took him away in a tumbling, fabric-covered ball of curses. He vanished into a nearby grove of thorn trees. There was more screaming.

Liberating the feet was more difficult. Lando finally pulled his suit-boots off, scraped his way past the restraints, and had begun to gather up his shoes and wits and Mutdah's money, when a silvery snake appeared in the grass before him. It had fingers for a face and a red glassy eye in the palm.

It couldn't bite; it was programmed not to.

"Vuffi Raa, you've got to pull yourself together!" There was no response; the independent appendage couldn't talk, and vulgar gestures were beneath the robot's dignity. "I don't know exactly what's going on around here, but it's our chance to get out! Move!"

Behind the uptilted table, Lando found his suit helmet. He also found a complex pile of electronic equipment, cables leading to a large flat, complexly braided coil that had been situated at the back of his head.

"I'm a little disappointed," he said to the tentacle. "And here I'd thought he was doing all that spellbinding by sheer force of personality!"

Somehow the chromium appendage managed to convey impatience as Lando dawdled. It lay on the ground fidgeting while he pulled on his boots. Overhead—directly overhead—there was a resounding bellow. Jagged sheets of curved plastic began falling.

"Relax, old boy, I'm pedaling as fast as I can! I wish you could tell me what the deuce is going on!"

As he shoved his foot into the boot, snapped the vacuum clasps tight, Lando saw the lightning flash of high-powered energy-weapons above them.

And several of the fighter-craft he'd battled on the way to 5792.

"Edge take me, *that* makes things a little clearer!"

Together the gambler and the disembodied tentacle hurried into the deceased trillionaire's deserted mansion, robot appendage in the lead and seeming to know where it was going. Inside, they took an elevator down into the planetoid. Even as they let it bury them, they could feel the asteroid shake and shudder from the assault overhead.

In the blink of an eye, the carriage passed the ruined door of the library, swung on its gimbals, turning at least one startled occupant on his head, and whisked onward in this new orientation. Adding injury to insult, Lando was nearly dashed to the floor as the machine crashed to a stop inside the spaceport service building.

Rasping on damage-distorted ways, the pneumatic door ground halfway open, then froze. The gambler squeezed through, chrome snake underfoot, and the pair leaped from the building a fraction of a second before it collapsed in flames.

Fire and explosions rocked the airport as more fighters strafed and bombed it. A scarlet beam lashed the waiting *Millennium Falcon* as they approached her. The back-splash nearly fried the gambler. But her shields held.

Gasping, Lando ran up the boarding ramp, pausing only to punch buttons to retract it, then sprinted forward around the corridor, momentarily outdistancing even the tentacle as it hastened back to its owner. Vuffi Raa had climbed down out of the ceiling access, and was strapped into the pilot's seat.

Lando took the right-hand position without complaint. "Let's get the devil out of here!" he screamed above the chaos roaring outside.

Reclaiming his leg, Vuffi Raa spared a split-second of attention for the gambler while he helped it connect itself. "You're a hard being to rescue, Master. You don't wait for help. I'll ask you how you got loose from Rokur Gepta later, if we live. Meanwhile, hadn't you better man the quad-guns?"

"*You* suggesting an aggressive act? I think you're right." Lando was gone before he'd finished the last sentence. Sliding into the gun chair, he flipped switches and pushed buttons, grabbed the handles of the ungainly weapon, and rested restless digits on the triggers.

A fighter made a pass at the larger ship as she lifted, her thrusters glowing blue-white.

Lando made life hell for him.

The *Falcon* soared into the multicolored sky, two of the fighters harrying her like angry hornets. They were fast, maneuverable, and *good*. Too good: Lando hadn't any easy dodge available there, as he had at the fissured asteroid. Nor was he experiencing much success smoking his tormentors. But his steady, accurate, occasionally inspired shooting kept them from having very much luck, either.

Another frantic pass, another exchange of energy-bolts, to little effect except in generating adrenalin on both sides.

Oseon 5792 dwindled rapidly beneath them.

Then somebody manhandling a fighter made a mistake, zigging when he should have zagged. Aboard the *Falcon*, crosshairs rested firmly on his midsection, waiting for exactly such an error. They were still on him as

Lando mashed both triggers, tracking all the while, following through.

The fighter burst into a tumbling ball of sparks and greasy smoke.

Vuffi Raa rolled the *Falcon*, skidded, bringing Lando's guns to bear again. He poured her fury into the remaining fighter as it swerved to avoid the fate of its companion.

Freighters weren't supposed to be able to do that!

The unnaturally agile saucer suddenly performed a maneuver that, in another place and time, would be called a Luftberry Circle, placing her smack on the fighter's back again. Her quad-guns pounded.

The enemy wriggled off the hook once more, but this one made an error, too: he got sore. Veering in a wide, angry, predictable loop, he came back to have his vengeance. Instead, he got four parallel pulsed beams of raw fusion-reactor output straight in the helmet visor.

And exploded, showering space with incandescent atoms.

Beneath them, there was a sudden streak of light.

Something left the asteroid *faaassst!*, headed for interstellar space. At very nearly the same instant, the surviving three fighters, having reconnected themselves with their battleship engine, bored directly for Bohhuah Mutdah's miniature world, fanatically intent on taking their victim with them—and unaware that (whoever it was) he was gone. Detaching themselves at the last second, they slung the giant, throbbing power plant at Oseon 5792.

One of them had a mechanical failure. His cable wouldn't release. He was pulled down with the engine into hell.

The other two sheered off frantically.

Vuffi Raa raced tentacle tips over the *Falcon*'s keyboards. The resulting acceleration could be felt by her captain even through her powerful inertial dampers. His gun seat slewed around violently, slamming itself and its occupant hard against the stops as the guns swung wildly. The asteroid dwindled to a pinprick—

—and blossomed into a glowing cloud, consuming one of the fighters who thought he'd gotten away, tumbling the other. Even the Flamewind paled momentarily as the ravening fireball expanded, growing brighter, brighter.

Then, from the inside out, it began to dim.

Lando took a deep breath—discovered he'd already taken one he didn't remember—and let it out.

"Brace yourself, Master!" screamed the intercom beside his ear.

BLANG! ZOONG! GRAT!

It was like being inside a titanium drum being beaten by a tribe of savages. Debris showered past the *Falcon*, mostly ricocheting off her shields, some pieces actually getting through at a reduced and harmless velocity.

The freighter shook and danced, then steadied.

Lando released a second breath he didn't recall taking, unstrapped himself from the quad-gun chair, rubbed a couple of sore places on his back, and shambled forward to the cockpit.

Deep in interstellar space, far from the Oseon and getting farther by the nanosecond, a brand-new one-seat fighter, bruised and battered by the Flamewind and the destruction of a world, took its badly shaken pilot home.

Rokur Gepta laughed bitterly. The best deception is the one that first deceives the deceiver. Blood stained the voluminous gray robes he wore, and agony pulsed through his ruined eye—another debt he owed Lando Calrissian. Yet Rokur Gepta was a being who took precautions, too.

For example, his private fighter, one of the tiniest craft capable of interstellar flight ever constructed. It had saved his life in the Rafa System; now it guaranteed his continued existence once again.

In a universe that was all illusion, deception was a double-edged sword. As Bohhuah Mutdah, he had nearly sunk into that flaccid degenerate's depression, so thoroughly had he absorbed the role. Only an all-consuming passion for vengeance had helped him to maintain his true identity. Similarly, when attacked by Calrissian, the disguise that he had worn for centuries had nearly been his undoing.

He endured the pain a while longer as a lesson to himself. There was no truth, no objective reality. Yet it would serve him, as a master of deception, to keep his illusions sorted out better. He would meditate upon this lesson while waiting at the Tund System for the scheduled arrival of the *Wennis*, due to rendezvous with him after the passing of the Flamewind. He'd left her and her crew on Oseon 6845 and flown the fighter to 5792 to assume the role of Bohhuah Mutdah.

A pulse of raw anger nearly overwhelmed him, and he concentrated on the pain again to maintain self-control. He'd lost his pet on 5792—another debt he owed the vagabond gambler, one which he would pay with interest when the opportunity presented itself again. Correction: when he *made* the opportunity.

Well, enough was enough. He set his tiny ship on automatic, let the gray-swathed form he usually assumed fade. At long last he occupied the pilot's seat in his true appearance.

The tinklewood rod dropped to the floor of the small cabin, the bloodsmears along its length vanishing before it hit. Gepta's pain, fully as illusory as his common worldly manifestation, vanished even more quickly.

Then another rearrangement, another shift of shapes and colors. Once again the charcoal-cloaked, mysteriously masked entity appeared, clean of bloodstains, free of pain.

He cut out the autopilot, took the grips of the fighter's controls, and punched in the overdrive.

The ship became a fading streak against a starry sky and was gone.

"There it is, Master!" an excited Vuffi Raa called.

Lando peered into the transparent canopy of the *Falcon*'s cockpit. The radar and proximity indicators were still nonfunctional and would remain so as long as the Flamewind raked the Oseon. He longed for an old-time primitive optical telescope. The electronic magnifier aboard the *Falcon* was worse than useless here.

"You've got a sharp eye, little friend. But keep the shields up—we don't know whether he's really helpless or just faking." Lando took another puff on the crudely rolled cigarette. Someday he'd get the chance to buy some more cigars.

The *Falcon* swayed and dipped, matching the velocity of the tumbling fighter. Not only had the droid insisted on rescuing its occupant—if said occupant had survived the beating his craft had received—but Lando had agreed in the hope that it might answer a few nagging questions.

Exactly *whom* had he offended sufficiently to merit the fantastic vendetta that—he hoped—was drawing to a close this very minute? He'd certainly never won enough money from any single individual to make it understandable.

The streamers of the Flamewind and the starry background began whirling crazily as Vuffi Raa rolled the ship to match the motion of the disabled fighter. Lando took a final drag, groaned, and cranked himself out of the seat, staggering a little at the disorienting sight. The *Falcon*'s artificial gravity and inertia compensators were functioning perfectly, but his sight was fooling his middle ear. He squinted.

"I'll get topside. Hold her steady, will you?"

"Be assured, Master—and be careful. I'll join you as quickly as I can."

"Right."

On the way to the upper hatch, Lando reclaimed his helmet. He hadn't had time to take off his pressure suit, which was just as well. He placed the bubble on his head, gave it the slight push downward and the fractional turn that locked it into place, and checked the telltales on his arm to make sure he had a perfect seal.

One more stop. He seized a meter-long breaker bar from a socket-wrench set in the engine area. He'd lost his stingbeams on 5792, kept no other small arms aboard the *Falcon*. Hefting the length of titanium, he swung it experimentally. Not as good as steel would have been, too light, but it would do to crack a helmet faceplate or a skull.

A muffled *clank!* reverberated gently through the entire ship. Almost as quickly, the robot's voice crackled in his earphones. *"We're locked on, Master. I'll just stabilize our attitude and be right with you."*

Lando didn't feel the maneuver. When things were working right (and he couldn't see out a window), he wasn't supposed to. In any case, he was busy turning a large metal wheel set in the hatch over his head. The seal was supposed to be tight with the escape aperture of the fighter; his suit was only a precaution. But he had closed an airtight door behind him when he entered this area of the ship.

Lando was a man who took precautions.

The wheel hit its stop, the door slumped downward a

couple of centimeters, and Lando swung it aside. Pocked and abraded metal greeted him, a circle of it, set in a broader area that matched it in long, hard wear. The circle had an inset ring at its edge. Lando dug a gloved pair of fingers under it, pulled hard, and a strip of sealant followed it down through the *Falcon*'s hatch.

The circle popped out—slightly higher pressure inside the fighter. Lando tossed the emergency access plate down to the chamber floor, stuck a cautious wrench handle through the port, followed it with his head and shoulders. A booted foot hung on either side of his head. The boots were connected to a pair of legs that rose to a body slumped in an acceleration chair and strapped in. The body didn't move.

Straining a little, Lando stretched up and hit the harness quick-release. Tugging gently on the figure's ankles, he got the body started down through the hatch, having to drop his breaker bar to the floor to make room and gain an extra hand. The shoulders jammed momentarily, then slid through.

Lando was glad he'd adjusted the gravity in the room to one-tenth normal. The guy would have squashed him on the way down the hatch ladder. He was huge.

With the rescued pilot lying unconscious on the floor, Lando heaved the hatch back into place, turned the wheel until a green light winked from a small panel beside it, and dropped back to the floor. He read what he could of the pilot's suit telltales. Appearances could be deceptive; the pilot looked human, but it could be ammonia he was breathing inside his suit.

That wasn't the case. As he detached his own helmet and began on that of the disabled fighter pilot, he heard another clank as Vuffi Raa cast off the ruined craft. Inside the helmet was an aged rugged face, elaborately scarred, and covered with a grizzled week-old beard. Even in repose the face looked tough and wise and experienced.

An eyelid fluttered.

Lando recovered the wrench handle, just in case, then had a second thought. This fellow looked strong enough to take the handle away from the gambler and shove it right up his—

A hiss sounded across the chamber. Vuffi Raa stepped through the door just as the pilot began to stir. The tough old man shook his gray head slightly, looked up groggily at Lando, blinked, and looked around the room.

His gaze stopped at the droid, froze there. A look of passionate hatred suffused the pilot's face, and his body tensed for combat.

"*You!*" the pilot screamed, "Destroyer of my world! Kill me now, or you shall surely escape death no more!"

EIGHTEEN

WITH A VICIOUS TENTACLE-SLASH AT THE BULKHEAD behind him, the robot launched himself across the room, straight at the astounded fighter pilot. The pilot leaped up just as four chrome-plated manipulators seized him in their mechanical embrace, joined by a belated fifth.

The pilot heaved his forearms up and outward in a hold-breaking maneuver, fended off a tentacle with a forearm block that would have snapped radius and ulna of a human antagonist, delivered a powerful turning back-fist blow to Vuffi Raa's pentagonal torso.

The little robot flew back the way he'd come, smashed into the wall, and was on the way back into combat again before Lando could so much as blink.

"Master!" the droid shouted, once again wrapping his limbs about those of the pilot. "Use your medikit!"

Fumbling at the belly of his suit, Lando grabbed the kit's injector, a flat thick coin of an object with a red side and a green side laminated over silvery plating. As Vuffi Raa held the fighter pilot momentarily, Lando slapped the injector on his neck.

There was a *hisssss*, the pilot slumped, and Vuffi Raa released him.

The robot seemed to slink into a corner, his red eye growing dimmer, his tentacles spreading and curling until the little fellow was a simple metallic sphere. The light pulsed feebly once, and went out.

"Vuffi Raa!" the gambler exclaimed, shaken with surprise and grief. He hurried to the robot's side, without the faintest idea what to do for his friend. A tiny hint of eye-glow still could be made out. Lando stood as anger began to fill him.

He walked over to the pilot. The sedation hadn't rendered him unconscious. He lay, breathing deeply, his eyes swimming in and out of focus, in and out of burning lunatic hatred for the helpless droid across the room.

Lando turned him over roughly, tore the somewhat antiquated blaster from the man's military holster, flipped him on his back again. Poking around in the small cramped chamber, he found some scraps, odds and ends from maintenance projects, among them a two-meter length of heavy wire. Holding it against the shield-saturated upper hull, he burned it in half with the blaster on its lowest setting, and, without waiting for the fused ends to cool, returned to the recumbent pilot, twisting one piece around his suited wrists, the other around his ankles.

Then, uncaring about what physiological damage he might be doing the soldier, he twisted the knurled edge of the injector until a small arrow was opposite the engraved legend STIM, and clapped it firmly to the man's face.

The device made its subtle noise. The fellow flushed, groaned, but his eyes grew clearer immediately. Lando pressed the still-warm muzzle of the blaster against the man's left kneecap.

"All right, Ace: tell me your story and make it short. By all means *don't* cooperate. I'd love an excuse to use you up, one joint at a time!" The knuckle of his index finger tightened on the trigger, and the pilot saw it.

"I'm Klyn Shanga," the trussed-up figure said with a sigh. "I'll tell you anything you want to know, as long as you promise to use that blaster on me afterward. One clean, effective shot for an old soldier, what do you say?"

Taken aback, Lando let the muzzle drop to the floor. "I say I'll let you know after I hear what you have to say. 'Klyn Shanga': what kind of name is that?" He squatted on the deck beside Shanga, one eye on Vuffi Raa. The robot didn't stir.

Shanga shook his head and sighed again, trying to accept defeat. He'd had a good deal of practice. "It's the name of a dead man, friend, the name of a dead man. Who in the Name are you, and what are you doing fighting *men* like yourself with that fiend over there?"

"I'm Captain Lando Calrissian of the *Millennium Falcon*," Lando replied evenly, "and that 'fiend' is my pilotdroid and *friend*, friend. His name is Vuffi Raa and he never hurt the tiniest insectoid in his life. He's programmed against it."

The pilot blinked. "A droid? Is that what it told you? That explains the fancy chrome—I almost didn't recognize it. But I *did*! You don't forget the devil that destroys your civilization!"

Lando scratched his head. "Be sensible, man. How

could one little droid...and anyway, what I've told you is true. He *is* a droid, I've seen him partially disassembled. Let me tell you, if he's been permanently harmed—do you know why he's curled up like that and deactivated? Well, it's because he was forced to attack and restrain a sentient being, I'd guess, to defend himself and me."

Shanga slumped back on the deck, laid his head down, and groaned. "I don't know what the Name is going on here! Partially disassembled? Programmed against aggression? You don't happen to have a cigarette, do you?"

Lando smiled grimly. "I was about to ask you the same thing, Klyn Shanga."

"Klyn Shanga?" said a small voice from across the room. "Is that what you're called? Master, I believe I can clear up some of this confusion, now."

"*Vuffi Raa!*" Lando shouted joyfully. The pilot stiffened.

"You don't know me, creature, but I know you! Remember the Renatasia System?"

The robot uncurled himself, stepped slowly and gracefully toward the two men, and lowered his torso to the floor, letting his tentacles relax. It was one of the few times Lando had ever seen the robot rest. It was one of the few times he had ever needed to.

"Yes, Klyn Shanga, I remember it very well. And with more shame and regret than I can ever express. Master, the Renatasia is a prehistoric colony. No one knows how long ago human beings settled there. Long before the Republic, certainly. Long before any historian is willing to admit there was spaceflight. But it *exists*, and was totally isolated from the rest of civilization, not aware of it, any more than we were aware of them."

* * *

"You will recall," the droid explained, "that my former master, the fellow you won me from in the Rafa, was an anthropologist and government spy. Well, I was with him for many years, a condition of mutual discomfort and dissatisfaction, I assure you.

"An independent trader, much like yourself, Master, had stumbled across the Renatasia, and my master was designated to check out his findings, reported because there is a standing reward for such discoveries.

"Forgive me, Freeman Shanga—oh, it's Colonel, is it?—well, forgive me, sir, but the Renatasia was a backward place in the technological sense. My master surmised that, sometime after the original colonization, it had been cut off from whatever system the settlers had come from, and, over the next dozen generations, had slid back into barbarism—perhaps even further. As it turned out, they had climbed back high enough to have commercial interplanetary travel within their own system, but had not discovered faster-than-light modalities.

"It was this which was their undoing. The government had classified them as socially retarded and suitable for forcible redevelopment—a variety of wholesale 'therapy' that is a thin euphemism for ruthless exploitation. The Renatasia System, unable to defend itself, was to be *used*. To be used *up*, if desirable.

"But first it had to be surveyed, analyzed, inspected for hidden strengths.

"My master believed that the best deception was the truth—suitably edited. He ordered me to cover my metallic surface with a latoprene coating of an organic appearance, had me make suitable clothing to fit over my admittedly rather unconventional shape, and accompanied me to the surface of Renatasia III in an open, highly conspicuous landing. We announced ourselves to the local government—the system was divided at the time into separate nation-states that often fought vicious wars with one another—as representatives, envoys, from a galaxy-wide civilization.

"Renatasia, after a suitable interval, was going to be invited to join.

"There were parades, Master, and celebrations. We traveled widely in the system, the honored guests of a people who hoped that this fresh contact with a higher civilization would put an end to war and poverty among them. We went to banquets, we made speeches. And always, always, *I* was the Chief Delegate. My master played the role of secretary and assistant.

"We were there for seven hundred standard days, during which we helped them organize a single system-wide government, organized their defense force under a unitary command, then greatly reduced its size. We gave them new technology—trivialities that would aid them not at all when our true purposes were revealed.

"The government Fleet arrived on the seven hundred first day.

"In the beginning, the rejoicing was only redoubled—until the fleet began collecting slave levies, demanding taxes, closing schools and forcing the Renatasians to teach their children the major galactic tongues to the exclusion of their own. Whole cities, whole nations resisted. Whole cities, whole nations were leveled.

"Two thirds of the population was exterminated in the bungled pacification operations that followed.

"Stunned and embarrassed, the government left the Renatasia System. The entire matter was covered up and what was termed an 'incident' was forgotten as quickly as possible."

"*We* didn't forget!" Klyn Shanga cried from his supine position on the deck of the *Millennium Falcon*. "We had nothing left but our dreams of retribution! And now we have failed!"

Vuffi Raa propped himself a little higher, began untwisting the wires around Klyn Shanga's wrists. "You gathered warcraft. I didn't recognize you for what you were. There were fighters from at least twenty civilizations in your squadron, and that booster engine was from a scrapped dreadnaught."

"Yes! It took us a decade to put the operation together, cost us everything we had! And in the end, it came to nothing!" He turned his face to the floor; his shoulders shook briefly.

Lando untied the soldier's ankles, helped him to his feet. "I trust, old man, that you understand: Vuffi Raa is many things, but he is only a droid. He has no choice but to do exactly what he is ordered to do. Did you ever see him personally harm anyone?"

Shanga turned to face the gambler. "No, no I didn't. What has that got to do with it?"

"A very great deal. You saw how he reacted, simply to passively restraining you?"

The warrior set his mouth grimly. "So what? You can kill a man by *ordering* it done. You don't have to bloody your own hands. Yet you'll be just as guilty!"

Lando took a firmer grip on Shanga's blaster. "Then I suppose that means you won't give your word not to—"

"You're bloody well *right* it doesn't!" roared Klyn Shanga.

"Very well." Lando, holding the weapon on the man, reached up and reprogrammed the airlock hatch. "Come along, Vuffi Raa."

Stepping through the bulkhead door, the gambler spoke again. "We'll bring you a cot and some food. I intend to drop you off at the nearest system, and you won't be harmed. I hope to convince you on the way, sometime in the next few days, that this vendetta is irrational. Vuffi Raa is a thoroughly good being, and would have died rather than destroy your culture, but he is also a robot who, even in the vilest of hands, must obey. I'm trying to do something constructive about that, too."

"You are?" a dazed Vuffi Raa asked from the corridor outside. "What, Master?"

"Don't call me Master!"

He shut the door, programmed it to restrain the fighter pilot, and shoved the blaster into a slash pocket on the outside of his suit. "Let's get forward, old thing, we need to decide where next to head for."

"That would depend, Master, on whether we are freight haulers or gamblers, wouldn't it?"

"Indeed it would, except that, at the moment, we are gentlebeings of leisure. We have a hundred seventy-three-odd thousand credits I won on Oseon 6845, after all."

Halfway to the cockpit, the droid turned and looked at Lando. "I hate to say this, Master, but from past experience *that* won't last very long."

Lando stopped in midstride, a scowl on his face. He wanted desperately to shuck out of his increasingly uncomfortable spacesuit, get a shower, and lie down for a couple of eons. "Thanks for the vote of confidence. But we also have twenty *million* credits I sort of accidentally brought along with me from Bohhuah Mutdah's place. He won't be needing it anymore!"

They continued along to the control deck, where Vuffi Raa began the procedure necessary to setting a course. Lando was glumly rolling another cigarette with crushed cigar tobacco and highly unsuitable paper.

"Twenty million credits, and I don't have any decent smokes!"

The robot paused. "Master, may I ask you a question?"

"As long as you don't call me master when you do it."

"I'll try. Lando, Klyn Shanga's people, the Renatasians—I feel responsible for them. Their civilization has been all but obliterated. If they recover at all, it will be centuries before they're finished."

Lando nodded solemnly. "That's true. On the other hand, everybody has to start again, fresh every day, from wherever they are."

"Well, Mas—I mean, Lando, we have your winnings from the Oseon. Wouldn't the Renatasians recover a good deal more quickly if they had some help? After all, we're gamblers and adventurers. Being rich would only get in our way. I think we ought to give Klyn Shanga the twenty million."

Lando looked at Vuffi Raa, lit his cigarette, and leaned back in his acceleration couch. It was a long time before he spoke.

"Vuffi Raa, you're a decent, humane droid at heart. And, when you get right down to it, I'm not too bad a sort myself. Compared to the rest of the universe, we're the good guys.

"But as far as the twenty million is concerned, my little mechanical friend, forget it.

"I'm going to *enjoy* being rich."

ABOUT THE AUTHOR

Self-defense consultant and former police reservist, L. Neil Smith has also worked as a gunsmith and professional musician. Born in Denver in 1946, he traveled widely as an Air Force "brat," growing up in a dozen regions of the United States and Canada. In 1964, he returned home to study philosophy, psychology, and anthropology, and wound up with what he refers to as perhaps the lowest grade-point average in the history of Colorado State University.

L. Neil Smith's previous books—all published by Ballantine/Del Rey—are *The Probability Broach, The Venus Belt, Their Majesties' Bucketeers, The Nagasaki Vector,* and *Lando Calrissian and the Mindharp of Sharu.*

THE ILLUSTRATED MANUAL
OF SEX THERAPY

THE ILLUSTRATED MANUAL OF SEX THERAPY

Helen Singer Kaplan, M.D., Ph.D.

Drawings by David Passalacqua

Quadrangle / *The New York Times Book Co.*

Drawings Copyright © 1975 David Passalacqua.

Book design: Tere LoPrete

Second printing, July 1975

Library of Congress Cataloging in Publication Data

Kaplan, Helen Singer, 1929–
    The illustrated manual of sex therapy.

    1. Sexual disorders. I Title. [DNLM: 1. Psycho-
therapy. 2. Sex disorders—Therapy. WM610 K17i]
RC556.K32   616.6   74-26016
ISBN 0-8129-0545-8

To Aphrodite

Contents

INTRODUCTION   *The Concept of Sex Therapy*   3

I BASIC ISSUES

CHAPTER 1   *The Nature and Causes of the Sexual Dys-functions*   11

CHAPTER 2   *The Sexual Evaluation*   17

II THE SEXUAL EXERCISES

A. An Erotic Technique Used for Many Dysfunctions

CHAPTER 3   *Sensate Focus I—Pleasuring*   29

CHAPTER 4   *Sensate Focus II—Genital Pleasuring*   46

B. Erotic Techniques Used for Specific Dysfunctions

CHAPTER 5   *Frigidity—Female Sexual Unresponsiveness*   60

CHAPTER 6   *Female Orgastic Dysfunction*   72

CHAPTER 7   *Vaginismus*   99

CHAPTER 8   *Impotence—Erectile Dysfunction*   111

CHAPTER 9   *Retarded Ejaculation—Ejaculatory Over-control*   131

CHAPTER 10   *Premature Ejaculation—Inadequate Ejaculatory Control*   152

III CONCLUSIONS

CHAPTER 11   *The Role of Psychodynamics in Sex Therapy*   169

List of Illustrations

Chapter 3 Sensate Focus I—Pleasuring

    1. Woman face up   31
    2. Woman face down   35
    3. Man face down   39
    4. Man face up   43

Chapter 4 Sensate Focus II—Genital Pleasuring

    5. Masters and Johnson position for stimulating the woman's clitoris and vagina   47
    6. Masters and Johnson position for stimulating the man without erection   51
    7. Woman touching man's erect penis   53
    8. Man touching woman's nipples   57

Chapter 5 Frigidity—Female Sexual Unresponsiveness

    9. Female superior—nondemanding thrusting   63
   10. Male inside female from rear—touching her clitoris   69

Chapter 6 Female Orgastic Dysfunction

  A. *Totally Anorgastic Female*

   11. Female alone masturbating with finger   75
   12. Female masturbating with vibrator—male is present   79
   13. Male stimulating female's clitoris   83
   14. Male orally stimulating female's clitoris   85

  B. *Coitally Anorgastic Female*

   15. Bridge—male stimulating female's clitoris while he is inside   89
   16. Bridge—female stimulating her own clitoris while male is inside   91
   17. Bridge—male is kneeling—female is stimulating herself with vibrator while male is inside   95

Chapter 7 Vaginismus

    18. Female inserting her own finger into vagina   101
    19. Female inserting catheter into vagina   103
    20. Male inserting his finger into woman's vagina   105
    21. Male inserting an object into woman's vagina   107

Chapter 8 Impotence—Erectile Dysfunction

    22. Female stimulating male when he is partially clothed   113
    23. Couple stimulating each other—she is partially clothed (fantasy)   117
    24. Female is stimulating male orally   119
    25. Female is stimulating male manually with petroleum jelly   123
    26. Female superior—female stimulating male's erect penis   125
    27. Female superior—inserting his penis into her vagina   129

Chapter 9 Retarded Ejaculation—Ejaculatory Overcontrol

    28. Male masturbating—female's back is turned   135
    29. Male masturbating—female in his arms   137
    30. Female stimulating male—his hand is on hers   139
    31. Female stimulating male's penis near her vaginal entrance   141
    32. Female touching male's penis during coitus—male superior   145
    33. Female touching male's penis during coitus—"doggy" fashion   147
    34. Coitus with female's legs tightly closed   149

*Chapter 10 Premature Ejaculation—
Inadequate Ejaculatory Control*

    35. Semans' maneuver—female is stimulating male's penis manually   155
    36. Semans' maneuver—female superior coital position   157
    37. Side-to-side coitus   159
    38. Squeeze   163
    39. The kiss   179

THE ILLUSTRATED MANUAL
OF SEX THERAPY

The Concept of Sex Therapy

The prescription of specific erotic experiences constitutes a distinctive feature of the new sex therapy. Various other forms of psychotherapy—notably analysis, marital therapy, and behavior therapy—have also been used to treat sexual dysfunctions. All of these rely exclusively on the therapeutic transactions which take place in the doctor's office. The analytic process produces an intense emotional interaction between the analyst and his analysand. The analysis of this relationship is used to foster insight into the unconscious conflicts and fears and desires which may lie at the root of the patient's sexual difficulty. The marriage therapist uses his observations of the interactions between the troubled couple as the basis of his inferences regarding the unconscious sources of a sexual problem. He confronts the couple with the destructive effects of their behavior on one another and also attempts to bring to their awareness the unconscious infantile and transferential forces which presumably have given rise to their neurotic behavior toward each other and also to the impairment of their sexual fulfillment. The behavior therapist does not deal with the concept of unconscious motivations. Rather he attempts to understand the behavioral conditions which have shaped and perpetuated a man's impotence or a woman's failure to reach orgasm. He tries to improve sexual functioning by changing the maladaptive reinforcement contingencies which have produced the sexually destructive anxieties and antierotic behavior patterns. Various techniques such as systematic desensitization to diminish anxiety, reinforcement of desirable erotic behavior, and adversive conditioning to eliminate patterns which are sexually destructive are used to implement this objective.

3

Sex therapy may employ all these various forms of psychotherapeutic interventions which are conducted in the doctor's office. However in sex therapy these are used in conjunction with prescribed sexual tasks which the couple practices in the privacy of their bedroom. It is the integrated use of systematically structured erotic experiences together with psychotherapeutic exploration of each partner's unconscious intrapsychic conflicts, as well as of the subtle dynamics of their interactions, which constitutes the unique feature and basic concept of sex therapy. In all probability the key to its effectiveness lies in this amalgam of experiential and dynamic modes.

The concepts and techniques of psychoanalysis, marital therapy, and behavior modification, which all have important places in the new sex therapy, are well documented and have been amply described in the literature. For these reasons these topics will not be covered in this volume. Indeed, practitioners of sex therapy should really be familiar with this material before they embark on the treatment of sexual dysfunctions.

Rather it is the objective of this book to describe the *erotic techniques* which are commonly employed in sex therapy, and also to offer some hypotheses regarding their rationale and the mechanisms of their action. In addition, the emotional impact of these exercises on patients, as well as the therapeutic implication of these emotional reactions, will be explored.

These tasks which are prescribed for sexually troubled couples, are not inhumane mechanical exercises. To the contrary, the erotic and sensuous interactions structured for the couple in sex therapy frequently evoke highly emotional responses from one or both partners. These responses are of profound significance for the psychotherapeutic process because they reveal crucial dynamics of the clinical problem which thus becomes immediately available for exploration during the psychotherapeutic sessions. For example, an impotent man cannot lie back, as he was instructed to do, and enjoy the tender caresses of his wife because he is made anxious by this experience and he becomes obsessed with ideas of rejection: "She is not enjoying this. . . . She will get tired. . . . She will think I am sick. . . . I must give her an orgasm. . . ." His fearful reactions to receiving pleasure from his wife and his defenses against this fear will become apparent both to his

4

therapist and to the couple themselves. Often engagement in such previously avoided experiences serves to confront the individual with the hidden insecurities which have been producing the failure of his erective reflexes at the very moment that he is so eager to function.

In this book I will describe some typical patient and spouse responses to each of the prescribed sexual tasks. In addition, I will explore some of the implications of these emotional reactions in terms of the causality of the sexual problems.

The couple's emotional responses to the prescribed sexual exercises represent a therapeutic challenge in that they constitute resistances and obstacles to therapy as well as a unique opportunity for effective therapeutic intervention. Therefore, I will also discuss some of the therapeutic strategies which may be used to deal with these emotional responses.

Finally the book contains illustrations of the techniques. In the past, both in training others to do this work and in prescribing sexual tasks to my patients, I have had to rely on my verbal descriptions. Often these do not convey the various positions with sufficient clarity and I have had to make sketches to illustrate what I was asking them to do. On some occasions members of the staff have actually had to demonstrate some of the more difficult positions during training seminars. It is the objective of the drawings contained in this book to provide clear illustrations of commonly suggested positions and erotic activities both for the didactic purposes of training and also for the instruction of patients. The drawings will, apart from merely illustrating specific positions, also, I hope, convey the beauty and humanity of sex, fundamentals to successful sex therapy.

The book, thus, is primarily an illustrated manual of the experiential aspects of sex therapy. In order to understand this material in a meaningful way, however, it is necessary to go into a little background regarding the nature of the sexual responses of men and women, the dynamics of sexual dysfunction, and some basic concepts of causality. These topics have been described in depth in my book, *The New Sex Therapy* (Quadrangle, 1974). These basics are summarized herein only for the purpose of setting the material on the tasks in its proper perspective.

I have also included a chapter on evaluation, i.e., the sexual examina-

5

tion and history. This is the structured interview by which one obtains the data which is necessary to formulate the problem. A sensitive multidimensional formulation is necessary to enable the therapist to make rational treatment decisions. Practiced in this manner, sex therapy is highly individualized and flexible. There should be no standardized treatment routine to be applied mechanically to all sexually dysfunctional couples. Each procedure, each task, each interpretation should have an explicit rational basis. Such an individualistic approach requires a rather special assessment technique, one which is focused on evaluating a couple's sexual *experience* rather than relying exclusively on obtaining descriptive mental status type of data.

Sex therapy, effective as it is for appropriate cases, is not indicated for all sexual difficulties. Some persons' sexual problems are too deeply rooted and some relationships are too hostile to be amenable to brief intervention. It is useful for the therapist to be aware of the limitations as well as of the strengths of this approach. Therefore some of the prognostic factors which seem to influence the outcome of sex therapy are also discussed in this book.

One of the serious limitations of sex therapy is that, with the exception of totally anorgastic females, treatment entails the participation of two cooperative individuals. As described in this book, the prescribed exercises which are a crucial ingredient of sex therapy are essentially structured interactions between sexual partners. They simply cannot be conducted alone. This poses a problem for the single person with a sexual dysfunction.

Some clinics have attempted to deal with this dilemma by providing surrogate partners—e.g., strangers who for a fee partake in the sexual exercises with the patient. There are advantages and disadvantages to this approach. The chief advantage is that it provides an opportunity for some inadequately functioning single persons to attain self-confidence and security in sexual functioning which will then enable them to seek a relationship. However, one of the prime objectives of sex therapy is to humanize the sexual relationship. Sex with a paid stranger, no matter how perfect it is mechanically, will not accomplish this. A preferable approach perhaps is by means of psychotherapy, to bring the person to that level of self-esteem where he will be free to engage in a relationship with a woman even if he does not function perfectly. In my own clinical practice, when a dysfunctional patient who has no partner seeks help I do an evaluation and share my formulation with the patient. I also describe and explain the treatment which might be helpful in his case. Sometimes psychotherapy is offered as a reasonable alternative to sex therapy for the single patient, but sometimes it is not likely to be effective, at least in terms of the sexual symptom. The patient is of course not cured by this kind of consultation and counseling, but he is given a rational understanding of his problem and also the hope of resolution when and if he can form a suitable relationship.

In any work on sex therapy a word should be said about its narrow objective of improving sexual functioning. We should not feel apologetic for this because a person's erotic well-being is an extremely important aspect of human experience. Admittedly, however, it is only a limited aspect, and sex therapy should take cognizance of larger human issues. While we focus on sex, we should also be responsive to the wider psychic matrix of which sexuality is an integral and beautiful part.

I

BASIC ISSUES

I

The Nature and Causes of the Sexual Dysfunctions

The sexual responses in men and women transform the quiescent genitals into effective reproductive equipment. "The flaccid urinary penis is transformed into the erect reproductive phallus, while the dry potential vaginal space becomes an open, lubricated, and engorged recepticle."* On first inspection the sexual response of men and women appears to be a single event. In the male, erection proceeds to ejaculation. In the female, lubrication and swelling of the genitals culminates in orgasm. However, evidence suggests that the sexual response of both genders actually consists of two separate phases. These are analogous both anatomically and physiologically in both genders. They may be inhibited separately to produce different dysfunctional syndromes.

The first part of the sexual response consists of genital vasocongestion. The second, orgasm, is essentially a series of involuntary clonic contractions of the genital musculature.

In the male, erection is produced by a vasocongestion of penile blood vessels. Penile capillaries expand and special veinous channels close. Blood is trapped in special caverns of the penis, and this essentially hydraulic mechanism extends that organ. This response is mediated by the autonomic nervous system: arteriolar dilation is parasympathetically mediated, while closure of the veinous valves is probably controlled by sympathetic nerves. Orgasm is a separate response. In the male it comprises two components: emission and ejaculation.

* *The New Sex Therapy.* Helen S. Kaplan. Quadrangle, 1974.

Emission (which is perceived by men as the sensation of ejaculatory inevitability) consists of the reflex contraction of the internal reproductive organs. Contractions of the vasa deferentia, prostate, and seminal vesicles squeezes ejaculate into the posterior urethra. Emission is a sympathetically mediated response. A split second later ejaculation occurs. This consists of 0.8-second contractions of the striated muscles at the base of the penis: the bulbo and ischio cavernosi muscles.

Two analogous events occur in women. In response to sexual arousal there is a vasocongestion of the blood vessels of the labia and tissues surrounding the vagina. This swelling is more diffuse than in the male. Females do not have special caverns, and instead of erection, female genital congestion produces the "orgasmic platform," localized perivaginal swelling. Genital vasocongestion is also responsible for vaginal lubrication which is actually a transudate of the fluid that accumulates in the pelvis during this arousal phase in females. In addition the smooth muscles of the internal vagina expand, causing an internal ballooning and extension of the vagina and a rise of the uterus. In contrast to the male, the female orgasm only has one component. Women lack the emission phase. However, the clonic phase is strictly analogous and consists of the 0.8-second contractions of the ischio and bulbo cavernosi muscles as well as of the pubococcygeal muscles. Peripheral innervation of the female sexual response has not yet been studied, but it may be speculated by analogy that the female sexual responses are also governed by the autonomic nervous system.

When these responses or any of their component phases are impaired, sexual dysfunction results. There are six dysfunctions: three of the male and three of the female.

When the erectile response is impaired the man is *impotent*. The inhibition in impotence is confined to the erectile, vasocongestive component of the sexual response. The ability to ejaculate may be retained in impotence. There are also two ejaculatory disorders: *premature ejaculation* and *retarded ejaculation*. The premature ejaculator fails to acquire adequate voluntary control over his orgastic reflex. As as result he climaxes very rapidly. In contrast the patient with retarded ejaculation suffers from involuntary overcontrol. He has difficulty in releasing his ejaculatory reflex even though he receives adequate stimulation.

12

Vaginismus is a uniquely female complaint which has no analogy in the male. In this disorder the muscles guarding the vaginal entrance have been conditioned to respond spasmodically when any attempt at penetration is made. This condition makes intercourse impossible.

The other two female dysfunctions are analogous to impotence, on the one hand, and retarded ejaculation on the other. The *generally unresponsive* woman, like the man with erectile difficulty fails to respond to sexual stimulation with lubrication and genital vasocongestion. The woman who suffers from *orgastic dysfunction* like the man with retarded ejaculation experiences various degrees of difficulty in releasing her orgastic reflex, but is otherwise sexually responsive.

A Psychosomatic Concept of Sexual Dysfunction

The sexual responses are delicate and can easily be disrupted by negative affect or by psychological conflict and inhibition.

When a man is frightened or angry or tense at the moment that he is making love, his erectile or ejaculatory reflexes are likely to be impaired. For proper sexual functioning to occur a person must not only be free of intense negative affect, but must also be free of excessive cognitive control. In other words good sex requires a calm emotional state and *abandonment* to the erotic experience. This is also true of all other biological functions which are controlled by the autonomic nervous system. Digestion, respiration, and cardiovascular functions are similarly innervated by the visceral nerves and are similarly subject to impairment by emotional and cognitive factors. In other words these functional systems are also subject to psychosomatic disorders.

In the past it was believed that only profound neurotic conflict was capable of impairing the sexual responses. Severely pathogenic and regressive conflicts centering on unconscious, delusional, and infantile fears of injury if one were to enjoy sex were believed to be the sole vectors of sexual dysfunction. These conflicts were believed to originate in the patient's childhood before the age of five. Pathological interactions with parents which resulted in morbid fears and insecurities and the defenses erected against these were believed to hold the key to all sexual difficulty. Not surprisingly, analytic treatment was designed to clarify these issues and bring them into the patient's conscious awareness in hope of resolving them. Only the resolution of deep unconscious conflict was believed to be capable of curing the sexual symptom.

Masters and Johnson and the behaviorists taught us that the roots of psychopathology often originate in far simpler ground. Performance anxiety, superficial insecurities, tensions due to poor communications with one's mate, anxiety born of misconceptions about the human sexual response also can and do cause a large proportion of the sexual difficulties we see in clinical practice. And this is eminently logical. For physiologically speaking, sexually disruptive anxiety is identical whether caused by return of oedipal taboos and fears of castration, or whether a man panics because he is afraid that a bout of alcohol-induced erectile difficulty will be repeated.

Actually, causality lies on a continuum which reaches from superficial anticipation of failure to the profound psychopathology which causes the sexual response to acquire dangerous symbolic meaning on an unconscious level. Concomitantly, effective intervention also can be described as falling on a continuum: from sex education and counseling, to sex therapy, to extensive reconstructive psychoanalytic treatment.

Our sexually repressed society, has until recently, failed to regard sex as a natural function. Thus accurate information about the sexual response has not been freely or widely available. This curtain of ignorance plus the highly emotional attitudes about erotic matters provide a fertile culture medium for the growth of ignorance, myths, and misconceptions. Myths are prevalent about ever-ready male functioning, vaginal orgasms, mutual climax, masturbation, fantasy, frigid women, and so on. A great deal of anxiety and guilt can be generated when there is a discrepancy between real experience and unrealistic expectation. Such misconceptions along with the emotional reactions which accompany them can produce sexual maladjustments and dysfunctions.

In addition, anxiety and guilt may cause a person to avoid sex and/or to restrict his or her sexual behavior. This deprives him of the oppor-

14

tunity of exploring and learning sexual techniques and attitudes which will please him and his partner.

Persons who suffer from ignorance about sexual techniques and malignant misconceptions can often be helped with simple sex education and counseling. This treatment mode entails dispelling misinformation and guilt and giving instruction in effective sexual techniques.

The causes of another group of dysfunctional patients run somewhat deeper. The sexual responses of this group are impaired by the fear of sexual *failure*, by a tendency to remain under *conscious control* during the sex act, by haunting fears of *rejection* should they fail to please the partner or to *"perform"* adequately. Yet they are free of deeper guilts and fears and marital hostilities. This group of patients are highly amenable to brief sex therapy which aims to create a secure, open, and comfortable sexual ambiance. The course of treatment in such cases tends to be uncomplicated. Interpretations are mainly supportive, aim at opening the couple's routes of communications, and are not often profoundly analytical. Results of sex therapy with this group of patients is excellent. Fortunately these constitute a sizable proportion of the patient population.

The next group of patients are more difficult to treat. They, too, suffer from fears of rejection and from performance anxiety. But in this group these fears are related to deeper insecurities. The sexual problem is associated with profound conflicts. Sex therapy must contend with fundamentally disturbed relationships between the genders. In this group of patients the self-esteem is more fragile; guilt arising from sex and pleasure is more tenacious.

These more difficult patients are still amenable to sex therapy, but only if the sex therapist is prepared to contend with disturbance on a deeper dynamic level. The therapist must be cognizant of the psychodynamics of unconscious conflicts and of the relationship of such conflicts to sexual difficulty. He must be skilled at working on the level of unconscious motivation. He must have the clinical judgment to decide: when to *bypass* such conflicts by providing the patient with defenses against anxiety and thereby sever the connection between deeper conflict and sexual functioning; when to attempt to *resolve* such conflict by active interpretation and confrontation; when to *shift the emphasis* of treatment away from the experiential symptom-focused sex therapy into *psycho*therapy designed to resolve intrapsychic and marital dynamics while the therapist postpones actual sex therapy.

Finally there are some patients suffering from sexual dysfunctions which are not amenable to brief active intervention. Fortunately these seem to be relatively rare. The sexual problems of this group are tenaciously connected to profound marital and individual psychopathology. Their depressions are so deep, their paranoia so pervasive, their marital hostilities so malignant and antisexual, and their defenses so rigid and successful that they first need more extensive psychotherapeutic intervention, either analytic which aims to change basic emotional attitudes or marital: the goal of which is to resolve profound dyadic (couple) conflicts, before they can benefit from sex therapy.

2

The Sexual Evaluation

Assessment in medicine employs two main tools: history and examination. In diagnosing a patient's sexual problem we also rely on history and examination. However, the examination in sex therapy does not primarily employ physical inspection, palpation, and auscultation. Of course in some instances when it is indicated, physical examination of the sexual organs needs to be done, and the diagnosis may in some cases also depend on input from laboratory examinations. However in our sexual examination in contrast to examinations for other ailments, we rely most heavily on a sensitive and empathic assessment of the couple's *sexual experience,* as it is communicated to us by them in the consultation room. It is in this manner that we capture the signs, symptoms, and antecedents of the sexual dysfunction and obtain the data we need to assess the determinants of the person's problem. Perhaps some time in the future sex therapists will observe their patients in the act of lovemaking or inspect video tapes of their sexual activities. Until such a time the interview which is designed to assess the couple's sexual experience in detail and depth is an exquisitely sensitive and highly effective diagnostic tool.

After I obtain a couple's names, ages, address, and marital and family status I ask for the nature of the chief complaint and events of the onset of the problem. Then I evaluate their sexual experience.

Please tell me exactly what happens when you two make love. [They are often embarrassed and evasive.] I am sorry if this is embarrassing, but I can't really help you until I know exactly what is going on.

I pursue gently but firmly. My own attitude of sexual openness is transmitted and eases the inquiry. I encourage and reinforce openness, frank participation. Sometimes one partner is more able to communicate than the other. I note this for later reference, but for the sake of my inquiry I encourage the communicative one to begin. I continue until, in my mind's eye, I have a crystal clear and detailed picture of the physical acts which transpire between the couple. I persevere in order to also understand the emotional reactions of the partners, their fantasies, and the interplay between them.

If there are obscure areas I will persist and question until these are cleared up.

Yes, but *when* do you initiate actual intercourse? When *you* feel a certain level of excitement? When you think *he* is getting impatient? Both?

The process is very much like auscultating and percussing again and again until one has a clear mental picture of the inner anatomy and pathology of that coughing patient's chest.

Usually there has been a change in sexual responsiveness. Then I will conduct a similar assessment of both partners' prior sexual experiences.

What was it like before you had intercourse? When you were only necking? Before you had orgasm? Was it different with other women? With a prostitute? How are your masturbatory experiences different from when you are with your husband? Tell me what you experience when you masturbate.

When I have a clear image of the couple's sexual experience, as it exists now and as it evolved, I can begin to formulate their problem in my mind. This is a tentative formulation, but one which guides my questions toward particular pathways. For clinical purposes (as opposed to investigative objectives), the psychosexual history is most effective if it does not consist of a routine set of questions, but instead is problem oriented.

18

Medical and Psychiatric Evaluation

In the course of the sexual evaluation I always conduct a brief psychiatric examination as well as a medical history and drug survey. This is an essential part of the total evaluation, because medical and psychiatric problems such as diabetes or depression can be the major determinants of a sexual dysfunction.

MEDICAL SURVEY

One cannot assume that a sexual problem is psychogenic unless a possible physical etiology is ruled out. Some dysfunctions are seldom associated with organic factors. These include situational orgastic dysfunction and primary prematurity. But it has been estimated that low libido and impotence in 10 to 25 percent of cases are caused, at least in part, by medical and pharmacologic factors.

Any generally debilitating and/or painful *illness* will affect sexual functioning adversely. In addition endocrine disturbances which interfere with testosterone production or utilization also impair libido in both genders, and erection in the male. Therefore during my medical history I will always specifically question about the signs and symptoms of hepatic disease, pituitary and gonadal difficulties, and the like. Any illness which impairs blood supply to the pelvis and any interference with the pudendal or autonomic pelvic nerves interfere with sexual functioning. For this reason review of systems must be done to rule out circulatory disturbances, neurological illness, or surgical procedures which interfere with genital nerves and blood vessels, for example, perineal prostatectomy and sympathetetomies. Diabetes even in its early stages is the most common physical cause of erectile difficulties. For this reason a 2-h. glucose tolerance test is always ordered in all cases of impotence. In addition I always order a serum testosterone level and sometimes an estrogen and progesterone level as well in order to determine whether treatment with androgens as part of the sex therapy is indicated. Often a thyroid function test is also ordered.

Drugs and medicines are common unsuspected culprits in the sexual dysfunctions. Four categories of medication are capable of impairing the sexual responses: antiandrogens, antiautonomic drugs (anticholinergics and antiadrenergics), narcotics, and excessive use of sedatives and alcohol.

These drugs act by a variety of mechanisms. Narcotics are general sedatives and also seem to exert a specific depressive effect on the sex areas of the brain. Alcohol is a general central nervous system depressant which like sedatives in general impairs sexuality along with other functions. When chronically ingested in high doses, it also causes neurologic damage which may be sexually destructive. The female hormones estrogen and progesterone, cyproterone, and the antihypertensive agents aldectazine and aldectone are antiandrogens which produce a chemical castration. These may lower libido in both genders and cause erection problems in males. Aldomet and other hypotensive agents paralyze the adrenergic nerves which mediate ejaculation and one aspect of erection and cause impotence in a large percentage of the patients who ingest them. The drugs used in the treatment of hypertension are particularly apt to contribute to sexual dysfunctions.

It is clear therefore that a sexual evaluation should include a survey of all medication taken by the patient. It is not wise to commence sex therapy if a patient is on medication which impairs the sexual response. Often medication can be changed to drugs which act effectively on the medical target symptom without producing sexually destructive side effects.

PSYCHIATRIC EXAMINATION

A brief psychiatric examination is conducted on *both* partners as part of the initial evaluation. This examination should yield three types of information: (1) The presence and nature of any psychopathology in either partner must be determined, (2) the quality of their relationship must be assessed, and (3) the therapist should emerge from the initial evaluation with a good idea of the precise role that the sexual symptom plays in the intrapsychic dynamics of each partner and in their marital interactions. These three factors must be understood before intervention can be conducted on a safe and rational basis.

Psychopathology

Many persons who seek help for their sexual dysfunctions are free of significant psychopathology. And their mates are also basically healthy emotionally. Prognosis with sex therapy is generally excellent with emotionally healthy couples, and the therapist can expect a fairly uncomplicated and rapid course of treatment.

But of course neurotic and psychotic persons also suffer from sexual dysfunctions, and the mates of dysfunctional persons may be emotionally disturbed. Psychopathology in either partner exerts strong influences on sexual functioning and on sex therapy: emotional difficulties affect the outcome, complicate treatment, and sometimes even preclude sex therapy altogether.

Sex therapy is contraindicated when *either* partner is in an active stage of a major psychiatric disorder. Clearly, florid schizophrenic reactions, blatant paranoia, and significant depression in *either* partner make sex therapy unfeasible. In fact injudicious intervention with a marginally compensated person may even precipitate a serious adverse reaction.

Sex therapy with persons who harbor major psychiatric disorders but *are well compensated* is not contraindicated providing the therapist is sensitive to and careful not to tamper with crucial defenses against the emergence of open illness. In fact, improved sexual functioning and a better marital relationship may result from successful sex therapy in such cases.

Neurotics and persons with personality disorders frequently are afflicted with symptoms of sexual dysfunction, and this group will make up a large bulk of patients in sex therapy clinics.

While, in general, neurotics with neurotic partners have a more guarded prognosis with sex therapy, many such couples can benefit from sex therapy in terms of improved sexual functioning. In evaluating such patients, in addition to assessing the specific sexual problem it is important for the therapist to formulate a picture of the deeper structure of the unconscious dynamics of both partners. He needs a clear concept of his patient's personality structure and his unconscious conflicts and defenses to guide his therapeutic intervention during sex

21

therapy. He especially needs to know how to avoid mobilizing neurotic defenses and resistances. An astute assessment of which of his patient's conflicts must be resolved, and which ones can be bypassed, in order to liberate sexual functioning is very important in dealing with the neurotic segment of the patient population.

The Relationship Between Sexual Symptoms and Neurotic Conflicts

Effective sex therapy requires an understanding of the precise relationship *between the patient's unconscious neurotic conflicts and his sexual symptom.* In the past it had been assumed that all sexual symptoms were direct products of deep conflicts and that these conflicts had to be resolved before sexual functioning could improve. Our experience with sex therapy has shown that this concept is erroneous for practical purposes. The relationship between sexual symptoms and neurotic conflict is highly variable and complex. While it is, of course, true that some sexual dysfunction is a direct expression of neurotic conflict, this is certainly not universal. Sexual dysfunction often results from more superficial sources of anxiety—such as anticipation of failure to perform. This may occur in persons who also suffer from deeper problems. However, often there is *no direct* connection between the presenting sexual complaint, which may be caused by simple performance anxiety, and the patient's deeper neurotic problems. In such cases the prognosis with sex therapy is excellent. However, the sexual functioning and symptoms can in neurotic individuals acquire symbolic meaning or become utilized as a psychologic defense. When such is the case, the therapist can expect a difficult and stormy course of treatment. For example if a man's premature ejaculation unconsciously expresses his rebellion against his "wife-mother"; if a woman's failure to respond to her husband is a symbol of her yearning for a "superdaddy" whose love will repair her self-esteem, and so on; then the brief active intervention of sex therapy may meet tenacious obstacles and resistances. Fortunately sexual symptoms do not always serve as psychological defenses. Even those cases are not hopeless, however, because therapeutic techniques exist whereby such connections between unconscious conflict and sexual symptoms can sometimes be bypassed. In such cases the benefits of sex therapy are limited to improvement of sexual functioning while the patient retains his basic neurosis. Finally the confrontation with deep sexual conflict which occurs in the process of sex therapy frequently opens the way for reconstructive psychotherapeutic resolution of the patient's basic problems.

The Relationship Between the Couple

The quality of the relationship between the couple who seek help for sexual problems is an important prognostic factor in the outcome of sex therapy. The therapist needs to understand the nature of the bond between them on both a superficial and a deeper level. A true love bond even in the presence of superficial bickering and petty differences improves the prognosis for sex therapy immensely, regardless of the specific clinical problem. Couples who love each other deeply really wish to function, to experience each other fully on a conscious as well as an unconscious level. For such loving couples sexual improvement poses no threat and creates no conflict. On the contrary the opposite is true if the relationship is essentially hostile, even if on the surface the interactions appear tranquil. In such cases the expressed wish for good sexual functioning runs counter to the unconscious need to hurt and to keep the mate at a distance. Such unconscious fears and angers will mobilize serious resistances and obstacles to therapy. How *can* a woman lovingly caress and pleasure a man at whom she is deeply angry? How could a man possibly be patient and gentle with a woman and allow himself to become aroused by her when he is fearful of intimacy and involvement with her? The depth and seriousness of such negative feelings and transactions must be assessed and dealt with in therapy. Sometimes they are insurmountable and preclude sex therapy, which after all requires the unambivalent cooperation of both partners. In other cases when negative feelings are based on resolvable fears and resentments, the therapist can deal with negative interactions successfully. In fact sex therapy provides a splendid opportunity to help a couple resolve marital difficulties when they are so motivated.

Apart from the quality of the couple's bond, a sexual dysfunction may play an important role in their marital system. Impotence may be a means of controlling the wife, and for her it may mean security in the relationship. When sexual dysfunction provides secondary gains in terms of stabilizing the marital system, one may expect intense emotional reactions and obstacles to treatment from either partner or from both.

THE PSYCHOSEXUAL EXAMINATION

The sexual inquiry is designed to give the therapist a detailed mental picture of the superficial as well as the deeper structure of the couple's sexuality. What "turns each on"? What "turns each off"? What are the fantasies and the unconscious hopes and fears of each?

Each partner is questioned in great detail about his sexual development. "Did his sexuality develop normally? When and how did he first experience erotic feelings? Was childhood sexuality suppressed? Was it associated with negative contingencies? At what age did masturbation commence? What were the early fantasies? What were his feelings about this? Any early overt sexual experiences? What was the family attitude toward masturbation? Toward sex? What was the first sexual experience like? Was it exciting? Guilt provoking? Did she "turn it off" or "go with it"? How did he function? What sorts of erotic situations have excited him in the past? When and under what circumstances has he failed to function? Or functioned well? How does *he* experience orgasm? How does *she?* How does she feel about clitoral stimulation? What vaginal sensations does she have on coitus? How does she feel about oral sex? About receiving stimulation? About giving stimulation? How about semen in her mouth? About her genital odors? What excites her most? What sorts of fears does she have? How does she feel about her body? breasts? How does she think he feels about her body? Does she think she takes too long to climax? Can he hold out long enough? Does he get an erection by touching her body? Does he need physical stimulation of his penis? How does she feel if he doesn't get an erection? How does he feel when she doesn't climax?"

It is the main purpose of this evaluation to provide a conceptual blueprint for therapeutic action. It is the strategy of sex therapy to modify the couple's sexual transactions so as to eliminate fear, guilt, and anxiety, and to maximize excitement and gratification. These are highly variable and individualistic matters. Only if the therapist has a clear image of the specific sources of stress which had impaired the free expression of the couple's sexuality can he intervene in a rational and individualistic manner.

The initial sexual evaluation no matter how skillfully done yields only a first approximation, a tentative hypothesis of the structure and dynamics of the couple's sexual difficulty. This view is refined, clarified, and corrected as therapy proceeds. The couple's reactions to the assigned sexual tasks illuminate hidden features of the couple's sexuality which are seldom totally revealed on the initial evaluation. I consider an initial evaluation successful if I feel secure in what I am doing in devising and prescribing the first structured interaction. If the issues are not sufficiently clarified by my verbal inquiry, I will often use a behavioral sig* as a *probe*. How do they respond to a sensate focus sig? With anxiety, pleasure, or eroticism? Much is learned from such responses and also from the couple's association to the structured interactions. The deeper and more subtle issues of a case usually do not become completely resolved in my mind until I have had the opportunity to observe the couple's experiences with some of the assigned tasks.

---

* Sig means "signa," the symbol used on pharmacists' prescription to note the directions to the patient about the use of medication.

II

THE SEXUAL
EXERCISES

A. An Erotic Technique Used for Many Dysfunctions

3

Sensate Focus I – Pleasuring

The term "sensate focus," invented by Masters and Johnson, is a rather clumsy term for a simple and beautiful activity. It means that the couple desists from intercourse and orgasm for several days or weeks during which time they gently caress each other's bodies and genitals. I prefer the term "pleasuring" (which was also introduced into the literature by Masters and Johnson). Many authorities believe that these exercises are among their most significant clinical innovations.

Application of Sensate Focus—Pleasuring

Masters and Johnson state in their book, *Human Sexual Inadequacy* (Little, Brown, and Co., 1970), that all the couples they treated, regardless of the nature of their complaint or of the psychodynamics of their problem, start the experiential aspect of their treatment regimen with the sensate focus exercises. This is usually prescribed on day three of the therapeutic procedure, after the nature of the sexual problem has been discussed with the couple by the cotherapists during the "roundtable" meeting. I have also been impressed with the profound therapeutic impact the sensate focus experience has on many persons, and I use it extensively in sex therapy. However, I do so in a more flexible and individualistic manner. I prescribe pleasuring only when it seems specifically indicated by the nature of the dysfunction and by the requirements of the dynamics of that particular case. Thus for example I do not routinely prescribe pleasuring at all for couples whose chief complaint is vaginismus or premature ejaculation or for totally inorgasmic women.

For these dysfunctions I employ the specific indicated therapeutic tasks which will be described later: dilatation, Semans' maneuver, and self-stimulation respectively. However I may of course also prescribe pleasuring in such cases but only if it is really needed. The timing of the prescription is also flexible and dictated by dynamic considerations. Therefore, I may not use pleasuring as the initial experience, but only after the case has progressed. Thus for example I might prescribe sensate focus for a couple after the man has already attained a good degree of ejaculatory control by means of the Semans' exercises, or if the couple continues to avoid tactile contact, or if they are too orgasm-oriented, or if they need to be confronted with their anxiety about intimacy, and so on. For other dysfunctions sensate focus is employed more often.

I commonly prescribe pleasuring in the initial stages of the treatment of erectile disorders, general nonresponsivity of women, and relative orgastic inhibitions. But I do not do this routinely because often other types of experiences seem to be more rational. For example in treating some particularly defended impotent patients, I might avoid gentle, slow stimulation because in some men this causes excessive anxiety. I might use other forms of stimulation such as erotic films or art literature to promote arousal in such cases.

Rationale

The mechanism of action of sensate focus is not completely clear. Probably there are various dynamics to account for the profound effects which these seemingly simple and gentle exercises frequently evoke. These effects may be understood on several conceptual levels.

30

Pleasuring—Woman face up

The pleasuring prescription often (though by no means always) produces a reduction of tension in the sexual transactions. Each partner is freed of the expectation that he/she must produce an adequate response in himself and in his partner. He doesn't *need* to have an erection, it is *not her duty* to *make* him have one. Neither is *allowed*, much less pressured, to reach orgasm. Failure is practically impossible under these circumstances. Furthermore medical authority has given permission, indeed *prescribed* pleasure. From the perspective of learning theory this creates conditions ideal for the *extinction* of sexual anxiety. Under such relaxed, easy conditions old fears can be extinguished. Anticipatory anxiety related to failure and injury can gradually be reduced. Under these circumstances the emergent pleasurable responses also reinforce more adequate sexual behavior.

Apart from their teaching function, the sensate focus exercises are also intrinsically enjoyable and provide the couple with the opportunity to give and receive pleasure from each other. Gentle stroking and nuzzling and caressing seem to evoke highly pleasurable emotional responses from most persons, providing there is no significant conflict about the pleasuring experience. This is true on the infrahuman as well as on the human level. Petting a dog is highly rewarding and may be used as reinforcement, and "gentling" young laboratory animals is a well-known technique for producing tame and cooperative experimental subjects. Clinical evidence suggests that mutual, gentle, tactile stimulation can enhance the affectionate *bond* between people. Again on an infrahuman level, Harlow found tactile contact to be an important component in the affectionate bonds developed by baby chimps. One tends to respond with love to a person who gently caresses and pleasures one. Tender, tactile contact seems to increase intimacy and mutual involvement. Stringent experimentation is of course needed to support these clinical impressions.

Thus sensate focus is a learning experience whereby pleasurable responses are reinforced and sexual anxiety is diminished because the fear of failure is removed. An additional feature apart from the intrinsic value of this experience relates to psychodynamics of the couple's psychosexual problems. In gently caressing each other the couple may be confronted with an experience which they have previously avoided because physical intimacy arouses anxiety in one or both partners. With the arousal of such anxiety and of the defenses this anxiety elicits, both become subject to psychotherapeutic exploration, and this is very important for the therapy of all but the most simple cases of sexual dysfunction.

It is the clarification of such negative emotional responses which is the crux of intervention in the therapy of most cases of sexual dysfunction. This point will be elaborated in a later section of this chapter which deals with some typical patient responses to sensate focus.

Directions

If a therapist is open and essentially conflict free about sex and pleasure, he is likely to give the pleasuring directions in an effective manner. Conversely, patients are likely to respond negatively to a therapist's lack of ease or to his own anxiety.

Here is the usual way I give these directions. They vary of course with the couple, their level of anxiety, the nature of psychopathology, if any, and their socioeconomic and cultural backgrounds. My method should not be imitated unless it seems natural. Each therapist should develop his own individual style of communication.

"First, I do not want you to have intercourse or orgasm for a little while. How do you feel about that?" (The therapist should then deal with any feelings expressed.) "You *will* have physical contact however, of a very special kind. After dinner tonight, when all your responsibilities are done, I want you both to take showers and then go to bed without any clothes on. Then I want you to caress each other. First you caress her." (The choice of who does the pleasuring first is sometimes of little importance and at other times it is crucial, depending on the dynamics of the couple's problem: for example, if one spouse has an inhibition about *asking* the other for pleasure. If she is so afraid of rejection, so insecure, so guilty that she is heavily involved in giving as opposed to taking some share of pleasure for herself, then I will—after I point this out—ask her to pleasure her husband first. That way she is more likely to be able to relax and abandon herself to her pleasure,

34

Pleasuring—Woman face down

because she has already "paid." On the other hand if a partner is paranoid, and if he feels controlled and demeaned that he must "serve" his wife, that his beautiful erection is not sufficient to stimulate her, then I will—again after *gently* pointing out some of the fallacies of his attitude—suggest that he be the initial receiver. *After* he has been duly caressed, it might be easier for him to give himself to the task of caressing his wife without experiencing anger.)

"You [the man] lie on your stomach. Then I want you [the woman] to caress him as gently and tenderly as you can. Start with the back of his head, his ears, his neck. Go slowly down his back and sides. Down his buttocks, the insides of his thighs. Gently, his legs and his feet. You [the receiver] must try just to concentrate on your feelings. This is very important. Don't worry if she is getting tired or bored. Try to stay with your feeling. And give her feedback. If something feels unpleasant, if she is doing it too fast or too light tell her. If something feels particularly good, tell her or show her.

"When you both have enough of the back turn over. Now do the front the same way. Start with the head and face and neck. Slowly and gently with as much sensitivity as you can find, caress his chest, belly, sides, but not the penis this time. Do the thighs, legs, and feet. Do it till he and you have enough. Then it is your turn. Now you [to the other] do her the same way. Skip the nipples and clitoris and vaginal entrance. Just concentrate on caressing the rest of the body. Any questions? Either of you?"

Reactions to Pleasuring

It is very important to evaluate both partners response to pleasuring in detail and depth. The next therapeutic session usually starts with an inquiry about their experience. Couples are likely to respond briefly: "It was great," "It didn't work," and so on. That is insufficient. A detailed discussion which clarifies the actual experiences of both must be elicited in order for therapy to proceed rationally. In addition, there is a therapeutic value in an open discussion of such feeling as it begins to facilitate authentic communication between the couple.

All behavioral prescriptions elicit *emotions* of which the partners may have varying degrees of awareness. These emotions in turn motivate certain patterns of behavior.

An open probing discussion of the experience helps clarify the affective as well as the behavioral aspects of the experience to both the therapist and to each partner. In order to evaluate the unconscious meanings of these experiences in addition to getting the partners to describe their behavioral and emotional reactions in detail, I also ask for any dreams or fantasies which they may have had during this period. Dreams and fantasies are an excellent means of getting insight into the unconscious significances of these experiences. It is a matter of judgment how this material is to be used clinically. In some cases I will make profound interpretations; at other times insights into more superficial and supportive material is all that is indicated. In general one is governed in one's clinical transactions by the need to avoid the mobilization of profound threat and resistances in both partners.

POSITIVE RESPONSES

Many couples respond very positively to sensate focus. The experience is deeply pleasurable. Some persons enjoy receiving more than giving and vice versa. Often the bond between the couple is enhanced and they are more tender and loving towards each other. Often couples who have had a positive response come to the next therapeutic session holding hands. Often the spouses are relieved to learn that they can give pleasure to the other with their hands and lips, that they do not have to "produce" an erection or lubricate or have intercourse to please their partner. Usually the experiences are sensuous rather than erotic. Occasionally however, one or both may experience intensely erotic feelings and the couple may "disobey" and proceed to orgasm and/or intercourse "against orders." Such behavior is sometimes a resistance born of anxiety, but sometimes such sexual enthusiasm is a healthy expression of growing freedom. Again only a detailed, clear, gently but persistently probing discussion of the physical and emotional responses of the couple can help the therapist evaluate patient responses.

38

Pleasuring—Man face down

NEGATIVE RESPONSES

When the responses are clearly positive, therapy proceeds to the next behavioral prescription which is indicated for that individual case. Often, however, especially if a significant degree of psychopathology or marital pathology exists, persons have negative responses to sensate focus. Adverse emotional reactions vary in intensity from mild and transient to extremely intense and potentially disorganizing. All of these negative responses must either be resolved or bypassed before treatment can proceed.

Some degree of anxiety or discomfort is frequently elicited by engaging in intimate touching and feeling. This is especially true if such contact has been previously avoided for years, and sex had been primarily orgasm-and-performance-oriented.

Negative emotion may be experienced per se, or it may be expressed by avoidance and rationalizing or obsessive behavior:

We didn't have time to do it more than once.

It is too mechanical.

We did it but found it boring, ticklish, silly, and so forth.

I liked doing it to him, but I felt anxiety when he pleasured me.

I thought her arm was getting tired. I couldn't relax. I thought she would get bored.

When he got an erection I felt I had to bring him to orgasm or he would be frustrated.

I just couldn't keep my mind on it. I kept thinking about the kids and dinner.

I felt awful. I am so fat. I thought he would find me repulsive. I just couldn't let him touch me.

I kept wondering if this should give me an erection.

He is so goddamn clumsy. He tickled me, I didn't like it. He is just a lousy lover.

Do I have to go through all that to get laid? Other women just have orgasms without all that fuss.

Causes of Negative Reactions

The causes of the anxiety and anger which may be elicited by mutual pleasuring are many.

If a person has been deeply injured during his formative years, he may protect himself against further injury with alienating defenses. He becomes detached and *avoids intimacy*. Such a patient may experience profound anxiety and anger if his defenses are threatened by the pleasuring experience which compellingly promotes involvement, intimacy, and love.

Guilt about pleasure in general and sex in particular is ubiquitous in our society. When some persons are caressed and stroked the resulting pleasure evokes guilt, and defenses against such guilt must be resolved in the therapy sessions before such a person can be free to enjoy sex.

Hostility toward a spouse may interfere with giving him/her pleasure. If a person is deeply ambivalent about a relationship; if he/she feels exploited, gypped, trapped; there may be a deep resistance to giving the spouse pleasure so that the *giving* part is abortive, clumsy, or sabotaged in some manner. Other hostile and ambivalent persons do not allow themselves to be aroused by the partner. Arousal to such persons is tantamount to involvement, to which they are essentially resistant.

Fear of rejection is often evoked by sensate focus. Some persons feel unless they are giving they will be rejected. They can't ask for themselves. Such persons are likely to experience obsessive thoughts: they are unattractive, the spouse doesn't like doing this, grocery lists or tax obligations and the like nag while they are being caressed. The therapeutic handling of such obsessive defenses includes confrontation with the anxiety which was experienced, as well as interpretations of its unconscious meaning. Specific behavioral prescriptions may also be helpful. For example, one might instruct the couple that the anxious partner must *ask* for what she desires and that the partner must only do what is specifically asked for. The couple is also instructed to share their feelings and reactions to these transactions. In this manner she learns that she will not be rejected if she "dares" to ask him for something. She learns to take responsibility for her own satisfaction. Again, anxiety and defenses evoked by asking are then dealt with in the therapy sessions.

Although this exercise is specifically structured to insure against failure, the *fear of failure* may nevertheless be evoked by sensate focus. An insecure partner will be afraid that he is clumsy and insensitive and feel hopeless about ever being able to please his partner. Reassurance

Pleasuring—Man face up

and corrective experiences can usually diminish this obstacle to sexual abandonment.

Finally deeply neurotic fears and defenses against sexuality are occasionally elicited by sensate focus. For the male these include unconscious fears of injury if one touches and enjoys a woman's body. Such castration fears have a deep long history in the patient's childhood. Fears of homosexuality and of sadistic and masochistic impulses are also occasionally evoked by the open touching and fondling entailed in the process of sensate focus.

Therapy

A negative response to sensate focus on the part of either partner is an obstacle to further therapy which must be resolved or bypassed.

If the negative response is relatively mild, simple *repetition* of the experience along with an interpretive but essentially supportive and reassuring discussion is very often enough to improve the emotional response.

> Do you think you might have been feeling a bit of anxiety when you had those thoughts about your coronary? It is natural to feel a little ill at ease at first. You never allowed yourself to experience such physical intimacy before.

Deeper anxieties such as fear of injury and terror at intimacy often require interpretive kinds of psychotherapeutic intervention, because a certain degree of *resolution* is necessary in order to permit the sexual response to emerge. Resistance to pleasuring often has its roots in a neurotic fear of sexual functioning. If such is the case, resistances must be worked through for a successful outcome. Sometimes, however, when the *process* of sensate focus, and not the *outcome* (i.e., relief of the sexual symptom) evokes anxiety, it is possible to *bypass* this aspect of the process and proceed with other aspects of the treatment. Thus when a person is anxious about touching and intimacy but does not have severe conflict about sexuality per se, the therapist may choose to skip sensate focus and go on to a more genital-oriented task and still obtain a good result in terms of sexual functioning.

4

Sensate Focus II – Genital Pleasuring

Sensate focus II is usually the next step after sensate focus I, but in some cases treatment may begin with this task. When the couple has successfully experienced mutual pleasuring, or when it is the therapeutic decision to omit or detour this experience, they are instructed in genital pleasuring. This refers to gentle, teasing stimulation of the genitals, the objective of which is to produce arousal, but *not* orgasm:

"I want you to experiment with taking turns giving each other genital pleasure. Do as much of the general body caressing as you need to arouse your partner. Then play with his penis. Play gently with the tip and the shaft and the testicles for a little while. Then go to another part of his body. One which he likes. Caress his belly or ears or thighs. Then get back to his penis. Use your fingers or your lips as you and he please. How do you feel about using your mouth on the genitals?"

(Feelings about oral-genital sex must be dealt with explicitly at some point in therapy. This subject is often intensely invested with emotion and there may be a temptation to avoid this. However it should be confronted or it may become an obstacle to openness and a potential source of anxiety. It is easy for the spouses as well as therapist to be biased in either direction with regard to oral sex. Some persons feel oral sex is disgusting and neurotic and a person who is healthy sexually does not need such "extreme" stimulation. Other prejudices run to the opposite. Some persons feel that oral sex is a necessary prerequisite for a full sex life, that anyone who objects is inhibited and neurotic, and this issue must be resolved in order to have fully satisfactory sex. Actually there is no proof to support either position. Some persons can have

46

Genital Stimulation—Masters and Johnson position for stimulating
the woman's clitoris and vagina

a fully satisfying sex life without oral stimulation. Oral stimulation is certainly *not* a necessary product or process of sex therapy. On the other hand oral sex, both giving and receiving the stimulation, is found exquisitely pleasurable and gratifying by many perfectly normal couples, and sometimes in the course of sex therapy inhibitions to oral sex are resolved with very happy results. The most challenging therapeutic situations are those in which one partner ardently desires oral stimulation and the other is repelled or feels guilty about this sexual technique. Such an impasse often presents opportunities for effective therapeutic intervention whose benefits extend substantially beyond an improvement in sexual functioning.)

"I want you to use a teasing tempo. Do not use the rhythmic, driving stimulation which leads to orgasm. If he gets no erection, that's fine. He will still feel pleasure. If he gets one, play with him for a little while, then caress another part of his body. Don't worry if the erection goes down. That is natural and normal. It will come up again if you don't worry about it. You [to the man] while she is caressing you, try not to become distracted. Stay with your feelings. Enjoy the feelings.

"After you have enough, it is your [to the woman] turn. I want you to play with her whole body first. Then when you feel she is ready, or when she tells you, play with her breasts. Gently kiss and pinch the nipples. Play with the pubic hair around her clitoris. Do not touch the clitoris right away. Play around with the vaginal entrance. Do not put your finger all the way into the vagina. That doesn't feel good to most women. Touch the clitoris lightly. Go somewhere else. Go back to the clitoris. Be as gentle and sensitive as you can. Try [to the woman] to give him a little feedback. He has no possible way of knowing what you are feeling. Men have erections, but our responses are internal. He cannot tell "where you are" unless you tell him. Let him know what feels good. You have to tell him what you are feeling if you want him to give you pleasure. Again [to the man] do *not* at this point use the rubbing, driving kind of rhythmic stimulation which produces orgasm. There is a lot of pleasure in just being touched and aroused. One doesn't have to have an orgasm to have pleasure. There are several positions in which this is comfortable. Some people like the position shown in Figures 5 and 6 others have found 7 and 8 to be particularly good. Other couples prefer to find their own positions."

49

Reactions

Many persons who have sexual difficulties when they attempt to have intercourse or when they are striving for orgasm are able to experience intense erotic pleasure and also to respond physiologically when genital pleasuring is the goal of the interaction. This is not surprising because by structuring the situation in this manner many sources of fear and tension which are produced by intercourse are eliminated. Neither partner has to perform. They are "taking turns," so one's response is not contingent on the other's. When the humane goal of pleasure is substituted for the pressured goal of performance, the sexual situation often becomes relaxed enough for the erotic responses to develop freely. The man becomes excited, and before he knows it has several erections. The woman may feel intense erotic pleasure for the first time in her life, or more commonly for the first time since her pre-coital "petting" days. She may lubricate and desire intercourse. Again couples may "break training" at this point. And again this may be a healthy or a resistant manifestation depending on the underlying emotion.

When the responses to genital pleasuring are positive one proceeds to the next step in treatment, which may be extracoital orgasm or coitus. As always, prescription is highly individualistic. It is the negative responses, which frequently occur, that represent the therapeutic challenge.

NEGATIVE REACTIONS

Genital pleasuring may evoke special kinds of negative emotional reactions in one or both spouses. Whereas sensate focus is likely to evoke anxiety about intimacy, trust, sensuousness, and feelings associated with a negative body image, genital pleasuring is more likely to evoke specific sexual anxiety. The anxiety may range from mild and transient to severe and phobic. The anxiety and guilt evoked by mutual fondling of genitals may be experienced per se or may become obscured by a myriad of defenses and avoidances. Just how the negative affect is experienced depends on the degree to which the person is in touch with

Genital Stimulation—Masters and Johnson position for stimulating
the man without erection

Genital Stimulation—Woman touching man's erect penis

his feelings. If he is not aware that his lack of feelings, his obsessive ruminations while he is being stimulated, the late TV watching which prevents the experience from being carried out, and similar phenomena are expressions of the anxiety evoked by genital play, then this is what I discuss with the couple during the therapy session. How deep the interpretations should be made, how much insight into unconscious sources of anxiety is necessary for sexual functioning to improve is a matter of clinical judgment and personal therapeutic style. I tend to make interpretations on rather deep unconscious levels and balance these with enough support to keep resistances from mobilizing. Other therapists (who also get very good results in therapy) tend to stay on a more superficial "counseling" level in their interpretations.

Thus for example, when a patient complained that he started to think about his business as his wife was caressing his penis, he was confronted with the possibility that this is an obsessive defense against some sort of anxiety.

THERAPIST: What do you suppose might be making you anxious? What were you experiencing when you started to ruminate?

MAN: Well it was feeling good. I started to have a fantasy. . . . then I thought, don't have a fantasy that is bad . . . the doctor said stay with your feelings . . . I don't know . . . I often think of business during sex."

Later it developed that the patient used to guard himself against "impure thoughts" as a young and religious man with school problems. Through interpretation he came to understand that he had harbored intense conflict about masturbation. It was not surprising that the present sexual experience evoked his old guilt and anxiety about masturbation and also the old defenses against this. In the therapeutic sessions his early masturbation was reevaluated in a positive light as a sign of healthy struggle against the efforts of others to suppress his healthy sexuality. This support enabled him to accept and work through his masturbatory guilt. Unless adequately balanced with genuine support this sensitive sort of material may be difficult to handle within a brief therapy since one can hardly rely on a long-standing trusting therapeutic relationship to counterbalance the anxiety mobilized by recognition of threatening unconscious material.

Genital fondling often evokes negative feelings and defenses against the appearance, odors, and secretions of the partner's and the person's own genitals. This material is openly worked through in the therapeutic sessions. These frank discussions of previously taboo and shameful topics are of immense value in improving the communications between, and security of, the couple, above and beyond the immediate goals of sex therapy.

Certain specific negative feelings recur again and again and are typically evoked by genital pleasuring prescriptions. These are guilt about feeling and showing pleasure, covert hostility toward one's partner, and fear of rejection by one's partner. The first two have already been discussed in connection with the negative responses to sensate focus while more will be said of the fear of rejection when the tasks used for the treatment of impotence and frigidity are described. On a deeper neurotic level the castration anxieties, homosexual conflicts, and threatening sadomasochistic impulses, which have already been mentioned in the previous section on sensate focus, may also be elicited by genital touching.

Therapeutic Management

Repetition, insight, or bypass are the three therapeutic strategies which may be employed to manage negative responses to any of the prescribed sexual tasks. This is also true of genital pleasuring.

When anxiety and defenses are mild, mere repetition combined with some interpretation and support are usually sufficient to propel therapy forward.

Go home and try it again. Tell him the way you like him to touch you best and do it again. It is hard to shed the anxieties of a lifetime in just a few weeks. You will probably be more relaxed this time.

56

Genital Stimulation—Man touching woman's nipples

When feelings run deep I try to promote insight. This is possible only if rapport and understanding are sufficiently developed so that interpretations of unconscious material can be made incisive and yet supportive enough to foster insight without mobilizing resistances.

Sometimes when pathology is too tenacious and profound for any reasonable hope at rapid resolution I try to bypass the anxiety. I try to lower the defenses against sexuality, while providing defenses against the associated anxiety.

First, one usually confronts the patient with the fact that obsessive ruminations are a manifestation of anxiety. One admonishes the patient to be temporarily "selfish" and to concentrate solely on his own feelings.

> Be selfish—her turn will come next. You have to abandon yourself to your feelings if you want to function. Everyone does. She does, too.

At this point I often encourage the spouse to talk about her own "selfishness," i.e., her ability to stay with her feelings and her fantasies as her sexual arousal builds up. This does much to liberate the more guilty and controlled spouse.

Another excellent method of bypassing resistances is by suggesting that the patient distract himself with erotic fantasy while he is being stimulated. The use of fantasy as a method of overcoming resistances to sexual abandonment will be dealt with when the orgastic dysfunctions of women and of men are discussed.

Finally resistances can be bypassed by changing the sexual prescription. If his partner's fondling of his genitals arouses too much anxiety in a man, he might be instructed only to caress his partner and bring her to orgasm during the next week. Her arousal together with his growing frustration might be reassuring and stimulating enough to bypass his anxieties and allow him to function.

B. Erotic Techniques Used for Specific Dysfunctions

5

Frigidity—Female Sexual Unresponsiveness

The unresponsive woman feels no erotic sensation or sexual pleasure. She does not show the signs of physiological arousal, i.e., she remains relatively dry even though she is stimulated by her partner and has intercourse. Her conscious attitudes towards sex vary. She may loathe sexual activity, feel neutral, or even enjoy the physical contact.

The truly unresponsive woman is rare, and this is fortunate because she is difficult to treat. In our experience general unresponsiveness—particularly when it is primary, i.e., the woman has never been responsive to any man in any situation—has of all the dysfunctions the poorest prognosis with brief sex therapy. The prognosis is much better if the woman has been responsive in other situations but is now unresponsive to her husband. Even in situational frigidity however, extensive psychotherapy is often necessary before the patient is amenable to sex therapy and before sexual functioning can be obtained. Nevertheless, even in this difficult dysfunction, which often requires prior resolution of tenacious unconscious intrapsychic and marital conflict, the prescribed sexual tasks play an important role in therapy.

Sometimes these are not employed until the patient has resolved basic conflicts by means of psychotherapy. At other times the tasks may be used concurrently with psychotherapy in order to facilitate rapid resolution of obstacles which arise during the course of treatment.

Perhaps one can formulate the basic dynamics of unresponsivity as follows: The woman harbors an unconscious conflict about allowing herself sexual pleasure with a man. There does not seem to be one specific conflict in this disorder. It may involve deep oedipal fears of injury, hostility towards men in general or towards the specific man in question, fears of rejection if she "lets go," performance anxiety, erotic guilt, and so forth. The defenses against these conflicts specifically prevent the woman from responding. She either avoids receiving adequate stimulation, or if she doesn't actually prevent her lover from stimulating her, she erects *perceptual defenses* against enjoying this stimulation. She literally does not allow herself any erotic feelings. She unconsciously does not allow herself to respond. She prevents herself from abandoning herself to the sexual experience.

Treatment Strategy

The basic strategy in therapy is to attempt to structure the sexual situation so that the woman is able to respond to adequate and heightened sexual stimulation while she is in a relaxed, nonanxious and loving state. Under such conditions, she must learn to resensitize herself to the sensations she has defensively suppressed for a long time. Again the creation of a tranquil sexual system between the partners often requires considerable psychotherapeutic intervention but with this in mind, the following is a typical (but not universal) sequence of events which we employ at the Cornell Sex Therapy Clinic to treat the generally unresponsive female.

1. Sensate focus I
2. Sensate focus II
3. Nondemand coitus
4. Coitus to orgasm

Among this group of patients there is a very high prevalence of negative responses to the sensate focus exercises. These reactions are of course incorporated into the psychotherapeutic process. In addition to the psychotherapeutic explorations, when the history reveals that the woman experienced high levels of arousal in precoital and premarital "petting" situations, we might initially prescribe such activity while the couple is clothed, instead of the traditional nude and more exposed and therefore more threatening, pleasuring.

Nondemand Coitus

This exercise is optimally employed after the woman has shown a positive response to the sensate focus exercises which were described in the previous chapters. However, if genital touching arouses insurmountable resistance, it may occasionally be bypassed and nondemand coitus introduced at this time.

The couple is told to caress each other until the man has a good erection and until the woman has some degree of lubrication. If she fails to respond with adequate vasocongestion he is instructed to lubricate his penis with petroleum jelly.

Then the woman mounts in the superior position. She inserts his penis into her vagina. She allows it to rest there for a little while, while she gets the "feel" of the erect phallus in her vagina. She contracts the pubococcygeal muscles against his penis, again to acquaint herself with the vaginal feelings of which such women are often not aware. Then she starts to slowly move up and down on her husband's erect phallus. She plays and experiments with different motions and excursions. She should be moved solely by her own feelings and *not* by a regard for him. She must *temporarily* suspend her usual concern for his pleasure. She must be temporarily "selfish" so she can learn to feel her vaginal sensations.

He lends his erect penis and his gentle encouragement to the enterprise. If he should become too excited, he indicates this, and the couple "rests" for a while. This can be done with the penis inside the vagina or he can withdraw and later, after he has regained control, he can re-enter. The in-and-out interrupted coitus has a teasing effect which often heightens the woman's arousal.

62

Female superior—nondemanding thrusting

During the rest periods, the couple may be instructed to desist from stimulation. In other cases he stimulates her clitoris during the rest from intromission. In still other cases she is instructed to stimulate herself during these times.

The end of the exercise is reached when she is tired or when she has an orgasm, [which is exceedingly *unusual*, especially in the early phases of therapy]. More commonly they stop when she feels tired and satisfied that she has learned some additional vaginal sensations. Sometimes the man's ejaculatory urge becomes insistent and he does not wish to continue without climax. At any rate, at the termination of the exercise the man is usually provided with an orgasm, either by thrusting to orgasm on coitus, or by extravaginal stimulation.

It should be noted that even a well functioning, normal male may lose his erection during the course of the nondemand sexual exercises. This is no cause for concern for the male can easily be stimulated to another erection. The important subject of regaining lost erections is dealt with in the chapter on erectile dysfunction.

It is clear from the foregoing description that the nondemand coital exercises require the active cooperation of a functional male partner. He must have some degree of "erectile security" as well as good ejaculatory control. This is a good example of why sex therapy requires the participation of a cooperative couple, even when the partner has in no way caused or perpetuated his mate's sexual difficulty.

REACTIONS TO NONDEMAND COITUS

Women's reactions run the gamut from great pleasure and excitement and occasionally even orgasm—through a desired increase in vaginal sensations, erotic pleasure, and loving feelings—to the negative responses of anesthesia or to profoundly disturbing emotional reactions.

Male responses to this exercise also cover a wide spectrum. Some men are delighted to provide an erect phallus to help their wive's with their difficulty. They take pleasure and pride as well as sexual gratification from the experience. Other men have negative reactions—

anxiety and/or anger—to this previously avoided situation wherein the woman assumes control of the sexual interaction and is extremely active and "selfish." Again, these reactions reveal extremely valuable material for psychotherapeutic exploration.

When the reactions are positive the couple proceeds to regular coitus. If not, the negative reactions must first be worked through.

Many women who have sexual inhibitions are overconcerned with their partner's gratification to the neglect of their own. One must differentiate between the desirable qualities of generosity—sensitivity to one's lover and concern for his feelings—and the neurotic, immature, and compulsive neglect of one's own feelings, in the anxiety to please and serve. The latter is essentially a masochistic pattern of relating to the opposite gender. It is born of deep anxiety. Usually a masochistic person has profound feelings of inadequacy and self-loathing. She can not really believe that an attractive man can love her and accept her if she is merely herself: her sexual, emotional, real self. She must constantly serve and please and give him pleasure. She must not relax and enjoy herself. Such a person, whether female *or* male, has great difficulties in abandoning themselves to their erotic pleasures. It has been repeatedly emphasized that a substantial degree of abandonment is a prerequisite of sexual functioning.

The partner often unconsciously is attracted to and subtly perpetuates his wife's masochism. He permits her to serve, give pleasure, gratify him. This may allow a basically insecure man to function with a minimum of anxiety.

Some degree of sexual masochism, not in the extreme sense of being aroused by injury or physical violence, but rather in the form of sexual self-sacrifice, is very common in our male-oriented culture. We are taught from early childhood that sexual pleasure is the male's due. The woman must make herself as attractive and pleasing as possible. It is all right for her to have some pleasure too, but only really in the service of his. Beyond this cultural masochism, however, nonresponsive women often tend to be psychologically masochistic and compulsively giving— unable to ask or take. These insecurities spring from destructive and incorrectly perceived childhood experiences and neurotic adaptations to these.

66

It is not surprising that when unconscious masochistic patterns which serve one or both partners' deep unconscious needs are revealed by a structured behavioral task designed to give *control* to the woman, to govern the activity by *her* needs, to *neglect* the man's gratification, no matter how temporarily—a great deal of anxiety and defenses against this anxiety are evoked. Indeed, the nondemand coital exercises frequently provoke anxiety and deep insecurities in women and sometimes in the husband as well.

Management of such resistance consists of repetition of the task and active, vigorous psychotherapy. This is designed to reveal and resolve the self-destructive sexual behavior and most importantly also to correct the low self-esteem which often lies at its roots. In addition it is extremely important to be alert to any reciprocal psychopathology on the part of the husband. Some husbands and lovers of masochistic women do not have an unconscious investment in their wives' lack of pleasure. They really would be much happier if their wives were responsive. Others, however, because of their own insecurities derive some unconscious gratification from the lover's masochism. In such cases this dynamic must be dealt with or the partner is likely to sabotage the treatment. This can be done either by bypass or resolution. Bypass in such cases is psychotherapeutic and not strictly behavioral. For intercourse of course cannot be bypassed in most dysfunctional cases treated with sex therapy. When a sadomasochistic pattern is too tenacious to yield to brief intervention, bypass may consist of subtly communicating to the couple that they can retain the essential features of their psychological interactions, but at the same time they can still function sexually. They can fight and struggle if they must, but they can keep their neurotic interactions out of the bedroom.

Partner rejection is another common underlying cause for unresponsiveness in women, especially when this dysfunction is situational. Some persons can dissociate their sexual and affectionate responses to a great degree. They can enjoy and function in sexual experiences even when they have a detached or even a negative emotional connection to their partner. Other persons, especially women, cannot. Some unresponsive women who seek sex therapy are not aware that they are deeply angry or at least ambivalent towards their husbands. They feel exploited, cheated, and angry, and yet may be entirely unaware of their hostile feelings. Nevertheless these feelings inhibit their sexual responses to their husbands. At times partner rejection can be bypassed behaviorally, and the woman can learn to respond sexually in spite of her ambivalence. In other cases, the anger poses an insurmountable obstacle to sexual responsiveness and must be resolved psychotherapeutically before the patient can respond to the sexual exercises. Similar considerations apply to deep unconscious sexual conflicts which derive from oedipal problems and guilt about sexual pleasure which are also prevalent obstacles to female sexual responsiveness.

Orgasm

When the nondemanding, teasing coital exercises produce erotic responsiveness in the woman, the couple is instructed to proceed with ordinary coitus designed to lead to orgasm in both partners. Sometimes this produces orgasm in the woman. Other times it does not and other techniques designed to facilitate orgasm are prescribed.

Usually one does not specifically attempt to foster the unresponsive patient's orgastic response in the initial phases of therapy. It is the aim of this phase of treatment to enhance her general responsiveness. A goal oriented, orgasm-achieving orientation paradoxically is sometimes an obstacle rather than an aid to therapy. In some cases however, when the patient's unresponsiveness is secondary to repeated attempts and failures to reach orgasm, orgastic exercises are prescribed. These are described in the next chapter on the orgastic dysfunctions.

In unresponsive women with very low libido one tries to enhance her sexual response by other than tactile means. Low levels of testosterone, fantasy, and erotic literature have all been used to implement this objective.

PUBOCOCCYGEUS MUSCLE EXERCISES

Dr. Arnold Kegel has claimed that weakness and disuse of the pubococcygeus muscle is a factor in female unresponsiveness. He and his

Male inside female from rear—touching her clitoris

followers prescribe pubococcygeal muscle exercises. The effectiveness of this practice has not yet been evaluated systematically. However there is a certain rationale for this procedure and hence it is used by many sex therapists.

Essentially, proprioceptive sensations from the perivaginal muscles are an important source of pleasurable erotic vaginal sensation. Also the female orgasm consists of contraction of the ischio cavernosii, bulbo cavernosii and pubococcygeus muscles. Therefore, the reasoning is that strengthing the tone of these muscles would be helpful in producing stronger and more enjoyable orgasms.

If these muscles are found to be lax and atrophic on vaginal examination, or just on an empirical basis, the patient is directed to contract her pubococcygens muscles 10 times once or twice each day. If she has no awareness of these muscles she is told to start and stop her stream of urine. It is the pubococcygeus muscles which are contracted in the process of stopping the stream of urine. Thereby the patient learns to be aware of this group of muscles. The muscles can be exercised during routine daily chores.

An instrument called the perineometer enables a woman to contract her pubococcygens muscles against resistance which is measured by manometer via a device inserted into her vagina. Few sex therapists employ such an elaborate procedure.

6

Female Orgastic Dysfunction

A clear distinction should be made between the totally unresponsive woman and the woman who *is* responsive, enjoys erotic feeling, has a good vasocongestive response, but who has difficulties to varying degrees in achieving orgasm. In the past both were included under the rubric of "frigidity" and were considered to be a single disorder. This is an error, because while both syndromes have much in common and overlap to a certain extent, they are the product of different underlying mechanisms and respond to somewhat different treatment procedures.

The definition of orgastic dysfunction is a subject of controversy because the normal range and limits of the female orgasmic response has not yet been defined.

The orgasm is a reflex. All reflexes have a range and distribution of thresholds. In other words some persons need only a mild tap on the knee to elicit a kick, others will not respond until they receive a good sharp bang on the patellar tendon. Both are perfectly normal, i.e., the neural apparatus which mediates the reflex is intact. There is a normal *range* in the threshold of the patellar reflex. The thresholds of reflexes are also influenced by other factors such as psychological inhibition, drugs, and emotional states. Thus a nervous patient may have to be distracted by clasping his hands before the examining physician can elicit the knee jerk. These same considerations apply to the female orgastic reflex. However, we do not know where the normal limits of this important reflex lie.

Clinically, female orgasm seems to be distributed more or less along a bell-shaped curve. On one extreme are the women who have never climaxed at all. Next are women who require intense clitoral stimulation when they are alone and not "disturbed" by a partner. Women who need direct clitoral stimulation but are able to climax with their partners fall in the middle range. Also near the middle are women who can climax on coitus but only after lengthy and vigorous stimulation. Near the upper range are women who require only brief penetration to reach their climax and at the very extreme are the women who can achieve an orgasm via fantasy and/or breast stimulation alone.

Everyone agrees on criteria of normalcy and pathology at the extreme ends of the orgastic continuum. Clearly the woman who is totally anorgastic—i.e., the woman who has never had an orgasm at all—is inhibited and in the need of treatment. It is also clear that the woman who is rapidly and easily orgastic on coitus is normal. The controversy pertains to the middle range in the spectrum of female orgastic threshold.

Some workers in the field, including myself, consider women who are orgastic on clitoral stimulation when they are with their partners as normal. Others consider any woman who is not coitally orgastic, even though she is highly responsive and multiply orgastic on clitoral stimulation in the presence of a partner, as frigid. There is at this time insufficient data available to settle this controversy definitively.

On an empirical basis, until we have definitive evidence, we proceed as follows. We treat all women who complain of orgastic difficulty, coital or absolute. The totally anorgastic woman presents a special clinical problem. Such patients have an excellent prognosis for learning to have orgasms with sex therapy. We also accept coitally inorgastic women for treatment because they also can often benefit from therapy. For some women clitoral stimulation seems to be their normal response pattern and they and their husbands merely need counseling and reassurance to this effect. For other women, however, the lack of coital orgasm is indeed a product of inhibition or poor technique, and this segment of the patient population often learns to achieve the desired goal of coital orgasm with sex therapy. These two varieties of the orgastic dysfunctional syndrome, the total anorgastic and the situationally inorgastic woman, present somewhat different clinical problems and are therefore dealt with in separate sections.

Treatment Strategy

In general the basic treatment plan for orgasmic dysfunction is:

1. orgasm alone (masturbation)
2. orgasm with the partner—on clitoral stimulation
3. orgasm on intercourse

If orgasm on intercourse does not occur:
1. bridge maneuver

A—The Totally Inorgastic Woman

Approximately 8 percent of females in the United States have never had an orgasm. Some of these women are inorgastic because they have never been stimulated properly, others cannot respond with orgasm to even the most intense stimulation. For a variety of reasons these women have learned to inhibit their orgasmic reflex. This inhibition is entirely involuntary and such women often ardently desire the orgasmic experience.

MASTURBATION

The main principle of achieving orgasm is simple: maximize the stimulation and minimize the inhibition. To minimize inhibiting factors, it is often best to have the woman stimulate herself to orgasm when she is alone and free from the pressure of being observed and "timed" by her partner. To do this one must often help her resolve guilt and shame about masturbation. This is done during the therapy sessions.

Women who have never experienced orgasm are confused about the experience. Often they are frightened and anticipate injury. Such patients are asked to talk about their fantasies about orgasm. What do they think will happen? Women have varying degrees of awareness

74

Female alone masturbating with finger

about their fearful orgasmic fantasies. These must be explored in the sessions, and it is often useful to discuss their genesis in a reasonable and supportive manner. Some common fears which center around punishment for sexual pleasure include: "I will lose control," "I will go crazy," "It will injure me—I will get cancer—die—and so forth," "I will love it and become wildly promiscuous," "I must be in love before I can have an orgasm." Most of such fantasies clearly have their roots in childhood prohibitions against sexuality. Dreams and associations are often useful in working through such unconscious impediments to orgasmic release. And the patient must be reassured on the deepest level about the unrealistic nature of her injury fantasies.

At other times, if a woman is guilty about pleasure and success she may have the opposite fantasy—that orgasm represents the ultimate in success. In such cases she has to be reassured that orgasm is *not* the ultimate transcendental experience which will make her supremely happy. When she realizes that her other problems will not be dispelled by her achieving a climax, *then* it is sometimes possible for her to achieve her first orgasm. Ideally of course the basic success conflict should be worked through. This is a lengthy process but in sex therapy it is sometimes possible to confront the patient with this destructive dynamic and take the first steps toward its resolution.

Realistic understanding of orgasm is therapeutic. So I usually describe orgasm to the woman who has never experienced one:

It is a reflex, like a sneeze, only it is much more pleasurable. Orgasm varies very widely in how enjoyable it is, however. Sometimes it is really a great experience and you sort of get totally absorbed in it. Sometimes it is just a pleasant local sensation. Orgasm is a series of pleasurable contractions. There is no mistaking the sensation. It is unique, and you will definitely *know* when you have had an orgasm. When your sexual tension builds up, then there are suddenly some rhythmic contractions of the muscles in your vagina. Those contractions are the pleasurable part. You feel erotic pleasure in your clitoris as you build up to orgasm, but during the contractions you feel the pleasure around the vagina and deep in your pelvis. Sometimes you feel like thrusting your pelvis back and forth when you feel an orgasm coming on. That feels very good. But at other times you are moved to hold quite still and just enjoy the orgastic rush quietly. That also feels very good. You never really lose control or consciousness during an orgasm, but, as I said, sometimes you really can get lost in the cascade of pleasurable sensation. Do you have any questions about this?

After guilt feelings and fears and fantasies and misinformation about orgasm have been dispelled in the therapeutic session, the patient is advised to go home and try out digital masturbation. At this juncture her *erotic fantasies* are explored during the therapeutic sessions. It is important to reassure patients that fantasies, whatever their nature, are normal and indeed very useful in sexual functioning. They serve concomitantly to stimulate and to distract from anxiety. If the patient has sexual fantasies and daydreams she is encouraged to immerse herself in these images while she stimulates herself. If she is bereft of erotic fantasies, she is advised to purchase erotic literature and read it as a *probe,* i.e., to see what sort of scene or situation or picture or fantasy will stimulate her. Digital stimulation of the clitoris plus distraction by fantasy often produce orgasm within a few weeks. If it does not, the use of a *vibrator* is suggested. There are several suitable vibrators available for the purpose of female masturbation. The phallus-shaped battery powered machines are *not* good for producing orgasm because the vibrations are not strong enough, while almost any commercial *electric massager,* widely available in drug stores, can be effective.

It is suggested to the patient that she experiment with the vibrator by moving it around and near her clitoral area. Again she is advised to immerse herself in fantasy during the stimulation in order "to distract the distractor," i.e., distract herself from her own tendencies to exert conscious control over her orgastic response. In some cases she may be advised to read erotic literature or observe erotic pictures while she is in the very act of stimulating herself.

Some patients must stimulate themselves for long periods of time, occasionally up to *one hour* before they release into orgasm. The therapist's encouragement is important during this period.

Female masturbating with vibrator—male is present

There are several "tricks" or methods which may facilitate orgastic release. It helps some women to "bear down" when they feel orgasm by alternately tightening and relaxing the vaginal perineal muscles. A method which helps other patients is to thrust their pelvis actively and breathe pantingly at high levels of excitement.

Sometimes when a woman's orgastic response is inhibited, unpleasant tensions and sensations are produced when she is stimulated intensely. At such times it is best to advise her to cease stimulation for a second or so, then to resume again. Several repetitions of this "stop–start" technique often produce the initial orgasm.

All these mechanical techniques probably facilitate orgasm by distracting the woman from her inhibitory tendencies. Again a highly useful "distractor" is an erotic fantasy.

ORGASM WITH THE PARTNER

Reaching an orgasm on masturbation is a wonderful achievement for a woman who has never climaxed, but it is hardly a satisfactory end point of treatment. After a woman can reliably masturbate to orgasm alone, the next step in treatment is to have her have an orgasm in the presence of her husband. This is much harder to do because even though it is usually much more stimulating to be with a man than alone with one's fantasies, it is usually also far more anxiety-provoking. One has to perform, produce: "Will I be able to reach a climax? Will he get sick and tired of the tedious stimulation? Are other women quicker?"

There are various techniques to accomplish this next step. For one the couple may be advised to make love in their usual manner. After he climaxes, he stimulates her to orgasm manually. She is advised to use the same mental devices by which she was able to facilitate her orgasm on self-stimulation. She contracts her muscles, breathes pantingly, and above all immerses herself in her favorite fantasies while he stimulates her. This method often produces orgasm in the woman. Gradually it becomes less difficult and gradually she needs less and less fantasy as a distractor.

At other times self-masturbation in the presence of the husband is prescribed. This is indicated if the woman is very slow or if she has not yet worked through her reticence at asking for and accepting pleasure from him. Some couples are free enough to accept such a suggestion. Most often, however, women are embarrassed and ashamed and expect rejection from their husbands should they masturbate in his presence. Some husbands are indeed "put off" by this idea. But they are in the minority. Most often to the wife's surprise the husband does not react with the anticipated shock or disgust to his wife's masturbation. To the contrary, he is often intensely excited by the idea. Actually female masturbation is an exceedingly common theme in the erotic fantasies of normal men.

The experience of being open enough to stimulate oneself in the presence of one's mate most often has a salutary effect. It adds yet another dimension of depth and openness to the couple's sexual relationship.

B—The Coitally Inorgastic Woman

Failure to reach orgasm on coitus is the most common sexual complaint of women. This is not surprising when female anatomy and physiology are considered realistically. Experimental and clinical evidence indicates that the female orgasm is a reflex the motor expression of which consists of contractions of muscles surrounding the vagina, although it is triggered by sensory stimulation around the clitoral area. From a mechanical standpoint intercourse is actually a rather poor and indirect way of stimulating the clitoral area.

This point often evokes an intense emotional response from clinicians who for understandable psychological reasons would prefer that vaginal penetration were the best orgasm-producing stimulus. But unfortunately this is not so. Psychologically intercourse produces a highly arousing and emotionally satisfying erotic stimulus. Mechanically, however, clitoral stimulation during intercourse is limited to the traction on the clitoral hood produced by the thrusting phallus, and some pressure around the clitoral area by the man's pubic bone in some

82

Male stimulating female's clitoris manually

positions. This is not as strong a stimulus as direct manipulation of the clitoris. Given these facts it might be predicted that only women with a relatively low orgasmic threshold could reach climax on coitus alone, without any added clitoral stimulation. And indeed although definitive data is missing on this point, according to Fisher's surveys and estimates only one third to one half of women in the United States prefer to reach climax regularly on intercourse. It may be speculated that some of those who do not are not pathologically inhibited. Physiologically these women require more intense clitoral stimulation than is provided by intercourse. Others in this group most probably do represent a truly dysfunctional group. They probably have high orgastic thresholds because of psychological inhibition. The first group of physiologically, coitally anorgastic women need reassurance and counseling. The truly dysfunctional group often benefit from sex therapy.

THE BRIDGE MANEUVER

Sensate focus I and II and nondemand coitus are often used in the initial stages of therapy for coitally inorgastic women. The crucial task for this problem however entails the combination of clitoral stimulation and coitus, a technique which is called "the bridge maneuver." This technique is indicated for the woman who is clitorally responsive and who does not reach orgasm on coitus, but who wishes to do so.

Most coitally inorgastic women who are orgastic on clitoral stimulation can climax if they are stimulated at the same time the penis is contained in the vagina. Women often like techniques which provide such stimulation because the orgastic experience is quite distinct and highly pleasurable if the erect penis is in the vagina at the time of climax. However, use of this technique as a permanent adaptation has the disadvantage of being tedious for the husband. Also this practice seldom leads on to true coital orgasm. The bridge maneuver is different in that the basic idea is to provide the woman with clitoral stimulation *up* to the point of, but not actually to, orgasm, and then let coital thrusting trigger off the orgastic reflex. This is a "bridge" between clitoral stimulation and coitus.

Clitoral stimulation may be provided by the man or by the woman herself, depending on the dynamics of the case. If no specific psychological obstacles exist, there are advantages to advise the woman to stimulate herself, at least during the initial trials of the bridge. Her husband is less likely to find this tedious if stimulation takes a long time, he is apt to become more aroused when he is inside a woman who is stimulating herself, and finally the woman is often more able to relax and concentrate on her pleasure when she is in control of stimulation, and does not have to worry about "his arm getting tired," i.e., being rejected.

There are several positions wherein concomitant clitoral stimulation and intromission can be conducted with comfort. Side to side and woman superior and man kneeling are illustrated in the text in figures 15, 16, and 17. In addition, couples are encouraged to experiment on their own. The important principles in the positions to be used for the "bridge maneuver" are that there be free access for the stimulating hand to clitoris, and that the woman's hips be free for thrusting against the man's pubic bone.

This exercise should be used *after* the woman has experienced enhanced vaginal sensations. Methods to accomplish this include manual stimulation of the sensitive entrance to the vagina and the nondemand coitus exercises which were described in the preceding section.

There are two sources of erotic sensation in the vagina: tactile and proprioceptive. The inner two thirds of the vagina is not invested with touch fibers and is essentially anesthetic. However the entrance and outer one third is exquisitely receptive to touch and gentle manipulation of these areas causes exquisite pleasure in the receptive woman.

Muscle sensations supply another dimension of erotic sensibility. Vaginal muscle contractions can be experienced as intensely pleasurable during thrusting and during the orgastic contractions. The slow nondemanding coital thrusting which was described in the foregoing section along with pubococcygeal muscle exercises are useful in enhancing the vaginal sensations of some women who have defensively suppressed these perceptions in the past. Sometimes when vaginal sensations have been enhanced by these techniques, the woman spontaneously experiences coital orgasm. Most often however she does not and the bridge maneuver is then prescribed.

88

Bridge—male stimulating female's clitoris while he is inside

Bridge—female stimulating her own clitoris while male is inside

Directions for the bridge maneuver may be given as follows: "Play with each other in your usual way, until you [man] have a good erection, and until you [woman] feel quite aroused and desire to be entered. Then you enter her in the side-to-side, woman superior or kneeling, and so forth position." (The preferred position should be explored and described with the couple. Pictures are very helpful here.)

"While you [to the man] are inside, thrust slowly, with just enough rhythm and depth to maintain your erection. If you hold still altogether you may lose your erection. But do not thrust too intrusively. I want her to concentrate on her stimulation. In the meantime you [woman] stimulate your clitoris with your finger, just as you do when you are by yourself." (Directions can be varied so that the man stimulates the woman. This should only be done if she is easily orgasmic on his manipulation. Also a vibrator may be used for the bridge maneuver. Actually this is a highly effective means of promoting female orgasm during bridging. Its disadvantage lies only in that some couples object to this mechanical means of stimulation during coitus.)

"Concentrate on your favorite fantasy while you are being stimulated, just as you do when you are alone. When you feel orgasm coming on, *stop* the stimulation and actively thrust. This interruption may bring you 'down,' i.e., it may stop rather than trigger your orgasm. That is to be expected. Don't worry. Do it again. Hold still with your husband's penis inside and stimulate yourself to the point of orgasm. When it feels like it's just before, *stop*. Thrust fast and hard against him. You may have to repeat this several times before it works. If you [the man] get too stimulated to hold out, proceed to orgasm. That is natural. This can be a very exciting experience. You can try the bridge again next time you have sex. How do you feel about this assignment?"

REACTIONS TO THE BRIDGE

The bridge is often successful in allowing women to experience coital orgasm. Usually the couple's response to this is relief and enthusiasm, often to euphoric intensity. Women who have never experienced coital orgasm often feel very frustrated and tend to overvalue this experience. Often they feel inferior to women who can climax on intercourse. If they are insecure and do not value themselves as persons, they may develop paranoid defenses and may even fear that their lovers will abandon them and seek a woman who is coitally orgasmic. And indeed men also may have an intense emotional response to the coital anorgasticity of their wives. Insecure men in particular are apt to fear there is something inadequate in themselves if his partner doesn't climax "by his penis." Or they may project this anxiety and insecurity onto their wives and interpret this pattern of sexual response to mean that she is "sick" or expressing her hostility by "holding out."

For these reasons there is high prevalence of coital orgasmic simulation in our society. Women find it easier to forego orgasm and pretend, rather than to admit openly their clitoral pattern of responsiveness. The admission of truth on the part of the wife after many years of pretending to reach climax is often the initial and crucial step in the therapy of this condition.

The bridge maneuver almost always yields coital orgasm except when a woman has a specific and tenacious conflict about penetration. However the bridge does not progress to easy coital orgasm in all cases. Exact data are lacking on the outcome of this treatment for this complaint. In our experience fewer than half of coitally anorgastic women treated by this means become progressively more easily orgastic on intercourse to the point where they no longer require any clitoral "priming" to reach orgasm. The rest have learned a good technique for reaching orgasm with the penis inside, one which is potentially pleasurable for both partners. However these women continue to require some degree of direct clitoral stimulation before they climax.

When a woman remains essentially coitally anorgastic, the couple is in need of sexual counseling. Sometimes they easily accept this as a good and normal pattern of female sexual responsiveness. At other times, deeply emotional attitudes about coital orgasm must be worked through psychodynamically before a couple can relax enough to enjoy their sexual interactions on a realistic basis.

Orgasm is really highly pleasurable no matter how it occurs, providing neither partner considers noncoital orgasm as "second best."

94

Bridge—male is kneeling—female is stimulating herself with vibrator while male is inside

Secure and loving couples can have gloriously fulfilling sex lives even though the woman requires clitoral stimulation in order to climax.

The process of sex therapy for female sexual problems does not consist solely of mechanical exercises. It entails some striking changes of attitudes on the part of the woman. She must learn to accept her own sexual needs and wishes for erotic pleasure as a good thing and not just as a means of pleasing her husband. She must take responsibility for her own sexual gratification, i.e., she must actively make sure she is adequately stimulated and not depend entirely on her man's sensitivity and generosity. In practical terms this means that a woman who has always had intercourse in response to signals from her husband, who was largely moved by her husband's erotic needs, pace, and wishes, now sits astride in the female superior position and slowly moves upon his erect phallus according to the demands of *her* vaginal sensations!

Not surprisingly this move from passivity to activity may evoke intense emotions from the male partner. Some men, who are basically secure and loving, are relieved and delighted. Other men are deeply threatened and made angry by their wives' activity and growing strength. These changes may mobilize fears of being controlled and even injured by a powerful female. In analytic terms old oedipal and castration anxieties may be aroused in the man by the woman's more assertive role. Some are aware of these feelings and express them openly. Others are not in touch but suddenly become impotent or disinterested in sex.

It has been my experience that usually, if he is not deeply disturbed, the husband of a previously unresponsive or anorgastic woman who now becomes a more active participant in the sexual interaction can accept this and ultimately benefits in terms of his own sexuality. It is more gratifying for most persons of either gender to make love to a responsive partner who both actively stimulates and seeks stimulation— one who gently initiates sex and who expresses enjoyment. However the sexual system may be temporarily disjointed by the woman's transition to sexual maturity and the therapist must be careful to support the couple during the adjustment period. Activity must be differentiated from demand; initiation from aggression; the gentle expression of a wish from criticism.

SHE: I only said I would enjoy his kissing my breasts and he got mad.

HE: She is always putting down my lovemaking. I don't need instructions.

THERAPIST: Wouldn't you [to him] like to know what especially pleases her?

HE: Of course.

THERAPIST: How can she tell you without offending you? Tell her— now.

Successful resolution of female sexual difficulties depends on *both* partner's acceptance without guilt or shame or anxiety of her erotic needs and wishes. The husband's negative attitude, his inability to accept his wife's sexual autonomy may prove an obstacle to her sexual fulfillment which must be resolved during the course of therapy.

7

Vaginismus

Vaginismus is a disorder in which sexual intercourse is not possible because attempts at vaginal penetration evoke an involuntary spastic contraction of the vaginal entrance. This is a relatively rare condition. Response to sex therapy is excellent.

Evidence suggests that the essential pathology of this condition is a conditioned reaction of the muscles which guard the vaginal introitus. Apparently these muscles are readily conditionable to respond with intense spasm. The unconditioned stimulus responsible for the acquisition of the vaginismic response can be any source of pain associated with penetration. Physical disease, psychologically painful affect such as conscious or unconscious fear and/or guilt, traumatic sexual assaults all have been associated with the acquisition and perpetuation of vaginismus. Sometimes the traumatic source cannot be identified.

Vaginismus must be differentiated from physical obstructions of the vaginal entrance and also from simple phobic avoidance of penetration. The diagnosis of vaginismus can only be made on pelvic examination.

Treatment Strategy

Treatment essentially consists of extinction of the conditioned vaginal response. This is accomplished by the introduction, under relaxed and tranquil conditions, of objects of gradually increasing size into the vaginal entrance. When the patient can tolerate a phallus size object, she is cured.

This incredibly simple treatment plan is complicated by the fact that most vaginismic women do not present with a simple conditioned reflex which closes their vaginas. These women usually are also *phobic* of intercourse and penetration. The phobic avoidance must be dispelled before the deconditioning part of treatment can commence.

There are various techniques for managing phobic avoidance of intercourse. These include analytic interpretation of the unconscious elements which underlie the irrational fear; support and reassurance and encouragement to "stay with the fearful feelings" and attempt penetration in spite of these feelings; and such behavioral techniques as systematic desensitization and hypnosis. I generally employ an amalgam of the analytic and supportive methods. I try to explore the original source or trauma which led to the establishment of the vaginismus and work through the emotional responses to this. I quickly go beyond its genesis into the here-and-now destructive effects of the problem and support the patient's constructive and rational efforts to overcome this. However, others have used the more strictly behavioral approaches with reportedly good results.

In-vivo desensitization or insertion begins only after the woman's phobic avoidance of vaginal penetration has been diminished and after her ambivalences towards intercourse have been resolved sufficiently so that she is relatively free of conflict about the procedure. Clinicians use a variety of objects to be inserted into the vagina for deconditioning. Some recommend graduated glass catheters, others use rubber, and still others use a tampon. It is irrelevant for the purpose of conditioning what the nature of the object is. I use the patient's and the husband's finger only because I have found this to be most emotionally acceptable to patients and therefore less likely to mobilize therapeutic resistances than artificial objects.

Procedure

The patient is instructed to observe her vaginal entrance in a mirror while she is by herself. She is told to place her index finger at the vaginal entrance and see what it feels like to insert her finger tip into the vaginal entrance. These feelings and their meanings are explored in the

100

Female inserting her own finger into vagina

Female inserting catheter into vagina

Male inserting his finger into woman's vagina

Male inserting an object into woman's vagina

subsequent therapy session in a reassuring manner. In addition discussion of any dreams and fantasies which the patient may have during this period are frequently helpful in revealing and resolving the unconscious forces which in some cases serve to perpetuate the conditioned reflex.

When the patient can insert a finger tip, she is told next time to insert her entire finger. Then two fingers. Sometimes she is then instructed to insert a tampon without removing its covering into the vaginal entrance and to leave it there for several hours, or until it feels entirely comfortable. The therapist can facilitate the process of deconditioning by warning the patient that she can expect to feel some unpleasant anxiety and tightness but *not* pain when she inserts an object into her vagina. But neither the anxiety nor the tightness will increase. To the contrary, if she can tolerate the feelings for a little while they will diminish and she will soon feel perfectly comfortable during penetration.

After the woman can comfortably tolerate insertion of her fingers and/or tampon the husband is included in the procedure. He is asked now to inspect his wife's vaginal entrance in full light. Then he repeats the procedure which she has carried out on herself previously. First he inserts his finger tip into her vaginal entrance. Then, while she is guiding and controlling his hand, he slips the whole finger into the vagina. Initially he holds it there quietly. Next he gently moves it in and out— does the same with two fingers. All this time the wife is assured that there will be *no* attempt made at penile penetration. If the husband becomes stimulated during vaginal play, the couple is instructed to engage in sexual activity which will provide him with an extravaginal orgasm.

The occasion of the first penile penetration is important. The couple agrees to this beforehand. The husband lubricates his erect penis and penetrates while she is guiding him. He quietly leaves his penis in the vagina for a few minutes without thrusting, then he withdraws. The couple may or may not choose extravaginal forms of sex play at this time.

After initial penetration, gentle thrusting and, next, thrusting to male, orgasm usually follows rapidly.

109

Reactions

For some women desensitization is a relatively easy procedure, while others become extremely anxious. The anxiety is mostly anticipatory, it is usually most marked just *prior* to and leading up to penile penetration. After penetration has occurred there is usually a dramatic abatement of anxiety.

The positive outcome of treatment by deconditioning the spastic vaginal response is virtually universal providing the couple completes the course of treatment. However, there are great variations in the results in terms of the couple's sexual functioning after penetration becomes possible. It comes as a surprise to many that vaginismic women are usually quite responsive and also easily orgastic on clitoral stimulation. Most women continue this good response after they are able to have intercourse. Some even become coitally orgastic rather rapidly. For these treatment can be terminated. In other cases successful treatment for vaginismus reveals other sexual problems in the woman and/ or erectile and/or ejaculatory disorders in the husband. If such is the case further therapy is needed before the couple can enjoy good sexual functioning.

8

Impotence—Erectile Dysfunction

Erection is a neurovascular reflex which depends on a correct hormonal environment, a healthy penile anatomy, adequate vascular supply, and an intact and well-functioning nervous apparatus. Problems in any one of these components may cause potency disturbances on a physical basis. However, approximately 85 percent of impotence in the United States is strictly psychogenic. This is not surprising because even when there is physical integrity of the genital apparatus, the autonomic vascular reflexes which govern erection are delicate and subject to disruption by unconscious conflict and by emotion, i.e., anxiety and fear. Unless a man is in a calm emotional state and free of conflict while he is in the act of making love, his erectile reflexes are apt to be impaired.

In the past it was believed that psychogenic impotence is always the product of deeply neurotic conflict about sexuality. Specifically, according to psychoanalytic theory, unconscious fears of injury (castration) due to poorly resolved oedipal issues were the primary determinant of psychogenic impotence. More recently attention was focused on the dyadic (couple) causes of erectile difficulties and it was hypothesized that unconscious disturbance in the marital or love relationship, notably power struggles and contractual disappointments and mutual infantile transferences, were also capable of leading to erectile difficulties.

Clearly both unconscious and intrapsychic and dyadic conflicts can and do cause potency disorders. These conflicts are likely to emerge in the undefended man when he is about to engage in sexual activity. How-

111

ever many of the erectile disorders which we see in clinical practice are produced by simpler more easily correctible emotional factors. These include performance anxiety, fear of rejection by the woman, anticipation of impotence because of a past transient episode of erectile difficulty, overconcern with the woman's satisfaction, and culturally induced guilt about sexual enjoyment.

These concerns, as well as deeper fears, can intrude upon the man as he is making love and interfere with his abandonment to the sexual experience. Abandonment without interference by anxiety or by defenses against anxiety is a necessary condition for the smooth operation of the erectile reflexes.

Potency disorders which stem from such simpler antecedents are very often highly amenable to sex therapy, which always tries to humanize and demystify and diminish the anxiety which contaminates the sexual system between the partners. In this manner sexual abandonment becomes possible and potency is restored.

Treatment Strategy

The basic sequence employed in the brief active treatment of erectile dysfunction is as follows:

1. erotic pleasure without erection
2. erection without orgasm
3. extravaginal orgasm
4. intromission without orgasm
5. coitus

Each impotent patient's clinical situation must be individually evaluated in order to determine just what is causing the pathogenic anxiety and defenses at the moment of lovemaking. On the basis of these data, the sexual situation can be restructured to eliminate as many of the anxiety-provoking factors as possible. Some sex therapists do not structure the tasks on an individual basis, but routinely begin treatment with sensate focus I and II. There is a good rationale for such a pro-

Female stimulating male when he is partially clothed

cedure because these exercises are designed to eliminate much of the anxieties which operate in the average case. The prohibitions against having intercourse or orgasm eliminate performance anxiety, as does the therapist's suggestion that the reciprocal giving and receiving of pleasure be substituted for the goal of giving and eliciting a performance. Also "taking turns" eliminates the pressure created by making the man's response contingent upon his wife's. Usually a man will have spontaneous erections during sensate focus II. These may abate and return. This experience provides extremely important lessons for the couple, which should be made explicit by the therapist:

1. Under relaxed conditions erections will occur; i.e., the equipment is in good working order.

2. If an erection disappears it is not lost forever. It will come back in response to gentle stimulation. Indeed it is normal for erections to come and go during prolonged lovemaking, except at extremely young ages where they may persist for long periods of time.

SQUEEZE

Sometimes, in order to experientially confront an anxious man that he can regain a lost erection we use the "squeeze" technique which was originated by Masters and Johnson (see Figure 38). After a man has gained an erection the wife squeezes his penis just below the glans, with sufficient force that his erection abates. This does not usually hurt, but one third to one half of the erection abates, probably on a reflexive basis. Erections lost in this manner, return rapidly in response to gentle stimulation. Several repetitions of this maneuver generally suffice to cure a couple of the fear of losing the erection.

VARIATIONS IN STIMULATION

We also often start with sensate focus I and II but not invariably. Some men are actually inhibited by lengthy gentle foreplay. When the sexual evaluation reveals that there are some situations wherein the man is particularly potent we start with these. Thus for example some men who are troubled by erectile problems have excellent erections while they are "necking" with a woman while they are clothed. In such a case we might initiate treatment by having a man engage in love play while he keeps his clothes on. He is not allowed to have intercourse, but his wife stimulates his penis through his pants. At a later stage of treatment she may open his zipper and play with his penis, while he still keeps his pants on.

We also take advantage of the high morning androgen levels and the morning erection. It a man reports that he feels most aroused in the morning, and that he regularly wakes up with morning erections, we will prescribe sensate focus II in the early morning hours.

Sometimes we prescribe a lubricant, usually petroleum jelly. This substance is placed on the man's penis while his wife stimulates him, or while he stimulates himself in the presence of his wife. This is a most sensuous and arousing technique which seldom fails to produce an erection.

Oral stimulation is frequently used in this stage of treatment. For many men this is the most stimulating form of sexual activity and most likely to produce an erection. Naturally oral sex can be used only if the wife is willing and not repelled by the idea.

During stimulation whatever form this takes the man is admonished not to obsess, not to "spectator," i.e., watch if he is getting an erection or if he gets one to see "how hard it is."

If these techniques fail to protect him from anxiety, he is advised to immerse himself into a vivid erotic fantasy while he receives stimulation. Distraction from anxiety and from obsessive defenses against anxiety (self-observation or "spectatoring") by means of erotic fantasy has an important place in sex therapy. Erotic fantasies are ideal defenses against anxiety, while at the same time they facilitate the sexual response. The matter of fantasy must be handled with therapeutic sensitivity however. Couples often have intensely emotional reactions to their own and/or their mate's erotic fantasies. They are guilty and ashamed; they fear their content is "abnormal and sick"; they are jealous and/or guilty about the fact that someone or something else is

116

Couple stimulating each other—she is partially clothed (fantasy)

Female is stimulating male orally

being imagined during the sex act which is "supposed" to be just with each other.

If such emotional attitudes are mild and not deeply rooted in the couple's psychopathology, then an open discussion of each other's fantasies rapidly relieves guilt in each person and also promotes increased closeness between the couple and intimacy and erotic pleasure.

However, sometimes this is a difficult and delicate matter. An insecure spouse may actually experience a paranoid jealous reaction when she learns that her husband thinks of being fellated by a young stranger while he is making love to her. Such a response must be handled on a deeper level, one which transcends the narrow confines of a strictly symptom-oriented treatment. An adverse response to fantasy leads into important work with the patient's insecure self-esteem, into the fundamentally poor regard for herself, which is the root from which her lack of acceptance of her partner's normal erotic fantasy life grows.

Reactions

This regimen of intense erotic stimulation together with the relief of the necessity to perform frequently produces erection within a few days. Some men get irritable because they are not "allowed" to ejaculate during this period of time, but this does not pose any significant obstacle to therapy. There are some men, however, who fail to respond to these procedures. In such cases psychodynamic exploration of the anxieties and conflicts and marital difficulties may be attempted. However, in such cases the impotence is probably directly related to deep-seated intrapsychic and/or marital pathology and such patients are not usually amenable to brief treatment procedures. If a man fails to respond to behavioral prescriptions designed to produce erection without orgasm, his prognosis with sex therapy is poor.

Extravaginal Orgasm

After the man has gained confidence that he can have an erection, therapy proceeds to orgasm produced by manual and/or oral stimulation. The procedure is exactly as before except that he may ejaculate if he chooses to.

Some wives of impotent men are unable or unwilling to climax on clitoral stimulation and demand intercourse as their sole means of satisfaction. This demand places the man under great stress as he must perform with an erection or his wife remains unsatisfied. In such cases we shift the focus of therapy to the wife. We attempt to get her to accept extracoital orgasm as an alternative form of satisfaction. This may entail considerable psychotherapeutic work. But this is an extremely important aspect of therapy which usually does much to relieve the man's sense of pressure and need to "perform." He can now give pleasure to his wife with his hands or his mouth over which he has voluntary control. She is no longer dependent on an erect penis over which there is no voluntary control. She will no longer feel rejected if he does not erect—and he in turn will no longer fear rejection by her if he can caress her to orgasm and does not have to produce an erection to "prove" that he loves her or that he is a "real man."

Intromission Without Orgasm

Before actual coitus to orgasm it is often advisable to "practice" vaginal containment. The couple is instructed to engage in the same sort of erotic play which has produced erection during the previous week. When erection is secure, the man enters the woman for a little while. He may thrust a few times, but he may not ejaculate inside the vagina. Orgasm occurs extravaginally as before, after he has withdrawn. In some cases intromission should be under the control of the man, i.e., he enters and pulls out when he is moved to. In other cases, it is less anxiety producing and more stimulating for the man if his wife is in "charge" of his penis. In the female superior position she plays with his penis until he obtains a good erection. Then she guides his penis into her vagina. She thrusts a few times and withdraws the penis and plays with it again. This procedure may be repeated several times. Again ejaculation at this phase of therapy should be extravaginal.

122

Female is stimulating male manually with petroleum jelly

Female superior—female stimulating male's erect penis

Coitus

The initial coital experience may produce some anxiety and therefore should be structured so that it is as reassuring and stimulating as possible.

The man is usually given an "out." He is advised to engage in the same sort of sex play described in the previous section on "intromission without orgasm." He is told he now may ejaculate intravaginally if he is moved to. However if he is not moved to, if he has any doubts about his ability to function, he must withdraw and have his orgasm outside the vagina, or, in other cases, have no orgasm at all.

He is advised, in the presence of his wife whose feelings are of vital importance in this matter, to be "selfish." In order to function he must allow himself to abandon himself to his emotions and sensations to the exclusion of concern for his partner, *for that moment.* His "selfishness" is temporary, for if she is not satisfied by his spontaneous excitement and surge towards orgasm, he can satisfy her with a clitorally induced orgasm after he has ejaculated.

He is advised to employ fantasy, as well as any pace no matter how rapid, or any position or technique which is most reassuring and exciting to him. All these devices are temporary and tend to fall into disuse when coital security is reestablished. However, if in the future the man has some transient anxiety which again impairs his erectile response, he can avail himself of the techniques he has learned during sex therapy to help himself over his difficulties.

Reactions

The rapid relief of impotence, or for that matter the rapid relief of any sexual dysfunction, usually evokes relief and pleasure in the symptomatic patient. However, occasionally when the symptoms have served an unconscious defensive purpose, there is some anxiety or depression as sexual functioning is restored. It should be noted however that the partner may have an even more intense emotional response to her husband's sudden new potency. She may also have mixed reactions.

Some women are unambivalently happy at their husband's improvement and show this positive motivation in speech and in deed. Others, however, are threatened. These may verbalize their anxiety, or it may show in an unexplained depressed or anxious mood. Still others act out their conflict and unconsciously place obstacles in the path of their husband's treatment.

Sabotage of treatment and of a mate's sexual functioning can take many subtle forms. It can be as fleeting as a loss of interest, a lack of warmth and encouragement, a subtle critical attitude toward the husband. These attitudes usually become apparent during the therapeutic sessions. The wife's attitude may simply change from one of support to increasing detachment or demand. Or the wife's resistance may be blatantly obvious. She may become anxious or depressed, start drinking heavily, and/or complain that the exercises are tedious, boring, and mechanical. She may become openly critical, go on a spending spree. In one of my cases the wife started an extramarital affair just at the point where her husband began to get good erections.

The sources of negative partner reaction to rapid sexual improvement in the spouse are often unconscious hostility towards him and even more commonly the unconscious fear of losing him now that he is potent and virile. Some persons have psychological investments in their lover's inadequacy. Such women harbor deep feelings of insecurity. Unconsciously they believe, "I am not very attractive. He only stays with me because he is dependent on me for I tolerate his impotence. Now that he can function he will leave me and find a more adequate and attractive woman." The result of such an unconscious fear may be the sabotage of therapy in subtle or obvious ways. Sex therapy is not completed until such painful and sensitive issues have been adequately resolved and the partner is reassured. In the face of an unhappy and threatened spouse, one cannot expect a "cure" of the potency disorder to remain stable. There is a high probability of relapse unless both sexual partners' problems are resolved at least to the point of emotional stability.

Female superior—inserting his penis into her vagina

9

Retarded Ejaculation —
Ejaculatory Overcontrol

Retarded ejaculation is an involuntary inhibition of the male orgastic reflex. This condition is physiologically analogous to female orgasmic dysfunction. The retarded ejaculator is able to feel sexual excitement and have good erections, but even though he receives what should be ample stimulation, he has difficulty releasing this ejaculatory reflex. Severe overcontrol, i.e., the man who has never ejaculated at all, even on masturbation, is rare. This is fortunate because this extreme form of retardation is difficult to treat. In its milder forms ejaculatory retardation (or ejaculatory incompetence) is relatively common and has an excellent prognosis with sex therapy. In the moderate forms of this disorder the man can only ejaculate on masturbation when he is alone. Men suffering from milder retardation can climax in the presence of their partner but only in response to manual and/or oral stimulation. They cannot ejaculate in the vagina. Still milder forms are situational and some merely require excessively long and vigorous coitus in order to ejaculate.

The pathogenesis of ejaculatory overcontrol is similar to that of constipation, globus hystericus, and difficulty with starting the stream of urine. Defecation, swallowing, urination, and ejaculation or orgasm all depend on autonomically mediated reflexes which are normally brought under voluntary control. When the individual is in an emotionally aroused state or when he is under the domination of a psychological conflict, there may be an involuntary defensive reaction of inhibition of the reflex in question. The defensive reaction entails an overcontrol, i.e., the inability to release the reflex from cortical control.

The source of the unconscious conflict and/or the content of the emotional state seems to be nonspecific. In other words it has not been possible to identify a specific psychodynamic constellation which would discriminate ejaculatory incompetence from impotence. The same kinds of deeply unconscious castration fears and superficial performance anxieties, as well as fears about commitment to the partner will result in erectile difficulties in one man and ejaculatory overcontrol in another. The conflicts seem the same, but the *defenses* are distinct. The retarded ejaculator will unconsciously "hold back," i.e., exercise control and so avoid anxiety, while the impotent man allows himself to be flooded with anxiety which then ruins his erectile response.

The main purpose of brief, active sex therapy with retarded ejaculation is to *distract* the man from his excessive need to control, so that his orgastic reflexes can discharge unimpeded. Often this strategy works very well. At other times some of the underlying conflicts must be recognized and resolved, at least in part, before the patient can relax enough to allow himself to be so distracted. For these patients a very important factor involved in the anxiety and inhibitory defense against this anxiety is the relationship with the partner. Considerable resolution of unconscious problems in the relationship usually needs to be accomplished before the patient can relax and have easy and pleasurable orgasms.

Treatment Strategy

Two basic treatment principles govern the therapy of retarded ejaculation:*

1. progressive in-vivo desensitization to intravaginal ejaculation (i.e., desensitization in the presence of the partner);
2. stimulation with concomitant distraction.

PROGRESSIVE DESENSITIZATION

Most retarded ejaculators can ejaculate under some condition and the basic strategy of treatment is to gradually shape the patient's ejac-

* The treatment rationale of retarded ejaculation of men and orgastic dysfunction of women is analogous.

ulatory response toward the desired goal of ejaculatory freedom on coitus. Techniques are structured with this principle in mind. Therefore, the specific behavioral prescriptions will vary with the individual case.

For example, a patient can ejaculate only if his wife has left the house and he is alone. If he then masturbates with petroleum jelly to a fantasy of being orally stimulated by a strange woman, he can predictably reach orgasm. When he tries to make love to his wife, he has pleasure, a good erection, intercourse, she is satisfied, but he does not reach orgasm no matter if coitus lasts for one hour. His erection slowly abates and he goes to sleep.

This material is openly discussed with both partners. The first behavioral prescription in this case might be that he masturbate in his usual fashion with his usual fantasy behind locked doors while his wife is downstairs. If this is successful, several days later he might repeat the procedure while his wife is in the adjacent room. Next, while she is in the same room. Later on, they make love and after she is satisfied, he goes to the bathroom to masturbate to orgasm. This sequence begins to establish an association between the heterosexual act and orgasm. A key point in treatment occurs when the patient's wife can manually stimulate him to orgasm. She uses the petroleum jelly and he is advised to use his fantasy while he is being stimulated. These may be covert or openly talked about with his wife during the sexual act. [This use of fantasy is an expression of the second principle of treatment: *distraction* from excessive control and self-observation during stimulation.]

After the patient has been brought to orgasm by his wife, further lone masturbatory release is prohibited. He can only now ejaculate in the presence of and with the participation of his wife. Ejaculation progressively nearer the vagina is the next sequence of treatment.

The *male bridge maneuver* is employed after the patient can reliably have orgasm with her manual manipulation. The woman stimulates the man with the petroleum jelly until he is near orgasm. Then he enters. She stimulates his penis with her hand while he thrusts. Figures 32 and 33 illustrate two coital positions wherein this technique is comfortable and feasible.

After the man has penetrated the vagina with a combination of hand

Male masturbating—female's back is turned

Male masturbating—female in his arms

Female stimulating male—his hand is on hers

Female stimulating male's penis near her vaginal entrance

and vaginal stimulation, he begins to signal when he is at the point of orgasm so that she can withdraw her hand and let the coital thrusting bring about the actual orgasm. A position wherein the woman keeps her legs tightly closed during coitus (see Figure 34) increases penile friction and is sometimes useful at this stage of treatment.

STIMULATION AND DISTRACTION

The crucial principle which governs the treatment both of retarded ejaculation of the male and orgastic inhibition of the female is that the person be physically stimulated intensely, while at the same time mentally distracted from inhibitory vigilance. It has already been mentioned that mental absorption in erotic fantasy while genital stimulation is being experienced, is an ideal method of releasing the orgasm reflex. However, some patients require more complete or concrete distraction, because they are unable to lose themselves in their imageries and fantasies. In such cases I might advise that the patient read erotic literature or view sexually stimulating pictures while stimulation occurs. Thus for example, one woman has her first orgasm when reading an erotic novel while she stimulated herself with a vibrator.

Incompletely Retarded Ejaculation

There is a rare syndrome which conceptually belongs under the category of retarded ejaculation—which I have called *incompletely or partially retarded ejaculation*. In this syndrome only one phase, the ejaculatory component of the orgasm response, is inhibited, while the other component of the male orgasm, emission, is not impaired. The male orgasm consists of first, *emission*, which is a sympathetically mediated contraction of the vas deferens, prostate, and seminal vesicles. This gathers the ejaculate into the posterior urethra. This response is perceived without pleasure as the "sensation of ejaculatory inevitability." The ejaculatory component of this male orgasm normally follows a fraction of a second later. It consists of rhythmic contractions of

143

the striated muscles at the base of the penis. This part of the response is associated with the intense pleasure of orgasm and this produces the squirting action of ejaculation.

The man who suffers from incomplete retardation has good and pleasurable erections. But at the point of climax he only experiences the emission phase of the response. Perceptually he feels a "release" but *no* orgasmic pleasure. Physiologically there is only a seepage of semen and also a very slow detumescence (because the vasocongestion is not "pumped out" by the muscle contractions).

This extremely rare syndrome is sometimes confused with retrograde ejaculation which is quite different. In retrograde ejaculation the ejaculate empties into the bladder because the internal vesicular sphincter is paralyzed by anticholinergic drugs or by disease. The muscles at the base of the penis contract normally and orgasm is pleasurable in all respects but it is "dry," i.e., there is no external ejaculate.

The few patients with partial retardation whom I have treated have all had trouble abandoning themselves to the sexual experience. They tended to be overcontrolled, overly-self-critical, and performance oriented. These defenses were evoked by a variety of unconscious insecurities and conflicts. Treatment follows one of the same principles as retarded ejaculation: stimulation with concomitant relaxation and distraction.

One of my patients had his first complete and pleasurable orgasm when he was being stimulated by his partner while he was absorbed in watching an erotic film.

Another guide to the treatment of retarded ejaculation is to increase stimulation by structuring the tasks so that ejaculatory urgency builds up, while at the same time the obsessive defense of overcontrol is diminished. Patients who suffer from partial and total retardation tend to report that as pleasurable sexual tension builds up and they reach a stage premonitory to orgasm, they wonder "Will it be a good orgasm this time?" or "Will I have an orgasm soon?" If the patient experiences this, he is advised that he is *not* to ejaculate on that occasion. He is to withdraw his penis and desist from further stimulation. If it happens the next time he tries sex the admonition is repeated. He is only allowed to ejaculate if he does not stop to think about the process.

144

Position for female touching male's penis during coitus—male superior

Female touching male's penis during coitus—"doggy" fashion

Coitus with female's legs tightly closed

Reactions

Again there is no data to justify the conclusion of specificity in sexual dysfunction. In other words we can not say that impotence is specifically caused by unconscious castration anxiety or by performance anxiety. *Any* source of anxiety is capable of impairing the erectile reflex. And while castration and performance anxieties are frequently encountered in this population, they are by no means the universal causes. Similarly conflicts of any sort and defenses against these can produce inhibition of the orgastic reflex. However two conflicts do emerge with predictable frequency when treating the *retarded ejaculator*, namely: fear of involvement with the woman, and related conflicts centering around hostility and sadistic impulses toward women. During the course of treatment with these couples it is often revealed that the man is really "holding back" psychologically as well as physiologically with his orgasm. Frequently also a great deal of hostility to women is evident of which man is unaware. The patient must often be confronted with this hostility. And more important its sources must often be explored and resolved before he can enjoy orgastic freedom. Most such patients are extremely guilty about their aggressive impulses and therefore defend themselves against these in elaborate and tenacious ways. Resolution of guilt through reassurance that these impulses are not evil, that when people are angry there is a good reason, that anger is basically a constructive and adaptive impulse, are all important parts of the treatment strategy with this patient population.

10

Premature Ejaculation— Inadequate Ejaculatory Control

Premature ejaculation is the favorite dysfunction of sex therapists because although it is highly prevalent and troublesome, it is extremely easy to treat with sex therapy in most cases. Yet it is resistant to other forms of treatment.

The prematurely ejaculating patient reaches climax so rapidly that lovemaking is often disappointing for both partners. The essence of prematurity is lack of adequate voluntary control over the ejaculatory reflex. Some reflexes are subject to voluntary control and others are not. Erection in men and genital vasocongestion in women cannot be brought under voluntary control. Ejaculation and orgasm can. The normal person can delay orgasm and "let it go" when it is desired. The premature ejaculator cannot. He ejaculates reflexively as soon as he reaches a critical level of excitement.

I have hypothesized that the reason that the premature ejaculator has not learned ejaculatory continence is that he is not *aware* of the sensations that are premonitory to orgasm. That is probably because he experiences some anxiety at this time which distracts him. Conscious perception of the sensations leading to a reflex, as for example urination or defecation, are prerequisite for learning voluntary control.

152

Treatment Strategy

Successful treatment consists of fostering the patient's clear perception of the sensations premonitory to orgasm. This should be done under tranquil conditions, in the presence of and with the participation of his wife.

There are two methods which have proven successful in the treatment of premature ejaculation and they both seem to be governed by the same mechanism of action, namely fostering pre-ejaculatory awareness in the heterosexual situation. The first is the "squeeze" method of Masters and Johnson and the second is the "stop—start" technique. This technique was invented by James Semans and has been adapted for use in sex therapy by me at the Cornell Clinic.

STOP—START

Initially the patient practices control while he is being manually stimulated by his wife.

The couple is instructed to make love in their usual fashion until he has a good erection. Then he lies on his back, closes his eyes, and his wife masturbates him. He is told to keep his attention focused sharply on his erotic sensation. When he feels near orgasm he tells his wife to stop. In a few seconds the ejaculatory urge will abate and he then tells her to start stimulating him again. Again he stops short of ejaculation. This is repeated four times. On the fourth trial he ejaculates. The patient is admonished *not* to let anything distract him. In contrast to impotence and retarded ejaculation where *distraction* with fantasy is emphasized, in premature ejaculation the patient must *desist* from distracting himself. The essence of the treatment is that he stay closely with his experience of mounting excitement and learn to recognize the signs of impending orgasm.

After two successful trials the couple repeats the same procedure, this time using petroleum jelly as a lubricant. This is very arousing and closely simulates the vaginal environment.

Three or four successful trials with lubricant and the couple is ready

153

Stop–Start—Female is stimulating man's penis manually

Stop–Start—Female superior—coital position

Stop–Start—Side-to-side coitus

for coitus. This is also done within the stop–start format. The woman assumes the female superior position. The penis is inserted and he places his hands on her hips and guides her up and down until he is near orgasm. Then he stops her. A few seconds later, after the ejaculatory urge is gone, they resume. He does not thrust initially. On the fourth time he thrusts and comes. Again it is exceedingly important that he keep his attention focused on his sensations during this exercise. Three or four female superior stop–start exercises, with him thrusting more and more as they go on, and the couple is ready to do the same in the side-to-side position. The male superior is the most difficult from the standpoint of ejaculatory control and is done last.

Usually a man gains a good deal of ejaculatory control in from 2 to 10 weeks. Perfect control however is not usually attained until several months after termination of treatment. During this time the couple is advised to do one "stop–start" exercise per week.

SQUEEZE

The "squeeze" method advocated by Masters and Johnson contains essentially the same ingredients as the "stop–start" method described herein. The only difference is that instead of *stopping* the woman *squeezes* her husband's penis. Specifically she grasps the erect penis between forefingers and thumb just below the glans and presses hard until he loses a good part of his erection. Then she resumes stimulation.*

During the female superior coital exercises the squeeze technique is also employed. Here the woman removes the penis from her vagina and squeezes it until the erection abates. Then she stimulates him, and when the erection returns, she mounts him and resumes thrusting.

REACTIONS

1. *Boredom.* If the training period lasts more than a few weeks the routine is apt to get tedious for the couple. For this reason it is my

---

* Dr. Alex Levai who has been trained by Masters and Johnson has informed me that they are currently advocating that the female squeeze the man's penis, not on his request, but on a random basis.

practice to allow one "free," i.e., spontaneous, no stop–start lovemaking session during the week, after 3 weeks or so.

2. *Frustration by the woman.* She may become aroused and frustrated during the training period. For this reason, and if she desires it, the couple is encouraged to engage in sex play which provides her with orgasm through clitoral stimulation. This must never be at the cost of distracting the man from concentrating on his stop–start exercises. He must put all thoughts of his wife out of mind while he is being stimulated, or the exercise will not be successful. For these reasons clitoral stimulation for her occurs after the man has ejaculated. Both in the extravaginal and stop–start coital phases of the treatment program.

3. *Resistances.* The two phases of therapy, i.e., extravaginal and coital stimulation, tend to elicit different kinds of emotional responses from couples. Again, both provide a therapeutic challenge because they present obstacles to the progress of treatment. They also are a unique opportunity for significant therapeutic intervention in the couple's and each partner's deeper conflicts.

If the wife is hostile toward her husband she may react with anger at being used as a "Geisha girl" in the first phase of treatment when she is stimulating his penis. By contrast when the couple has an unambivalently loving relationship, the wife finds her help-agent role immensely satisfying, and she takes pleasure in her husband's progress.

The manual stop–start exercises have the potential for also evoking profound feelings and defenses against these feelings in the man himself. A man who is basically insecure about his worth and his essential "lovableness" often erects defenses of overconcern with his partner and compulsive attention to her needs. The stop–start exercise deactivates this defense. He is forced into the previously avoided position of having to receive and to accept stimulation from his partner. This change can give rise to considerable anxiety in some patients. Sometimes the anxiety manifests as fear of being rejected by the wife. More seriously troubled men will occasionally respond to this situation with paranoid defenses. Some are emotionally unable to go through the exercises without prior resolution of their basic insecurities by means of psychotherapy.

There are also some positive emotional reactions to stop–start. Often it enables men to enjoy the passive role in sexual relations for the first

162

Squeeze

time. They learn it is pleasurable to receive as well as to give. He learns that his wife loves him and will not reject him even though she is delaying her gratification for him and giving to him, and he is not "serving" her.

While the extragenital phase of treatment is apt to elicit emotional reactions related to giving and taking and the husband's passive-receptive role, the coital stop–start exercises typically elicit emotional responses which are evoked by the man's rapid improvement. By the time treatment has progressed to the female-superior stop–start, the man has gained a considerable amount of ejaculatory control. In uncomplicated cases this improved functioning elicits joy and relief in both spouses. However, improvement may also be very threatening to both. The woman, especially, is apt to become depressed or anxious at this time. She may be in touch with these feelings and their sources and experience them as such, or she may be unaware and act these out by sabotaging treatment. This can be done by refusing to cooperate, by communicating her boredom with the exercises or, worse, her growing loathing for them. Some women attack their husbands at this point. They criticize and discourage them, letting them know that even though they may gain ejaculatory control they remain inadequate and repulsive in other areas.

Such adverse emotional responses to a husband's improvement are most often rooted in the wife's deep insecurities. She feels inadequate and insecure and unable to hold on to her man. His disability and her tolerance of it made him dependent on her. Now that he is about to be functional, will he not seek out other, more attractive women? Clearly, reassurance that she is valued and loved for her own sake is therapeutically indicated at this time.

Another source of anxiety, now that the husband can function, involves the wife's own sexual adequacy. Many wives of premature ejaculators suffer from some measure of orgastic dysfunction. Not surprisingly they and their husbands attribute this to his difficulty. After all, how could a woman be expected to respond with orgasm when the man ejaculates so rapidly. However, this assumption is false in a large proportion of cases where the wife has an independent sexual dysfunction of her own. Her husband's ejaculatory problem has long served to obscure her problem, and the fact that he can now have intercourse for quite a long period of time and she does not climax confronts the couple with her problem. This can be quite threatening. Especially if it has been the family saga to consider him the problem and her the martyr.

To forestall such reactions I always make it quite clear during the initial session that premature ejaculation has a good prognosis. We will first treat the husband's premature ejaculation. But successful ejaculatory control on his part does *not* guarantee the wife's good functioning. It specifically does not. The woman's sexual functioning can only be assessed *after* he has gained control. If there turns out to be a problem, this will be treated at that time.

While the discovery of an orgastic problem in the spouse of a previously premature ejaculator occasions some adverse reactions, the ultimate outcome is good because it provides an opportunity for the wife to derive the benefit of treatment as well. However, such adverse reactions of a wife to a husband's improvement must be handled with therapeutic sensitivity or they can motivate the premature termination of therapy, before the man has gained ejaculatory continence.

On rare occasions, the symptomatic man may also be threatened by his own improvement. The symptom may serve an unconscious need, if, for example, it is his only "hold out" to a dominating mother-figure wife. Then treatment may reach an impasse at the point of coitus, or the man may become impotent. In such cases unconscious conflict must be resolved in order for the symptom to improve. In my experience the rare premature ejaculator who is not helped by the treatment procedure outlined above is likely to be troubled with unconscious resistance of this sort. Perhaps there is a small subgroup of premature ejaculators who are not amenable to a training procedure designed to provide sensory feedback of ejaculatory sensations. However, present evidence suggests that all premature ejaculators can respond to these measures except for those wherein ejaculatory incontinence serves a deep psychological need which cannot be bypassed by behavioral means.

III
CONCLUSIONS

I I

The Role of Psychodynamics
in Sex Therapy

As I review this manual of sex therapy I am uneasy because too much stress seems to have been placed on the sexual mechanics. It was the prime objective of the book to provide a clear description of the most frequently used exercises and when possible to conceptualize their underlying rationale. But in addition, I have also tried to stress the importance of the emotional reactions which patients have to these tasks.

Despite my efforts in this respect, the approach still seems too mechanical. I hope I have managed to place sufficient emphasis on the importance of integrating the tasks with psychotherapy. I hope there has been enough stress on the challenges and opportunities for dealing with deeper psychic issues provided by the emotional reactions of patients to these exercises. The beauty of this method of sex therapy lies in combining structured sexual interactions with psychotherapy. In actual practice *most* of the therapist's activities are psychotherapeutic and consist of active interpretation, support, clarification, and integration of the experiences with the couple in the office sessions. This dynamic interplay between experience and psychotherapy constitutes the essence of the new sex therapy. Often psychotherapy centers around the couples' resistances to the therapeutic exercises.

Resistances to Sex Therapy

It was Freud who formulated the concept of resistance. He observed that his patients resisted getting well in psychoanalysis. He explained this surprising phenomena as being caused by the patients' unconscious attempts to defend against conscious recognition of their anxiety-provoking unconscious conflicts. In order to avoid conscious recognition of unconscious conflict they attempted to sabotage analysis. But the concept of resistance has wider application. It pertains to anxiety generated by facing one's problems, giving up defenses, and changing one's behavior. Thus patients unconsciously resist sex therapy very much the same way that they resist psychoanalysis, and unless he is prepared for this, the novice therapist will be surprised and troubled when his patients fail to perform the prescribed tasks and come to the therapeutic sessions with obvious rationalizations.

A distinction must be drawn between resistance to the *process* and to the *outcome* of sex therapy. As has been repeatedly stressed, patients may have intense negative emotional responses to engaging in the prescribed exercises and erotic interactions of sex therapy. Other patients and their spouses are resistant to the outcome of sex therapy; i.e., good sexual functioning mobilizes anxiety and guilt.

RESISTANCE TO THE OUTCOME OF SEX THERAPY

Many persons are made anxious by success and pleasure. Fat persons are afraid to become thin, poor people are afraid to make money, and sexually dysfunctional persons are sometimes covertly afraid to achieve the sexual fulfillment which they so ardently desire on a conscious level. The unconscious roots of the fear of success vary. Sometimes anticipation of injury born of unresolved incestuous taboos play a role. Sometimes unconscious fears of loss of love and abandonment play a role. But whatever the unconscious roots may be, the anticipation or achievement of sexual success arouses a negative emotional response in some persons and so mobilizes resistance to the treatment.

Improvement of sexual functioning in a *mate* may also be deeply threatening because an insecure person may fear that a sexually adequate partner will abandon them. Again such feelings of threat may cause the mate to resist, i.e., to place various obstacles in the way of therapy.

170

Actually the dangers of a patient's sustaining emotional trauma as a result of successful outcome of sex therapy have been exaggerated by psychoanalytically oriented writers. Psychoanalytic theory predicts that *all* symptomatic improvement, unless it is the product of conflict resolution on an unconscious level, will be accompanied by significant anxiety and/or the development of substitute symptoms. These patients now express the same conflicts and/or guard against the same psychic "dangers" which were formerly the function of the sexual symptom. There are theoretic fallacies in this reasoning which are beyond this discussion. But from a practical perspective clinical evidence indicates that only a small segment of the patient population responds with significant anxiety to improved sexual functioning as predicted by analytic theory. However, *transient* improvement anxiety is very common and the therapist must remain alert for the possibility that the symptomatic patient and/or his spouse will resist getting sexually well because of such neurotic anxiety and guilt. Actually such transient improvement anxiety is not detrimental to therapy. In fact it provides an excellent opportunity for psychodynamic clarification and resolution of the patient's deeper underlying conflicts.

Learning theory predicts the opposite consequences of successful therapy. According to this frame of reference the patient will react purely positively when his symptom is removed. In fact his improvement will generalize and he will function better in other spheres of behavior as well. Accordingly there is no unconscious resistance to treatment. In actual fact *some* patients *do* respond as predicted by the behaviorists. Some patients and their spouses evidence undiluted joy at their improved sexual functioning and enjoy the process of therapy without ambivalence. But these patients are definitely in the minority.

Clinical observation of couples who undergo sex therapy reveals that the great majority show some degree, albeit mild, of adversive emotional reactions to a favorable outcome of therapy. For the healthier couples these tend to be transient and largely anticipatory. Once sexual functioning is established most patients feel wonderful and their relationships improve as well. Sicker patients are more likely to respond to a favorable outcome with a more serious or mixed or negative response. Once again skillful and sensitive psychotherapeutic management of improvement anxiety is crucial for favorable outcome in treatment with a major segment of the sex therapy population.

RESISTANCE TO THE PROCESS OF SEX THERAPY

Not only the outcome, but also the very *process* of sex therapy may mobilize resistance. The sexual techniques often force persons to experience behavior which they have previously avoided because this would mobilize anxiety, anger, or guilt. The techniques entail touching gently, kissing, displaying sensitivity to a partner's needs and wishes, and expressing tenderness—forms of behavior which promote involvement and intimacy and openness. This may be extremely threatening to a person who defends himself from hurt with distance, alienation, and control of his emotions. It is not surprising that patients will resist therapy when this occurs. They may admit their uneasiness to themselves, their spouses, and the therapist. More commonly, conscious awareness of these dynamics is too threatening. Instead they "act out." They avoid the tasks or do them in a clumsy or hostile or mechanical manner. They rationalize. They quarrel with their mates. They attack the therapist and/or the therapy, and so on. The therapist must remain alert to such resistance. Clarification and resolution or bypass is essential if therapy is to succeed.

This *process* of sex therapy not only may cause difficulty in either partner individually but it also frequently threatens the balance of the *marital dyad*. Sex therapy makes an effort to change the dyadic system which exists between the spouses. The sexual interactions of the couple must be changed in the course of treatment from alienating to human, from uncommunicative and secretive to open and authentic, from hostile to loving. Especially when each feels insecure with the other, changing interactional patterns may be temporarily painful. The pain may last until security is reestablished on a more realistic basis. The process of disrupting established interactions entailed in sex therapy can be very threatening and so mobilize resistance in either or both partners.

Prognosis in Sex Therapy

The outcome of sex therapy depends on three factors: the nature of the dysfunction, the structure and depth of the intrapsychic pathology of each partner, and the quality of the marital relationship.

The dysfunctions have different prognoses with sex therapy. *Premature ejaculation, vaginismus,* and the *total anorgasticity of women* all have excellent outcomes with sex therapy.

It is very seldom that a *premature ejaculator* doesn't learn good ejaculatory control within a few weeks to months. This condition seems to be relatively independent of intrapsychic and marital pathology and tends to improve even when it occurs in highly neurotic men whose marriages are troubled. As long as the relationship is stable enough for therapeutic cooperation, and as long as a man can concentrate on his premonitory sensations while he is being stimulated by his wife, in our experience, he will learn ejaculatory continence.*

The same can essentially be said for *vaginismus.* As long as the patient can be induced to tolerate progressively larger objects in her vagina she will be "cured" rapidly. The deconditioning seems to be relatively independent of any concomitant psycho- and marital pathology which may exist. However, mere deconditioning of a spastic vaginal introitus does not insure good and pleasurable sexual functioning. And indeed, after the vagina is open for coitus the couple's sexual adjustment varies greatly. Some couples function well and need no further treatment when penetration becomes possible. For other couples the newfound ability to have intercourse reveals orgastic or response problems in the wife and/or potency and ejaculatory problems in the husband. These then require further therapeutic intervention.

The woman who has never had an orgasm also has an excellent prognosis for learning to climax with sex therapy. Actually this is surprising because, in contrast with premature ejaculation and vaginismus, the other two dysfunctions which have excellent prognoses and which are relatively dissociated from psychodynamics, female orgasm is closely related to unconscious and dynamic psychic factors. Nevertheless, on

---

* There may exist a small subgroup of premature ejaculators whose disorder is the product of a different pathogenesis. These may account for the few failures which are reported.

173

an empirical basis, it is extremely unusual to fail to be able to teach a woman to reach orgasm in a brief period of time. However the ultimate outcome of treatment with this population varies greatly. Some women learn to masturbate to orgasm but go no further than this. Others progress to partner-related orgastic experiences and some become coitally orgastic.

Treatment of *erectile* and *situational orgastic dysfunctions* is more complex, and outcome is more variable. This is probably because these syndromes are intimately enmeshed in the psychic matrix in which they occur.

The *erectile dysfunctions* have a moderately good prognosis with sex therapy. Potency seems to be more directly related to a man's psychic and emotional state than does ejaculatory control. When emotional disturbances can be easily corrected or bypassed prognosis with sex therapy is excellent. When the negative emotional responses to sexual intercourse with a woman have deep and tenacious roots, prognosis is more guarded. In actual clinical practice the majority of secondary potency disorders have a favorable outcome. Sex therapy is highly effective in humanizing the sexual situation and reducing those superficial sources of sexually destructive tensions and anxieties which are so prevalent in our culture. However, sex therapy is only moderately successful (approximately 50 percent) in the primary erectile dysfunctions and also is of limited effectiveness in those dysfunctions which are clearly and directly related to profound psychopathology and marital disharmony. However, even neurotic patients should be given the benefits of a trial of brief, active sex therapy, because by using psychodynamic methods it is often possible to bypass even formidable psychopathology and get the patient to function sexually regardless.

Situational orgastic dysfunction has a mixed prognosis with sex therapy. In the course of treatment almost all women can learn to transfer their orgasm from self-stimulation to climaxing when they are together with their partner. But the outcome with coital orgasm varies. Actually when coital orgasm is not the universal goal outcome is excellent. With sex therapy those women whose physiologic orgastic threshold is sufficiently low to allow them to climax on coitus have a high probability of learning to do so. However, those couples wherein the woman's response pattern requires clitoral stimulation, learn to accept this and to have excellent mutually satisfying sex. To those who hold the belief that all women are capable of coital orgasm and that this is the only nonpathological pattern of sexual functioning the outcome of 25 to 50 percent of coital orgasm which can probably be achieved with sex therapy will be disappointing.*

Retarded ejaculation or the *orgastic dysfunctions of men* also have a mixed prognosis with sex therapy which varies directly with the severity of the condition. In its mild and partial forms, retarded ejaculation responds to sex therapy rapidly and almost universally. The more severe forms of this disorder seem to be inexorably linked with the patient's unconscious conflicts and resultant defenses, and severe forms of retarded ejaculation are often refractory to brief symptom-oriented forms of intervention.

The worst results with sex therapy unfortunately are with the totally *unresponsive woman.* Again, such a total suppression of sexual feelings is too often directly related to severe psychic damage and defenses against this to yield to brief intervention. The prognosis is better with secondary unresponsiveness, where it is often an expression of specific problems in the current relationship which can be resolved.

Intrapsychic Factors

It has been stated that superficial and surface anxieties such as performance anxiety often play a definitive role in the sexual dysfunctions. And this is true. Nevertheless, deeper kinds of psychic factors are also capable of producing sexual disturbances and often do.

In the analytic literature two basic unconscious conflicts which can produce sexual problems have been extensively considered and written about: unconscious fear of injury related to sexual behavior, and unconscious hostility toward the opposite gender. These are unquestionably important in producing sexual disturbances in some persons. When this is so, these issues must either be bypassed or resolved, at least to some degree, if the patient is to be able to function sexually.

* Again, evidence to support a definitive conclusion regarding the normalcy of coital orgasm is not yet available at this time.

Two other unconscious conflicts often contribute to sexual disorders. These have not been accorded as much attention and study as unconscious fear of injury and hostility. These are unconscious guilt about, and fear of, success and pleasure and the fear of intimacy and love.

Many persons in our culture are governed by an unconscious *self-destructive* pattern which makes pleasure and success somehow dangerous and forbidden. They are forever in conflict. On a conscious level they seek gratification. They strive for recognition, material success, beauty, pleasure in sex and love. But somehow, as they approach these normal and constructive human goals, they experience anxiety and/or guilt. These neurotic forces move them to sabotage their own efforts.

Such a self-destructive pleasure inhibition can act as a powerful obstacle to successful sex therapy. The outcome cannot be favorable in the face of such a dynamic if it is active. Guilt and anxiety about pleasure and success must be resolved or at least detoured in sex therapy before such a person can allow himself the intense pleasure of good sexual functioning. Of course, true resolution of this malignant conflict is the ultimate goal of therapy. When this can be accomplished, the patient's benefits extend considerably beyond his improved sexual functioning. However it is unfortunately not always possible to resolve pleasure conflicts, especially within the brief treatment format.

Sometimes when a patient is confronted with his pleasure inhibition in the course of sex therapy, he will then go on to seek reconstructive psychoanalytic therapy later on. Paradoxically if basic resolution is not feasible, it is sometimes possible to bypass this malignant and prevalent dynamic by fostering the patient's recognition of the fact that good sexual functioning is not equivalent to total happiness. Enjoyable sex is nice but will *not* really make him totally happy and successful. Sexual happiness is only a partial and limited kind of pleasure. He will still be able to suffer with his other inadequacies if he needs to. It goes without saying that this is a less than satisfactory outcome in terms of human values.

The fear of love, trust, and intimacy is also a malignant antitherapeutic force. Many persons are injured and disappointed early in life. Before they can deal with predatory attack on the basis of their own resources they must depend on parents and siblings to protect them. If

176

this protection is less than perfect, and if the parents are hostile, destructive, or ambivalent—in other words if there are painful contingencies attached to this early intimacy—defenses are developed. These defenses often take the form of alienation and detachment. The child has to protect himself from pain by detaching and alienating himself and becoming prematurely emotionally independent. To ask such a defensively alienated, detached patient to touch, relate, and be intimate, which of course is done during the process of sex therapy, is like asking a jungle fighter to give up his knife. Reestablishment of the capacity to love and to trust and to move close to another person again is often a difficult process which takes time. During successful sex therapy this process is seldom complete, but often is given a good start as obstacles to its natural flow are gently removed.

The Relationship

Are human beings basically a bonding species? What is the relationship between bonding and sex? We do not yet have the answers to such fundamental questions, and yet they are crucial to our complete understanding of human sexuality. Clearly there are complex correlations between human sexual functioning and the quality of the relationship between the partners. Indeed the nature of the relationship is an important prognostic factor in predicting the outcome of sex therapy.

Many subhuman species form a mating bond with a member of the opposite sex and have sexual intercourse only with that individual. In some species these bonds last only during the mating and/or breeding season, in others the exclusive sexual bond is for life. On the other hand other species including our nearest primate relatives do not form such bonds at all. Males mate with any female in heat.

Clinical evidence suggests that human beings are probably a bonding species, although it is not clear whether we are lifetime bonders or time-limited courtship bonders. Falling in love, the human correlate of bonding, is a highly predictable behavioral pattern which begins when the brain is flooded with sex hormones during adolescence. Most persons feel better and more secure when they are engaged in a love relationship. They enjoy sex with the person they love more than with a stranger with whom there is no emotional connection. However, some persons do not fall in love or their love and sexual relationships may show distorted patterns. Thus some men and women function best sexually with a variety of partners or with partners with whom they have limited relationships or who are emotionally unavailable. Most authorities believe that nonbonding or promiscuous sexual patterns represent a pathological inhibition of the natural human tendency to form love relationships, but definitive evidence on this matter is lacking.

Whatever our "natural" biologically programmed behavioral tendency may ultimately be found to be, it is only *one* of many determinants which govern our dyadic and sexual behavior. Learned or experiential components are, of course, of inestimable weight in determining of final love and sex responses.

Given our incomplete knowledge on this subject, clinical observation suggests that the healthy guilt-free person is not dependent on being in love for his sexual functioning and pleasure. He *can* function well sexually and experience erotic pleasure and lust in the absence of an intense affectionate or romantic relationship, as long as the relationship is neither destructive nor the sex object repugnant. However, a feeling of love between the partners makes sex an infinitely more satisfying, pleasurable, and human experience. Love is the only real aphrodisiac.

While love is not absolutely necessary, hostility and rejection and fear of the partner can be very destructive to sexual functioning. Indeed when an essentially hostile relationship exists between the partners who are seeking help for a sexual dysfunction, the prognosis is guarded. It is irrational to attempt sex therapy unless a reasonably affectionate relationship exists between the couple. It is difficult and perhaps not even desirable to attempt to foster a sexual relationship when such deep rejection of the partner exists that the idea of giving him or allowing him to give her pleasure evokes intense anger or fear. Such emotion may outright prevent cooperation in the treatment process. More subtly, if anger or fear is unconscious, there may be overt cooperation but, predictably, the angry or rejecting partner will covertly sabotage sex therapy.

However, it is possible to get couples to function sexually if they are

178

The kiss

not in love, if some affection exists even though they are relatively detached, just as long as they are not basically hostile to each other. This happens when surrogates are employed in sex therapy. However, while getting two "strangers" to function sexually with one another, whether they are married or whether they are paid surrogates, may have some merit, it is hardly emotionally satisfying for the patients or for most therapists.

The best prognosis in sex therapy exists when there is a real bond of love between the couple. If they truly love, if they are truly connected, if they truly feel for one another, then anything is possible. Even the most tenacious dysfunction is likely to yield when a real love bond exists.

Sex therapy cannot create love. However, in its process it frequently can remove obstacles to the experience and expression of love. And when such obstacles and defenses to love exist, their removal is the first order of business for the sex therapist.